Contemporary romance auka and still calls the frozen north ... found indulging her travel addicti... th her and she has written ... ov...

Lizzie has been honored to win the Golden Heart Award and HOLT Medallion, and has been named a finalist three times for Romance Writers of America's prestigious RITA Award®, but her main claim to fame is that she lost on *Jeopardy!*

For more about Lizzie and her books, please visit **www.lizzieshane.com**.

Praise for *The Twelve Dogs of Christmas*:

'Just right for animal lovers seeking a seasonal happily ever after' *Publishers Weekly*

'It has all the makings of a Christmas classic, and would be sure to warm the hardest of hearts' *Rachel's Random Reads*

'An irresistible blend of heart, humor, nostalgic moments, misunderstandings, family, friendship, tension, chemistry, attraction, spirited shenanigans, Christmas cheer, and a whole lot of puppy love' *What's Better Than Books?*

'A dog lovers dream come true, mixed in with Christmas and the most adorable romance' *Breakfast at Shelby's*

'A magical read . . . If you read one holiday romance this year make it this one, I don't think you'll regret it!' *Novel Gossip*

'All the other Christmassy books have a lot to live up to!' *Escapades of a Bookworm*

By Lizzie Shane

The Twelve Dogs of Christmas
Once Upon a Puppy

Once Upon a Puppy

LIZZIE SHANE

HEADLINE
ETERNAL

Published by arrangement with Forever
an imprint of Grand Central Publishing

First published in Great Britain in 2021
by HEADLINE ETERNAL
An imprint of HEADLINE PUBLISHING GROUP

1

Cataloguing in Publication Data is available from the British Library

ISBN 978 1 4722 7867 8

Offset in 11.65/13.86 pt Times New Roman by Jouve (UK), Milton Keynes

Printed and bound in Great Britain by Clays Ltd, Elcograf S.p.A.

Headline's policy is to use papers that are natural, renewable and recyclable
products and made from wood grown in well-managed forests and other
controlled sources. The logging and manufacturing processes are expected
to conform to the environmental regulations of the country of origin.

HEADLINE PUBLISHING GROUP
An Hachette UK Company
Carmelite House
50 Victoria Embankment
London EC4Y 0DZ

www.headlineeternal.com
www.headline.co.uk
www.hachette.co.uk

For Kali, who survived backpacking across Europe with me when we were both obnoxious teens. And Leigh, who shared some of my best adventures in Asia. And for the gentleman we met in Vietnam, who gave us the excellent advice about seizing the day.

Because you can't put more life in the bank.

Chapter One

In retrospect, a 140-pound Irish wolfhound mix might not have been his best impulse purchase, Connor Wyeth acknowledged when he stepped out of his home office and saw the wreckage of his six-thousand-dollar couch.

Not that he made many impulse purchases. Or any, for that matter.

Connor was a planner. Even Maximus—the canine culprit responsible for dragging the massive couch halfway across the living room and shredding the cushions until the entire room was littered in white fuzz—had been part of a plan.

Just not a particularly well-thought-out one.

Max's booming bark echoed off the high ceilings as the big dope galumphed gleefully between the front door and the living room crime scene. Spotting Connor, he slid to a stop on the polished hardwood floors and raced back to the entry. Maximus barked again through the glass that flanked the dark polished-wood door at whoever was on the other side, before looking over his shaggy shoulder at Connor, with his jaws gaping and his tongue hanging out the side of his mouth in that patented come-on-you're-missing-all-the-fun canine grin.

And Connor realized again how completely out of his depth he was as a dog owner.

Since he'd ostensibly gotten Maximus as a guard dog and early warning system to deter his friends from just waltzing into his house whenever they pleased, the trainer had told him he should praise Max when he barked at intruders. Connor was also supposed to scold Max when he did things like dismember the furniture, but scolding him now wouldn't do any good—not that it ever seemed to do any good—so Connor resigned himself to the loss of his couch and went to open the door.

He hooked a finger around Max's collar to remind him of the we-do-not-put-our-paws-on-guests'-shoulders-and-lick-their-faces rule and pulled the door open.

"No solicitors," Connor growled at one of his three oldest friends, standing on his doorstep with his arms bowing around a bulging bag and a collection of lawn signs. They were sideways, but the block print on them was clearly legible: BENJAMIN WEST FOR MAYOR. THE RIGHT CHOICE FOR PINE HOLLOW.

The signs made a good prop, but they both knew Ben wasn't here about the upcoming election. Not today.

Connor glowered—and Ben shoved past him, undeterred. "I brought lunch."

"And lawn signs."

Connor closed the door before releasing the hound. Max immediately lunged toward Ben, eagerly snuffling at the bag in his arms. It started to slip toward his eager jaws, and Connor swiftly rescued the food so Ben could kick off his shoes and prop the lawn signs against the window.

"I'm not putting those up," Connor warned. "I haven't decided who I'm voting for yet."

Ben ignored the blatant lie, reclaiming the lunch bag and starting toward the kitchen. "Tandy Watts put a banner on her porch. You can see it from space."

Normally Connor would give Ben a hard time—what else were friends for?—but there was a note of anxiety in his friend's voice that had him reassuring him instead. "No one is voting for Tandy Watts. She's only running because she wants to overturn the zoning decision you guys made against her last year, and the entire town knows it. You have experience on the council, and you're Delia's pick. Relax."

"I don't know why I wanted to run for mayor," Ben grumbled as he reached the kitchen and drew up short, staring past the island toward the fuzz explosion in the living room. "Redecorating?"

Connor put his body between Ben and the view, wishing, not for the first time since he'd bought the sprawling, open-concept house, that it was a little less sprawling and open concept. "Max was playing on the couch while I worked. I haven't had a chance to clean it up."

The dog chose that moment to race past, running the length of the house to leap onto the couch, sending it sliding across the polished hardwood floors, careening toward the—very breakable—glass coffee table. Luckily, the coffee table slid as well, rather than tipping and shattering—and Maximus gleefully flipped a pillow into the air.

"Max!" He tried to mimic the tone the trainer had used—the one that seemed to make all the dogs in the class sit up a little straighter. Maximus perked up, whipping toward the sound of Connor's voice. He sprang to his feet on the couch, his ears pricked forward, his jaws gaping in that dopey canine grin.

"Off!" Connor demanded.

The dog looked at him, cocking his head in confusion.

"Off!" Connor repeated, moving to drag Maximus off the couch—easier said than done when the dog in question weighed almost as much as an adult human and was eagerly licking every inch of Connor's face he could reach.

He finally ended up scooping the dog up in his arms and depositing him on the floor with a last firm *"Off."*

While Max licked him happily.

"Have you considered actually training him?" Ben asked, having set their lunch in the kitchen and wandered over to watch the show.

"I *am* training him," Connor snapped—his voice sharp enough that Max paused in mid-lick, his ears twitching.

"Uh-huh." Ben folded his arms. "You know you might have to *attend* the training classes you paid for in order for them to take effect. Though I'm sure Ally's happy to have your money either way."

Ben's girlfriend, Ally, ran the shelter in town, which offered training classes with a special discount for anyone who'd adopted their dogs from Furry Friends. The same classes Connor had had the best intention of attending every Monday. Before work had gotten busy, like it always did.

"I forgot to put them on my calendar."

Ben snorted. "You never forget anything."

"Fine." It was so annoying when his friends knew him too well. "I got busy."

"You're always busy. But I've recently discovered that being busy doesn't have to preclude you from having a life. It's a fascinating revelation. You should consider it."

"Having a revelation?" he drawled sarcastically.

"Getting a life."

"My life is fine," he growled—looking at Maximus

instead of Ben, since neither of them would be able to let the falsehood stand if Connor met his eyes.

His life wasn't fine. Especially not today. But he didn't want to talk about it.

Not with Levi, who'd dropped by this morning claiming to be "in the area." Not with his mother, who'd called him three times already today with made-up things she absolutely needed his input on. Not with Mac, who was sure to appear as soon as the Cup hit the afternoon lull.

And certainly not with Ben.

Ben was in that obnoxious smugly-in-love phase where he fixated on all the wonderful parts of being with someone and developed strategic amnesia when it came to the ripping-the-rug-out-from-under-you shit that happened when it all fell apart.

When you came home expecting to find a fiancée and found a Post-it note instead.

Maximus snapped at a piece of fuzz floating in the air, and Connor focused on the dog and the welcome distraction from his thoughts. "This is your fault," he growled at Ben, straightening to head back toward the kitchen and the promise of lunch. "You're the one who kept insisting I needed a dog."

"You did need a dog."

It was galling to admit, but Ben was right. Connor had isolated himself too much—starting exactly one year ago today—locking himself in his own head and dedicating himself to his work with what might have been a slightly unhealthy obsession.

Maximus had been the antidote to that.

Connor couldn't lose himself in work until one in the morning every day if he had a dog to feed and walk—

though walking Max was usually an exercise in being dragged around the neighborhood. The wolfhound mutt had never been trained as a puppy, and now he was a full-grown wrecking ball of love.

Connor wouldn't trade him for anything.

Ben unpacked the to-go containers from the Cup—and Connor tried not to wonder if he'd been the primary topic of conversation while Mac was packing up the order. The restaurant was a well-known gossip hub in Pine Hollow. It was probably too much to hope that the entire town didn't know what day it was. February first.

It would have been nice if Connor could have avoided the anniversary of his public humiliation without comment, but that wasn't how life in a small town worked.

He knew they supported him, but the pity felt like acid on his skin.

"You really should come to the training classes," Ben commented as he slid Connor's usual across the island toward him, and they both dug in. "Even Partridge is making progress, and he's not exactly a fast learner."

Ben and the niece he was raising had adopted the drooly bulldog around the same time Connor had adopted Maximus.

"Partridge has Astrid." Connor pointed out the unfair comparison. "Who would spend every waking second working on his training with him if she could."

"True. And I fully support her obsession. At least if she's working with Partridge she's not dropping not-so-subtle hints about me proposing to Ally."

Connor jerked at the words, startled. "Already?"

They'd been dating less than two months. Talking about marriage now was insane. But then he'd dated Monica for three years and been engaged for another two before she'd decided, thirteen days before the wedding, that she couldn't spend her life with him after all.

Maybe going fast was the way to do it. Commit before you had time to second-guess.

Ben swore softly under his breath, studying Connor's face. "Sorry. I shouldn't be talking about that today. I wasn't thinking."

And there it was. Today. The Anniversary. Ben wasn't usually that direct. Over the last year they'd steered well clear of She Who Must Not Be Named.

Connor took a firm left turn away from the subject. "You putting up lawn signs all over town, or are you expecting me to put all three of those in my front yard?"

Ben eyed him for a moment before accepting the shift in topic. "You do have a big front yard."

"Yeah, but three seems a little excessive, don't you think? I'm not sure I support you that much. There are limits to three decades of friendship."

"One sign for each decade. That seems fair." An alarm went off on Ben's phone and he silenced it, rising from the barstools at the island. "I've gotta get back to work. Will I actually see you tonight at Furry Friends?"

"Yeah, of course. I haven't been skipping the classes on purpose." Not entirely. "Things are just really busy."

Ben headed toward the front door, and Connor fell into step at his side while Maximus's snores echoed in the living room.

"How's the partner stuff going?" Ben asked, bending to grab his shoes.

"Too early to tell."

"Good luck." Ben hesitated after putting on his shoes—

and Connor resisted the urge to physically shove him out the door before he could start talking about the Anniversary.

Thankfully, Ben left without any more concerned looks, and Connor shut the door behind him, wondering if he could somehow head off Mac's inevitable visit. Mac was the most likely to come right out and ask him how he was *feeling*.

His friends and family were all checking on him, but he was *fine*. Or at least on his way toward it.

He had a Plan now.

The Plan was the reason he had Max. It was the reason he was *going* to make partner. And it was going to get him back on track for the life he should already be living. Perfect job. Perfect house. Perfect family.

He had the house. The job was all but guaranteed after the last twelve months of obsessively putting in more hours than any of the other associates at his law firm. And the family would follow, just as soon as he had a little more time to dedicate to finding the One. A woman who appreciated everything he had to offer—stability, loyalty, dependability. A woman who wouldn't just *say* she wanted those things and then run off to India two weeks before they were supposed to exchange vows. A woman who would stay.

Connor hadn't meant to avoid relationships for so long. He'd had a steady stream of steady girlfriends since he started dating. His high school girlfriend—whom he'd broken up with amicably to go to Yale. His college girlfriend—who had broken up with him amicably when they got into law schools across the country from one another. His law school girlfriend—with whom he had amicably parted ways when she wanted to stay in DC to clerk for an appeals court judge and he wanted to move back to Vermont to focus on corporate law and have a family.

And then Monica.

It was hard to describe his fiancée dumping him via Post-it two weeks prior to their wedding as anything resembling amicable.

So, yes, maybe he had been a little bitter, a little angry. Maybe he had thrown himself into work a little too hard and cursed the entire female half of the species with a little more enthusiasm than they probably deserved. Maybe he had avoided women except for the occasional Tinder hookup when he was down in New York for business—always casual, no expectations. But that was all behind him. He was starting fresh this year. Thanks to the Plan.

Impatient to get back to work, but knowing the mess would distract him until he took care of it, Connor went to clean up the fluff minefield that had once been his living room. He'd just shoved the couch back into position when Maximus snorted awake. He trotted over to "help," putting his front paws on the couch, his jaws hanging open in a happy canine smile.

"You pleased with yourself?" He took the dog's giant head between his hands, ruffling his ears. The dog groaned, leaning into Connor's hands, his soulful black eyes gazing adoringly into Connor's as Connor said the same thing he'd said at least five hundred times in the five weeks since he'd become a dog owner. "You aren't allowed on the furniture."

Or the counter. Or the roof of my car.

But how did he teach Max that when he couldn't physically wrestle him down?

"We're going back to obedience class tonight," he informed Max. "Even if everyone is going to be giving me pity looks."

Nudging Maximus's bulk out of the way, he brushed the fuzz off the couch. On closer inspection it looked like the couch had mostly survived whatever game Maximus had been playing. Only one of the throw pillows had exploded and rained its innards across his hardwood floors.

Considering that pillow had been one of Monica's additions, maybe Max had done him a favor.

His cell phone rang as Connor ruffled Max on the head. "Good dog. Never do that again."

He caught Max's collar, guiding him into the office and shutting the door so he could keep an eye on him as he worked. He started every day that way, but Connor had a tendency to get so engrossed in what he was concentrating on that when Max scratched at the door to be let out, he would automatically open the door for him without realizing he'd done it until he heard a crash in the kitchen. Or the living room. Or the bathroom.

Seeing his mentor's name on the caller ID, Connor quickly tapped to connect the call through his Bluetooth before it could go to voice mail. "Davis, how are you?"

The partner who had taken Connor under his wing at Sterling, Tavish & Karlson cleared his throat roughly, an affectation Connor had come to associate with bad news. He braced a hand on his desk—and Max looked up from his dog bed, concern in his liquid black eyes.

"Connor. I just had a chance to look at that Johnson contract, and I wanted to tell you how pleased the whole firm is with your work."

Connor frowned. Davis Aquino never called him just to give him an attaboy. No one had time for that. "You aren't calling to tell me 'good job.'"

The throat clearing came again, followed by a heavy sigh. "Look, Connor. You're our workhorse. Everyone knows how much you do for this firm, and I know you'd been hoping to make partner this year…"

Shit. Shit shit shit. "But?"

"We don't want to lose you. You're an incredibly valuable associate, but at the moment the senior partners are leaning in another direction."

"Is this a joke?" His unfiltered reaction burst out of his mouth—because this was Davis and not one of the other partners. "Who do they think does more for the firm than I do?"

"No one works as hard as you, but for some of the partners that's actually one of their concerns, that you'll burn yourself out. That you don't have work-life balance or any kind of a stress-release valve, and you'll be running on empty by the time you're thirty-five."

"I don't need a release valve," Connor said, trying to keep the sharpness out of his voice. "I'm good."

"Good," Davis replied. "That's good. But there are other concerns."

Connor forced himself to breathe. He'd carefully picked this firm. A place he knew he could rise. He'd been the perfect employee for *years* and there were *concerns*? "Such as?"

"Being a partner isn't just about being a workhorse. It's about representing us. Being a leader within the firm and the community. There's a social aspect, and with you working mostly from home—"

"We agreed that made the most sense. Less time wasted on an unnecessary commute when I can easily work remotely." The firm was based in Burlington, though so many of their clients also did business in New York that Connor was licensed in both states. He so rarely met clients in the office that Davis had *encouraged* him to work from home.

"That's true, but there's something to be said for being visible."

"I'll start working from the office." He would have to find someone to look after Max. Maybe Ally knew someone.

"It's not about being in the office more. It's also our events. You know STK prides itself on our engagement in the community, our charitable work—and you've been skipping most of our charity events for the last year or so."

Ever since he'd stopped being the golden boy. Stopped having the perfect woman on his arm and become the one everyone looked at with pity and asked how he was holding up. The events had gone from being chummy to excruciating. "I realize I haven't been as active, but I'm turning over a new leaf."

"Look, Connor, I love you. You'd be my pick every day of the week, but it isn't my call, and Brent and Lila especially are looking for something else. I figured you deserved a heads-up. I don't want you to feel blindsided. You're still incredibly valuable to STK."

Acid burned in his throat. "That's it then? It's a done deal?"

"Not yet," Davis assured him. "They still haven't made the final decision, but it would be an uphill battle for you, and maybe it's not the worst thing in the world if you take a different path. We want to keep you happy. You can do very well as an associate. Not everyone needs to be partner."

But that was The Plan.

It was all he'd been working toward for the last year. For his entire life, really, but it had only been an all-consuming obsession since Monica left—and apparently took his best chance of making partner with her.

If she'd stuck around, he'd still be going to the charity events, with his wife on his arm. She'd probably be pregnant with their first kid by now—concrete evidence of work-life balance. He'd be commiserating with coworkers about married life and impending fatherhood. He would have gotten to know more of the new associates, demonstrated his leadership abilities. His life would still be right where it was supposed to be instead of...

He looked around the office. *All work and no play.* Max rose from his dog bed and padded over, draping his massive head on Connor's desk next to his hand. Connor absently stroked his shaggy head, smoothing his thumb between his ears.

"Connor?" Davis's voice crackled through the earpiece.

"Yeah. Thanks for the warning. A lot to think about."

"You're really valued," Davis said—and Connor could almost hear his management training courses in the words.

Make employees feel that their talents and contributions are valued and appreciated.

And he did feel that way. But he wanted more. He wanted a stake. He wanted partnership. The security of knowing that he wasn't just an employee. That he *owned* his piece of the firm. He'd wanted that since he was nine freaking years old.

And he wasn't giving up now.

He said goodbye to Davis after a few minutes discussing the work he was doing for another client—a conversation he barely remembered, his thoughts were so thoroughly consumed by the partnership bombshell.

He knew it had never been a lock. There were always

more associates vying for partner than there were slots available—but he'd put in more hours than any of them. He'd *earned* this. And he wasn't going to let it slip through his fingers because the rest of his life had gone a little off track last year.

Making partner had been part of The Plan. Get a dog. Make partner. Find the One. Get married. Have kids. Five simple steps. But maybe it was time to shake up the order. Maybe he needed to start dating again right away. Find a nice girl to bring with him to a few of the firm's charity events to show the senior partners that he had balance, that he was a team player.

When he'd initially made The Plan, he'd intended to start dating right away—but then he'd gotten busy and his best intentions had fallen to the side. But now...now dating was a responsibility, and Connor Wyeth never shirked his responsibilities.

Max sat down, leaning his bulk against Connor's chair, so Connor had to brace his feet to keep it from rolling sideways.

He pulled up the app store on his phone, scrolling through and downloading several dating apps. He had work to do.

Then he'd take Max to obedience class tonight and figure out how to keep the dog from destroying his house.

It felt good to have a plan.

Chapter Two

Deenie Mitchell was at her best when she improvised.
It was part of what made her so successful at hosting princess parties for children—she never got too glued to a plan, always ready to adapt on the fly.

So when she walked into the farmhouse forty-five minutes before the Furry Friends Monday training session was supposed to start to find Ally in a panic because the trainer from Burlington had come down with food poisoning and wasn't going to make it, Deenie did exactly what she always did. She rolled with the punches.

"I have to cancel," Ally groaned, still gripping her cell phone and staring at the ominous food-poisoning text.

"No, you don't." Deenie took Ally's phone and flipped open the Magda's Bakery pastry box she'd brought home after visiting her aunt, shoving a piece of flaky raspberry–cream cheese decadence into Ally's hand instead. "Eat this. Magda's pastries solve all problems."

"I don't see how," Ally argued. "I have six paying customers arriving in less than an hour and no expert trainer to offer them. We promised them a certified professional every week." She took a bite of the pastry and groaned—though it was unclear whether it was with bliss at Magda's sinful skills or dread at having to cancel one of the classes in the pilot program designed to revitalize the Furry Friends Animal Shelter and turn it into a full-service pet mecca.

Deenie guided Ally to a stool, deliberately positioning her with her back to the windows that looked out across the gravel driveway to the barn that housed Furry Friends. Ally's grandparents had lived in the farmhouse and run the shelter for decades, before retiring and turning it over to Ally. The shelter had been hanging on by a thread for years, dependent on town funding, but Ally had come up with a plan to make the Furry Friends self-sufficient, and Deenie had moved in less than a week ago to help out.

They were still trying to establish themselves as the local source for all things dog—so the timing on losing their trainer was less than ideal. But not catastrophic.

"Focus on the positive—one of those paying customers is Ben, who's so sappily in love with you he probably won't notice there's no trainer," Deenie pointed out. "Another is Elinor, who'll be just as happy having Skinny Girl Margaritas with us in the storeroom. And a third is Connor—who can't be bothered to actually bring Maximus to class."

Not that Deenie minded Connor Wyeth's recent absence at the classes. The man had rubbed her the wrong way since the second they met.

He was just so *rigid*. He radiated the uptight vibes of all the people who looked down on her for her pink hair and unconventional life, and activated all her defenses—and when it came to fight or flight, with Connor it definitely seemed to be fight. She hadn't *intended* to goad him into adopting Maximus by arguing the wolfhound was too much dog for him, but she hadn't been capable of letting him win a single verbal sparring match.

Ever since, she always seemed to find herself sniping at him when they were forced to be near each other—something that had happened unfortunately often since Ben and Ally had gotten together.

"It's a sign."

Deenie refocused on Ally, evicting Connor Wyeth from her thoughts. "It isn't a sign. We've got this. We'll just make this week a bonus week—a practice session. I can lead it."

Ally's eyes flared with hope. "Really?"

"Of course. That's what I'm here for, right? Helping out with the shelter stuff? How hard can it be?"

Deenie had been following along with the class anyway, working with a little spaniel named Dolce so she'd be ready to be adopted as soon as her puppies were weaned and she was spayed. Though with the way Ally's grandmother had been fawning over the dog lately, it would be a minor miracle if Rita Gilmore didn't co-opt the sweet little dog for herself.

"I'm not certified or anything," she went on, "but if we explain about the food poisoning and promise people a real make-up class later, I can't imagine anyone will complain."

"They'll be thrilled. We all know you're the dog whisperer. That's even better than bringing in a different trainer."

Deenie held up a hand. "Don't get too excited. I'm just a warm body to fill in during emergency food-poisoning episodes."

"We both know that isn't true. I don't know how I would do this without you."

Discomfort swelled in the face of Ally's gratitude. Deenie loved to help—it didn't make sense not to step in and fix a problem when it was right there in front of her—but if she was actually *necessary*, that put a layer of pressure on her that she wasn't sure she wanted.

How messed up was that? Who else in the world *wanted* to be valued and then wanted to run the second she was?

As usual, she covered her discomfort with a flashy smile. "You'd fail miserably, of course. I'm indispensable."

It was a bald-faced lie—but Ally set down her pastry, looking at her as if it was the gospel truth. "I know. I never would have gotten that loan without you."

"Don't be ridiculous. Of course you would."

Ally shook her head. "I still can't believe you knew how to do all that small-business planning stuff."

"Shh, you'll ruin my image." Deenie took Ally's incredulity as the highest compliment. She'd carefully cultivated her persona as a feckless, glitter-coated fairy princess. It wouldn't do to have people realize she could write a profit and loss statement in her sleep.

A lock of hair fell into her eyes, and she raked it back. She needed a haircut—and to touch up the streaks. The blond roots had grown out, and the pink highlights had faded from their usual neon glory to a pale pastel shade, significantly decreasing the gratifying shock value.

"I'm just really glad you're here," Ally said with that unnerving sincerity.

"I have to be. I'm broke." The words were irreverent. Designed to make everyone think she was joking.

They were also true.

Deenie needed to replenish her funds after her last trip. She'd splurged on a few more experiences than had technically been in her budget when she was backpacking through New Zealand last fall. But how often did you get the chance to bungee jump into a gorge or walk in the footsteps of Hobbits? Sometimes you had to grab the opportunities life put in front of you—even if that meant coming home slightly closer to a zero balance than she usually preferred.

It didn't help that she'd also gone a tiny bit overboard on Christmas presents for her brother's kids, always trying to prove things to her family that couldn't be proven.

So she'd needed a place where the rent was low—offset by the hours she'd be putting in at the shelter.

It was a good idea, spending a few months hanging out in Pine Hollow, visiting her aunt, helping Ally, playing with the dogs, sewing custom princess dresses for her Etsy shop—once the demand picked up after the post-Christmas lull—and hosting princess parties whenever she could book them. All to replenish her depleted finances.

She *loved* this plan. She'd come up with the plan herself.

So why had she felt like she was going to crawl out of her skin ever since she moved in? Why did everything feel *wrong*?

It had to be the fact that she didn't know when she'd be leaving. She always had a vague destination in mind and date she could look forward to when she knew she'd be starting on her next adventure.

Her personal responsibility countdown.

Now the future stretched out in front of her in an uninterrupted sprawl of time. Everything was indefinite. And Deenie was discovering that even someone who rebelled against rules and schedules as much as she did really needed the structure of a known expiration date. An escape hatch.

It seemed to make the wanderlust worse—the ever-present itch beneath her skin grew that much more acute when she had no idea when she was going to indulge it.

Her sister would think she was insane. But then her sister had never understood that need to roam, to see the world. No one in her family had.

Well. No one except Bitty.

"Did you have a good visit with JoJo?"

"Oh, um..."

She hadn't *planned* on lying to Ally about why she kept going out to the Summerland Estates retirement community. It had just sort of happened. Not that it was a complete lie. She *was* going to see JoJo—she'd fallen in love with the sweet little papillon before the dog was adopted by Mr. Burke.

But she was also going to see Bitty.

She still hadn't told Ally about her great-aunt, not ready to have one more person asking how Bitty was doing. One more person she had to lie to, pretending everything was okay.

So instead she pretended it wasn't happening at all.

Nothing to see here, folks. Just Deenie Mitchell, master of illusion.

Guilt over the deception climbed up her throat, and Deenie didn't meet Ally's eyes, pretending to be absorbed in stealing a pinch of pastry. "Yeah, it was great. She's such a sweetie."

"You should have adopted her," Ally said. "She was so perfect for you."

"I can't travel with a dog. And Mr. Burke is a great fit. He adores her." Deenie pushed away from the counter. "I should get changed before the class." It was a flimsy excuse to escape the conversation, but Ally didn't seem to notice her evasion.

Deenie headed toward the stairs, detouring through the living room to pet the puppies.

The farmhouse wasn't fancy—a big box of a house with a wraparound porch—but what it lacked in design frills, it made up for in space. The living room looked even bigger now that half of the furniture had been moved to the Estates with Ally's grandparents.

A pen had been set up near the warmth of the fireplace for Dolce and her puppies. Most of them were asleep, but the adventurous one with a single black ear padded over for attention.

Ally's Saint Bernard, Colby, sprawled on a massive dog bed nearby, watching through slitted eyes to make sure he wasn't missing anything without exerting any unnecessary effort. After giving the puppy a final pat, Deenie moved to rub his silky head. "Hello, your laziness," she greeted him.

The dogs were excellent therapy after a day at the Estates—simple, uncomplicated affection after the inevitable complication of managing Bitty's care. Bitty's doctor had wanted a word with her today, a somber discussion of progress and expectations, the words swimming uneasily through her thoughts.

Leaving Colby, Deenie took the stairs two at a time in bouncing leaps in the hope that bouncy on the outside would translate into bouncy on the inside and bounce her right out of her funk.

The narrow stairs emptied onto a central hallway, where a row of basic square bedrooms jutted off to either side. Ally had claimed the one with the best light as her photography studio—electing not to use her grandmother's old art studio downstairs, since it didn't have a door to prevent her canine subjects from escaping.

And since it was still half full of Rita's clutter.

It had taken Hal and Rita Gilmore an entire month of yo-yoing back and forth between the farmhouse and their cozy new patio home at the Estates to move the things they wanted to keep with them. And Rita still popped by nearly every day because she'd thought of something else they'd forgotten.

Not that Deenie minded the regular visits. Rita's compass was a little off center, and Deenie had always loved that about her. It was why Rita and Bitty had been such good friends. And why Deenie had started volunteering at the dog shelter in the first place.

She pushed open the door to her room.

Unlike the Gilmores, it had taken her approximately thirty minutes and exactly one trip in her vintage powder-blue VW Bug—which wasn't exactly known for its storage capacity—to move all her worldly possessions into one of the farmhouse's empty bedrooms.

The bulging hiking backpack that had been around the world with her leaned against the foot of the bed. It hung open, the clothes she hadn't bothered to unpack a chaotic jumble of color erupting from the top.

In the far corner of the room, beneath one of the windows, she'd set up her bedazzled sewing machine. A hot-pink duffel bag sat on the floor beside the chair, overflowing with the satiny fabric and sparkling trim she used to make the princess dresses that were her primary source of income. Another oversized duffel partially blocked the closet—this one purple and containing all her princess party gear. Wigs and tiaras and glitter. So much glitter.

Everything she owned fit in that one corner.

She'd never been big on things. They only became anchors, weighing you down, tying you to places, making you feel like you couldn't pick up and leave easily.

The bed had already been in the room when she arrived, along with the little desk she'd turned into a sewing table. She always made sure to sublet furnished places—which usually meant she was in one of the vacation rentals out at the ski resort, but it worked well for her. Her life was nimble.

Just not now.

That forever feeling crawled like spiders under her skin. She should probably unpack, but part of her was fighting the comfort of this place. She didn't want to get too comfortable. She didn't want to get stuck.

She needed an end date. It kept her from getting stagnant—and helped her appreciate the moment she was in. It was always easier to live life to the fullest when you didn't take things for granted—and she never took anything for granted when she knew her time was short.

But right now she needed to stay. For Bitty. For Ally.

So she put that uneasy feeling in a box. Pushed it down beneath the glittery smile she'd perfected long ago.

The trick was to keep moving. To keep busy even if she was stuck here. And Deenie was an expert at that. Don't slow down. Don't get in a rut. Don't let the doubt in.

She looked out the window, across the gravel driveway, past her little blue Bug and the old green pickup with the Furry Friends logo painted on the side, to the big barn that housed the shelter dogs.

Tonight she had a class to teach.

And with any luck, aggravating Connor Wyeth would stay away and it would just be playing with dogs with her friends.

She could do this.

Chapter Three

The regular trainer wasn't there.

Deenie Mitchell stood in the center of the room, circled by a perimeter of chairs, spaced out so the dogs weren't distracted trying to socialize with one another when they were supposed to be learning. She was dressed in her usual a-rainbow-just-exploded-on-me style, with her pink hair matching her bright pink leggings and a tie-dye mini-dress completing the effect. But the look she shot Connor as soon as he stepped into the training room was more storm clouds than rainbows. That look seemed to say Connor was such a disappointment as a man that she didn't know how he could stand himself.

Though he might have been projecting.

Connor hated failure, and he hated being late—and to-night he was ten minutes late because he had completely failed in his efforts to wrestle Maximus into the car. Loading Max was always a battle, but today it had been Waterloo, and Connor had been Napoleon.

Then when they'd finally arrived at Furry Friends, Max had dragged him into the building and barreled into the storeroom, where the classes were held, with enough force to completely disrupt the class in progress.

When Max burst in, Deenie broke off midsentence, making a sharp "Eh!" sound. That tone somehow managed to say, "Stop right there, young man," and "What do you think you're doing?" and "I know you know better than that," all rolled into one syllable.

Max immediately stopped lunging, his ears pricked forward—and Connor resisted the urge to growl at how easy she made it look.

Deenie held up a finger. "Maximus, sit."

The dog's butt dropped immediately to the ground in the most perfect sit Connor had ever seen him execute—and a wicked flash of jealousy streaked through him as Deenie praised him and gave him a treat.

She raised her eyes from the wolfhound's and met his, judgment vivid in the blue depths. "Connor. How unexpected."

Okay, he might have missed one or two classes, but was that really called for? He narrowed his eyes, but she went on.

"Why don't you two take a seat?" She waved him toward the lone empty chair, midway between Elinor Rodriguez and her Australian shepherd and Kaitlyn Murray with her little French bulldog, who was so perfectly behaved he didn't know why she was even here.

"Come on, Max." Connor shortened up his leash, but it still took all his strength to muscle Max over to the open chair— Deenie's frowning gaze following him the entire way.

If Connor had known the pink-haired porcupine was going to be leading the class, he might have reconsidered coming tonight. But honesty forced him to instantly retract that thought. Max needed the classes too much. And Deenie Mitchell, for all her faults, was amazing with the dog. It was only Connor she appeared to despise.

They'd met at Christmas when he was adopting Max, and he couldn't recall a single conversation between them that *hadn't* started and ended with verbal jabs. But for everyone else—and all the dogs—she was all sunshine and glitter.

He maneuvered Max into a semblance of a sit at his side—pointedly not looking at the other dogs around the room who were sitting statue-still beside their owners like poster pups for good behavior.

Ben caught his eye and gave him a sympathetic grimace. He sat beside his niece, Astrid, who was carefully monitoring the behavior of the drooly bulldog at her side.

Deenie raised her hands to reclaim the focus of the room. "As I was saying, *consistency* is everything. Which is more a challenge for us than for them. Nine times out of ten, when a dog is developing a bad behavior, it's in reaction to something we're doing or not doing."

Her gaze slid right over Connor without stopping, but he felt like the words were poison darts aimed right at him.

"We'll practice the techniques we've learned in a moment, but right now let's take this opportunity to talk about what's been working and not working for us and see if we can find some solutions. What kind of obstacles have you been facing as you've practiced the methods we've been given over the last three classes?"

Ben urged Astrid to raise her hand, and Deenie smiled encouragingly at the girl, listening patiently as Astrid explained Partridge's obsession with drooling in Ben's shoes. Then it was Elinor's frustration with her dog's ability to open doors. The German shepherd's constant barking. The black

Lab who wouldn't stop pulling on walks. And Kaitlyn's little Romeo's refusal to shake with his right paw, no matter how many times she tried to get him to be ambidextrous.

Deenie nodded through each concern, calmly explaining that they were all totally normal and offering tips and tricks to try to correct the behavior.

Then her gaze landed on him.

"Connor? Any issues you've been having as you work with Max?"

He'd planned to tell the trainer everything and beg for help—but that was before he knew the trainer had been replaced by Deenie for the day. Connor kept his expression placid, meeting her eyes with steel in his. "Nope. Everything's been great."

The effect was somewhat ruined by Max's choice of that moment to lunge sideways in an attempt to greet little Romeo.

"Great," Deenie repeated, skepticism saturating the word. "You've had no troubles whatsoever?"

Max lunged again, nearly yanking Connor sideways off his chair—but he kept his gaze locked on Deenie's. "Not a one."

Irritation flashed across her face, before she abruptly turned away, facing the opposite side of the circle. "Great. Why don't we practice some of what we've learned? Did everyone bring their training treats?"

He didn't know why he had to antagonize her. Though the most immature part of him chimed in with a snide *she started it*.

He hadn't even known who Deenie Mitchell was two months ago. Their paths had never had reason to cross. Even in a small town like Pine Hollow, he didn't know absolutely everyone—and Deenie had only started visiting regularly a few years ago. Ben had hired her to throw a princess party for Astrid a couple summers back, but Connor hadn't met her until he ran into her at the shelter when he decided to adopt Max. The day when she'd antagonized him from the first word out of her mouth, telling him he wasn't man enough to handle the dog.

It was like she'd decided to hate him on sight.

He couldn't understand it. Elinor had once joked that he was a unicorn—attractive, solvent, loyal, never married, no kids, but wanting to settle down and make babies. She'd been trying to cheer him up after Monica left at the time, assuring him there were lots of women who would claw their way over a pile of Monicas to get to him, but she'd seemed sincere. He was a freaking *catch*.

So why was Deenie so determined to hate him?

She shot him another glare—and he realized he'd been ignoring her instructions. The others were all standing, their dogs seated attentively at their sides, ready to begin whatever it was Deenie had just told them to do.

Connor cursed under his breath and stood, trying to maneuver Max into the same position as the others. He didn't need Deenie to like him. He just needed Max to learn to behave.

"Deenie?"

For the fifth time in the last half hour, Deenie realized she was staring at Connor, and she yanked her gaze away, focusing on the adorable little drool machine in front of her. And the equally adorable girl holding his leash. Astrid was so eager. So determined to train Partridge right and prove she was a good pet owner.

If only Connor had half of her dedication. Or a hundredth. Honestly, she'd settle for *any* hint that he was taking this seriously.

It really was a waste of such an attractive man that he had to be such a massive pain in the ass. Tall and muscular beneath his I-dress-up-even-though-I-work-from-home suits, with the most ridiculously sculpted cheekbones, gorgeous amber eyes, and rich golden-brown skin that somehow managed to be sun-kissed even in the middle of winter. Though she wasn't watching him because he was good-looking. Absolutely not. It was like a train wreck. She couldn't look away.

He obviously hadn't worked with Maximus once. It was aggravating—that level of disregard. That *irresponsibility*. Her parents were constantly calling her lifestyle irresponsible—but she never, *never* took on a responsibility that she couldn't follow through on. She never left anyone in the lurch.

Sometimes that meant turning down opportunities she might have liked. She would have loved to adopt little JoJo when they were doing the big push to get all the shelter animals placed into forever homes before Christmas. The sweet little papillon had wiggled her way right into Deenie's heart—but Deenie knew herself. She knew that when her travel account was built back up and things with Aunt Bitty were to a certain point, she would need to get away.

Maybe Iceland this time. Or Fiji. The wanderlust never completely went away. She'd learned that right after college, when she'd decided to take a year off to get the travel bug out of her system before she started her grown-up life—and then hadn't wanted to stop.

But she'd needed money. She'd looked for work in her chosen field, but Theater for the Very Young wasn't exactly a growth industry, and she'd found herself hosting princess parties instead. She'd loved it—and the custom dressmaking had grown out of that—but she'd still had to work as a barista or an office temp to make ends meet. And when she'd been slogging through long hours at jobs that felt like they were slowly smothering her soul, she'd started fantasizing about a trip. She'd saved up two thousand dollars—and figured out how to stretch that shoestring into a seven-week adventure backpacking though southeast Asia.

Then back to the US for another meaningless job to shore up her travel fund. Lather, rinse, repeat.

So, no, she'd known she couldn't adopt JoJo. No matter how much she might want the dog in her life. And she'd known not to commit to helping Ally at the shelter forever—just until they got the new features off the ground. Building the agility course. Arranging all the new services.

And then Deenie would go to Iceland or Fiji or Norway—wherever the discount travel options led her. And forget all about Connor Wyeth.

Though at the moment, she was finding her plan to ignore him more impossible by the second.

Ally had volunteered to work with Dolce tonight so Deenie could focus more fully on helping the others, but it was hard to help anyone when Maximus was physically dragging Connor around the room, setting all the other dogs off with his desire to play.

Connor finally put the end of Max's leash beneath the leg

of his chair, settling all six feet three inches of himself onto the chair to pin it in place. Max lay down on the floor—

And proceeded to commando crawl across the room, slowly dragging the chair, with Connor on it, toward the German shepherd, who hadn't stopped barking since Max galumphed over to him. The sound echoed off the walls, making the room seem even more chaotic.

Deenie fixed Max with a firm look and a stern "Max. Stay."

The wolfhound stopped moving, his ears pricked forward. And the timer on her phone went off.

Guilty relief poured through her with the knowledge that the training session was officially over.

Deenie quickly thanked everyone for coming and promised that the usual trainer would be back as soon as he was recovered.

When this whole mess won't be my fault anymore.

"Remember to practice," she called out over a smattering of polite applause from the pet owners—not, she noticed, including Connor. "It's all about consistency and building good habits!"

The dog-and-owner pairs began filing out—the volume in the room dropping abruptly as soon as the barking German shepherd named Elvis left the building. Ally and Ben headed toward the front of the shelter with Astrid and Partridge and Dolce, exiting the large storage room they'd repurposed as a training studio.

Elinor hung back with Dory. The merle Australian shepherd had originally come to the shelter with the name Harry, as in Houdini, since she had escape artist tendencies. Elinor initially changed her name to the more feminine Dora, as in Explorer, but that hadn't quite stuck, so she'd asked her

students to vote and ended up with the hybrid Dory—
everyone agreed fit since the clever girl seemed to sp
most of her time disappearing and wandering around to
making friends.

"You're really good at this," Elinor told Deenie as Dory
sniffed at a spot on the floor—and Deenie tried not to look
at Connor, who was tangling himself in Max's leash. "I
think I learned as many good tips this week as I did from
the Burlington guy the last three weeks combined."

"I'm not certified," Deenie reminded her. "I'm just used
to dealing with large quantities of small children. You'd be
amazed how similar the skill sets are."

Elinor grinned. "You know that's a very useful way to
look at it." As a school librarian, she probably had more
knowledge than most when it came to keeping the young
and curious—of any species—entertained.

Connor swore, his shoulder slamming into the wall as
Max took his legs out from under him. Deenie grimaced. "I
should probably go rescue him."

Elinor's eyebrows arched high over her glasses. "Have
fun," she said, the words filled with laughter.

Then she gathered up Dory and made her exit, leaving
Deenie alone with Max and his aggravating owner.

For a moment, she watched Connor wrestle with the wolfhound, the muscles in his arms and shoulders working in a
display that was annoyingly sexy. He was the worst kind of
man. Materialistic. Judgmental. Arrogant. *Smug*. Everything
polished and perfect. Everything she tried to avoid. So why
did he have to look so *good*?

She found herself glowering as she approached, irritated
with herself for enjoying the show. And irritated with him
for being here at all.

She folded her arms, watching him struggle, until Maximus noticed her standing there and sat down, his ears pricked forward, eager to please. She looked up into the striking amber of Connor's eyes and let all of her frustration show.

"Connor…why are you here?"

Chapter Four

Connor felt defensiveness creep upward, along with his shoulders. He met Deenie's glare with his own. "Excuse me?"

"What are you doing here?" she repeated. "You obviously don't take this seriously. Are you *trying* to disrupt the class?"

"I take this very seriously," he snapped, shortening Max's leash, though the dog was behaving angelically now that Deenie was two feet away.

"Really." Her eyebrows arched high, though the haughty queen look was somewhat diminished by the spiky pink pigtails.

"Maximus happens to be a very difficult breed to train. I had a DNA test done."

She rolled her eyes. "Of course you did."

"He's mostly Irish wolfhound, but there's some Great Dane in there and something called borzoi, which is apparently one of the hardest breeds to train."

"So now you're blaming genetics? How many times have you practiced with him over the last three weeks?"

"I'm *busy*," he snapped. "My job is a huge responsibility—"

"So is a dog. You adopted him. You promised to be a responsible pet owner—"

"I am," he growled. "He's fed. He's walked. He has toys to play with." *And a couch to destroy.* "He's *happy*. And if he's a little unruly, that's my business."

"Then let me ask you again. *What are you doing here?* Because if you want an untrained dog, there's no reason for you to show up. And if you want a trained dog, you're going to have to go through the effort of actually *training* him. You can't just show up at class once a month and expect that to be the magic pill. He needs consistency—"

"I *know*. I heard that the first twenty times you said it today."

"Well then, at least one of you is on his way to being trained. Repetition is *necessary*."

"It doesn't work!" he snapped, and couldn't hold her gaze as embarrassment at the admission heated his face.

Deenie's aggressive posture softened a notch. "What?"

"I tried working with him at home that first week, and I couldn't get him to do anything. I don't know what I'm doing wrong, but every time we tried, it seemed to get worse."

Her blond brows pulled into a deep V. "So you gave up?"

"I didn't give up. I just… let other things take priority."

She sighed, and when she spoke again, there was none of the usual antagonism in her voice. "Well, that's a start."

"What's that supposed to mean?"

"Just that we can't fix things if you're pretending you're perfect all the time. We can all see Max is a bulldozer, and there you were today saying everything was going just great with the training."

"Maybe I didn't want to talk about what a fiasco it is."

"Connor, everyone has their struggles. There's always a learning curve."

"Right," he scoffed. "Like the dramatic struggle to get Romeo to shake with his right paw instead of his left. At least Romeo isn't capable of decimating my entire living room in five unsupervised minutes."

Deenie's eyebrows popped up again—but this time her eyes twinkled and he had the distinct impression she was trying not to laugh. "Max threw a rager in your living room?"

"One second he's with me in my office, and the next he's managed to drag my couch across the room and there's exploded pillow everywhere. I didn't even hear him do it."

Deenie nodded, her expression surprisingly sympathetic. "With dogs and children, silence is almost always a bad sign."

"Now you tell me."

"I would have told you before, but you kept insisting you knew everything you needed to know about pet ownership." She patted Max's head, rubbing down hard on his forehead just the way he liked. He leaned into the caress, groaning blissfully. "What did you do when you found him?"

Connor shrugged. "He'd already left the scene of the crime, so I put the couch back together. The trainer said they have short memories. What's the point of yelling at him?"

"Not yelling. *Correcting.* You're teaching him with everything you do. And when you don't correct him, you teach him that it's okay."

"I just don't want to—" He broke off, not sure how to finish the sentence. He didn't want to be the bad guy. Max looked at him like he was some kind of magical god. He needed to keep that.

Understanding flashed in Deenie's eyes. "He isn't going to hate you if you give him rules. Dogs like structure. And they *love* pleasing us. Let him know what makes you happy, and he'll try to do it. And be *consistent*."

"Yes. I heard that somewhere. I just don't have time. If I could hire someone—" Connor broke off, an idea crashing into his brain that was perfect in its simplicity. "I could hire *you*."

Deenie sighed and shook her head. "Connor…"

"It's perfect. You're already so good with him. You could practice with him. Give him extra walks so he doesn't go stir-crazy when I have to work. I'd pay you." He named a sum—and when she started to shake her head again, he doubled it.

Her jaw dropped, letting him know it was too much—but if it was too much, then she'd be less likely to let the fact that she hated him keep her from taking it. He was perfectly willing to overpay if it meant he had one less thing to worry about while he was trying to make partner and find the love of his life.

"Connor…I'm not a dog trainer. For that much you can get someone professional."

"I don't care if you're certified. Elinor said it. You're better than the guy they brought up from Burlington anyway. And Max knows you. He likes you. And I already trust you."

Her eyes flared and he flushed—both of them startled by the words. But perhaps the most surprising thing was that they were true. They might be incapable of being in the same room without bickering, but if he was going to be letting someone into his house to train his dog, he'd much rather it was her than some stranger.

"Just think about it," he urged—and then played his trump card. "You know it would be good for Maximus."

Deenie glared at Connor when he laid on that blatant emotional manipulation.

But he wasn't wrong. And the money was definitely enticing.

The amount he'd named was ridiculous. And would fund a spectacular trip to Iceland. Glaciers...volcanoes...hot springs..."I..."

"You said yourself it isn't a big-time commitment. A couple of sessions a day..."

"Stop trying to sell me on it, Connor. I'm saying yes."

"Yes?" His face lit, his smile absolutely devastating. The cheekbones, the granite jawline...Seriously, *why* did he have to be so good-looking?

"With conditions," she snapped.

"Of course." He held a hand up, like he was ready to agree to anything.

She narrowed her eyes. "This is not a get-out-of-jail-free card, absolving you of all responsibility. I'm not going to spend hours training him only to have you undo everything I've done. I'll train him. I'll practice with him, but you have to agree to three practice sessions per week—supervised by me, so I can see that *you* are learning the commands and how to enforce them, right alongside Max."

"One session. I'm paying you so I have the time to focus on work."

"Two," she snapped. "Plus you continue coming to these classes—no more skipping. *And* you bring Max into a social setting once a week so I can see how you are handling him around people and other dogs."

"Two sessions. Yes, classes. And one social outing every other week." He held up a hand when she opened her mouth to argue. "I really do have a lot of work responsibilities. That's all the time I have."

She narrowed her eyes, but nodded once. "Okay. Last condition. You have to acknowledge to me that even though I will be training Max, you are still responsible for him and won't do anything to undermine my training."

"Your opinion of me is so flattering."

"Verbally."

Connor's very square jaw locked. He had a hint of five o'clock shadow across that jaw. His amber eyes were heavily lashed—a fact that became even more obvious as they narrowed. She knew, from his earlier smile, that he had dimples, but they were nowhere in evidence now.

She thought he was going to balk, but then he ground out, "I acknowledge that you will be training Max, but I am still responsible for him, and I won't do anything to undermine you. Good enough?"

"Absolutely."

Connor nodded sharply. "Great. When can you start?"

Connor, Deenie noted irritably when the obnoxious man's sleek SUV *finally* headed down the Furry Friends driveway, was a scheduler.

He hadn't wanted to leave until he and Deenie had pulled up their respective calendars and "hammered out a time" when she could come by for an "orientation session."

When she'd told him she made it a point never to use her phone's calendar app, the expression on his face had been priceless.

But it hadn't deterred him from wanting to set a time. She practically had to sign a contract in her own blood promising that she'd be at his place at seven o'clock *sharp* the next evening before he would leave.

She tromped grumpily across the gravel driveway toward the farmhouse, reminding herself of the glorious pile of cash that would be coming her way if she played by Connor's rules for just a few weeks.

The lights were on in the living room as she let herself into the farmhouse. She found Ally sitting on the floor beside the pen they'd set up for Dolce's puppies. The little spaniel had shown up at the shelter in December, too pregnant to be a candidate for adoption—and Ally's grandmother had fallen in love with her.

Rita Gilmore had moved Dolce and the puppies into the farmhouse around Christmas—declaring that they must be lonely in the shelter with so many of the other dogs being adopted—and Ally and Deenie had decided to keep them there. The shelter didn't have any full-time residents for the moment—they hadn't been actively taking in dogs while Ally's grandparents were transitioning out to the Estates— and it cut down on the heating bill if they only had to keep the barn warm when they were hosting classes.

And it was hard to resist having the adorable puppies in the house.

Dolce slept quietly in one corner of the pen as the four pups tumbled clumsily over one another. At not quite eight weeks, they were nearly weaned and would be ready for adoption in another few weeks. Two of them had already been reserved by some of Astrid's classmates, but they were still looking for homes for the others—and Deenie had to constantly remind herself that she could *not* keep a dog.

"Did Astrid and Ben go home?" she asked as she sank down beside the pen, reaching inside to offer her fingertips for one soft little nose to sniff.

"School night," Ally explained. Colby snored nearby, his jowls flapping with every exhale, the sound oddly hypnotic.

"I thought you might go with them."

"And abandon you?" Ally pretended to be insulted, but she was blushing.

"You don't have to stay here with me just because you think you should." She drew one of the puppies out and cuddled it against her chest. "The whole concept of *should* needs to be outlawed. Do what makes you happy."

"I'm *happy* to be here with you," Ally insisted—and Deenie decided not to push it.

Ally and Ben had been officially dating for five weeks now, but there were still times when they seemed as tentative as newborn foals, all awkwardness and uncertainty. They were trying to take it slow—Ally had said that so many times it was practically her mantra and with Astrid in the picture it made sense—but it was obvious they were both so gooey over one another that the idea of *slow* was a struggle. At times, it almost seemed like Ally was asking permission to be as happy as she was—like she couldn't quite believe it wasn't going to be taken away.

Like now, when she blushed and wouldn't meet Deenie's eyes as she murmured, "Actually, I kind of wanted to talk to you about that..."

"About visiting Ben and Astrid on school nights? I

officially give you permission—but only if you've already finished all your homework."

"Ha. You're hysterical."

Deenie grinned. At least Ally was looking at her again. "What did you want to talk about?"

"It's Ben's house, actually. You know how he's been planning to fix it up so they can sell and move to someplace with a bigger yard for Partridge?"

I know how he's been planning to fix it up so they can sell and move in with you.

Deenie smiled. "Mm-hmm."

"Well, they were able to get a contractor lined up to redo the kitchen starting at the end of the month—but it's going to be torn apart for weeks. Construction dust everywhere. Ben said he and Astrid would just move a microwave up-stairs and live off takeout—which they mostly do anyway, because he's the world's worst cook—but I thought that's ridiculous when we have a perfectly good kitchen and so many extra bedrooms..."

And then Ally and Ben could move in together like they desperately wanted to without the entire town talking about the fact that they were moving too fast.

Ben and Ally cared *entirely* too much about what the town thought, in Deenie's unprofessional opinion. But she supposed that made sense. Ally was a people-pleaser, and Ben was running for mayor.

Deenie beamed in the face of Ally's nervousness. "I think that's an amazing idea. This house is way too big for just the two of us anyway—and we can foist all the puppy coddling duties off on Astrid. She'll be in heaven."

Relief washed over Ally's face. "Are you sure you don't mind?"

"Why would I mind? I love Astrid and Ben."

"But you just moved in. And the whole plan was for it to be you and me, upgrading the shelter and watching *Friends* reruns."

"We can still watch *Friends*. I'm pretty sure Astrid would love it. And it's good she'll be here to help. I might not be around as much as I originally thought."

Ally's face fell. "Oh no. This is not supposed to make you feel like you can't be around. This is your place first. Ben and Astrid can stay at Connor's—his house is massive."

"Well, that'll be awkward, since I'm going to be over there all the time."

Confusion twisted Ally's face. "What?"

"Connor just hired me to train Max."

"He did what?"

Deenie didn't bother repeating herself, since Ally had obviously heard her. Instead she cooed at the puppy in her arms, confirming that he was, in fact, the sweetest of sweet babies.

"You two hate each other. I always feel like we need to clear the area to avoid collateral damage when you start sparring."

"We don't *hate* each other," Deenie argued. "It's more of a strong natural antipathy. He represents everything I detest in the world, and vice versa. But otherwise I'm sure he's a lovely person."

Ally's eyes went round. "You're going to kill each other."

"I'm barely going to have to see him," Deenie assured Ally—and herself. "And he's paying me a small fortune. Money may not be able to buy happiness, but it does buy weeks exploring the hot springs in Iceland, which is practically the same thing." She shrugged. "And I love Max."

"Okay..." Ally said slowly. "So you're just going to train his dog and then run off to Iceland?"

"I'm not going to leave you in the lurch. But once we get all the new programs for Furry Friends up and running, you won't need me anymore. And you might want the space for Ben and Astrid..."

"We aren't... they aren't *staying*... We're taking it slow."

"Sloth speed. Got it." Deenie lay on the floor, setting the puppy on her chest so he could crawl across her. "But you know you don't *have* to, right? The entire town loves you two together. No one is going to shun you if you jump in with both feet."

"We're already in with both feet," Ally insisted. "But we want to be smart about this."

"Is anyone smart about love? Is that a thing?"

Ally rolled her eyes. "What about you? Are you ever going to tell me about the dating adventures of Deenie Mitchell?"

"I'm saving them for my memoirs," Deenie joked, dodging the question as smoothly as ever. Because talking about her failures in the love department was far too depressing. "Besides, I'm not looking for what you and Ben have. More power to you, but permanence makes me squirrelly."

"You say that now, but when you meet the right person—"

Deenie groaned, "God, you sound like my mother. 'Don't worry, Nadine. You'll grow up. You'll settle down. You'll *change*.'"

Ally lay down on the floor beside her so their shoulders bumped, bringing the other three puppies to scale them with their little paws. She linked their fingers together, squeezing gently. "Don't ever change." Ally turned her head so they were eye to eye. "But if you happen to fall in love—I can vouch for the fact that it isn't the worst thing in the world. It's actually..." She flushed, her eyes going gooey. "It's actually pretty amazing."

Deenie's eyes were misty, but she grimaced, feigning disgust. "Gah. Why are people in the honeymoon phase so determined to make everyone else disciples in the cult of romance? Some of us are perfectly happy without drinking the Kool-Aid."

Ally shrugged. "I'm just saying. It's *really good* Kool-Aid."

"I'll take your word for it," Deenie said—because she wasn't going to be swilling that stuff anytime soon. The last time she'd tried, her Love Kool-Aid had been poisoned. Better to avoid it entirely. Chase what made her happy, what made her feel whole, and not the things that broke her down.

Iceland. She just needed to focus on Iceland.

She might like these moments with Ally. She might have missed having someone she felt close to. But it never lasted. People with their lives tethered to one place always got frustrated with her wanderlust eventually. It had been years since she spent any real time with her two best friends from college—who had both long since drunk the Love Kool-Aid and put down roots. She was too different. That was what she'd been told her entire life. Until it had become a badge of honor. Stay different. Stay weird. Stay wild. It was who she was. And she wasn't giving it up for any man.

Unwelcome, a memory of Connor wrestling with Max's leash snagged in her thoughts and she shoved it away.

Especially not a man like him.

Chapter Five

Connor pulled into the driveway of the Craftsman bungalow on Tuesday afternoon and frowned at the blobby brown thing that had been hung on the door. If he squinted just right, it almost looked like a groundhog—which he had to assume was what his mother had been going for, since it was February second.

He grabbed the canvas shopping bag off the passenger seat and climbed out, maneuvering around Mitch's sedan. He lifted one hand in a wave when he saw Elinor walking her dog halfway down the block.

The houses in the neighborhood weren't quite identical, but they definitely rhymed—all Craftsman style, with tidy little front lawns and big fenced yards in the back. He and Elinor had grown up two doors apart from one another, and she'd bought a house on the same street a few years back. When they were kids, they'd run in a pack—Levi and Ben, Mac and Connor, Katie and Elinor—racing their bikes up and down this street, building snow forts, and defending their encampments.

He'd thought their kids would do the same, back when

he and Levi and Ben had all been engaged at the same time. But nothing had gone according to plan.

Though Ben was with Ally now. If he could get himself sorted out, maybe part of that vision of the future could still come true.

He took the two front steps in a single stride, narrowing his eyes as he got a closer look at the groundhog blob—and realized the construction paper monstrosity was signed with his own name, in wavering elementary school penmanship.

His mother opened the door while he was still staring at it. "Happy Groundhog Day!"

He nodded toward the construction paper monstrosity. "We're decorating for Groundhog Day now?"

"Why not?" His mother tipped up her chin, challenging him to dent her enthusiasm—knowing he would instantly back down. "It's adorable. I found a whole box of your old school projects. You were so talented."

He eyed the blob. "Anyone who didn't give birth to me might disagree."

She sniffed dismissively as he stepped over the threshold. "You missed a great festival today."

"It's Tuesday. I can't just skip work because a giant squirrel is predicting the weather."

She swatted at him and pulled him down to her level for a hug. He'd gotten his height from the paternal half of his DNA—though hopefully that was all he'd gotten. He had his mother's eyes—almond shaped and heavily lashed. His strong jaw and the golden tone to his skin could all be traced back to her Tongan ancestry. He was *hers*. And she was his.

Connor gently squeezed her shoulders, careful not to press

too hard. There was nothing frail about her—and she would give him a look that could melt steel if he implied she was weak—but she was getting older, and she'd been the sun and moon in his life for too long for him not to want to wrap her in Bubble Wrap and protect her. Even when she chafed against his attempts to take care of her. She'd laughed at him when he'd tried to buy her a bigger house.

"Here." He extended the bag to her as he stepped back. "Those chocolate marshmallow hearts. I saw them when I was at the grocery."

She peeked in the bag, tsking. "You spoil me."

"I try. I can't let Mitch be the only one showering you with presents."

Not that he begrudged his stepfather's presence. The man was a teddy bear. Quite possibly an actual saint. And he made Mele Wyeth—now Mele Cooper—giggle like Connor had never heard before.

He was happy his mother was so radiantly happy. She deserved to be freaking euphoric.

It was just annoying, those little reminders that she had a life he didn't know about. Inside jokes that he would never hear. It had been just the two of them from the time he was five until she started dating Mitch when he was twenty-four. He'd gotten used to being more than just her son. She'd been his best friend, the first person he told when he had a crush on a girl or got into law school—and she still was, but it was different now. And Mitch was so freaking *understanding* about his possessiveness that Connor had never had a chance to hate the man.

His mother ignored his comment for now. "Where's Max?" she asked, looking around him as if she might have missed the pony-sized dog.

"I corralled him in the mudroom, where he can't do any damage while I'm gone."

Her pursed lips betrayed a whisper of irritation. "You know you can bring him. He's welcome here."

"I know." Connor ducked under the chandelier that had always hung a little too low in the entry and stripped off his coat.

He knew why his mom kept inviting Max. He'd started using the dog as an excuse to head home during their almost-weekly dinners. He usually *was* at least slightly worried that Maximus might have wreaked some havoc in his absence—but it was a better excuse than needing to get back to work or wanting to escape a conversation that had grown awkward.

And there was no way he was bringing his wrecking-ball mutt to his mother's house. It was one thing for Max to run wild in his place, where at least he had the space for him to bound around, and quite another for him to ricochet off the cozy clutter of his mom's house, leaving a swath of destruction in his wake and probably knocking his mother into a wall in the process.

No. The dog wasn't coming over here until he was the picture of obedience.

Which, fortunately, he would be. Just as soon as Deenie got done with him.

Connor glanced at the watch his mother had given him when he passed the bar. He still had plenty of time before he was supposed to meet Deenie, but knowing his mother and her tendency to suck him in, he cautioned, "I can't stay long. I have an appointment after this."

He expected to see disappointment on his mother's face, not the gleeful flare in her eyes. "A date?"

He groaned. *Cue the awkward conversation.* "Not a date. I'm meeting a dog trainer."

He very consciously didn't mention said dog trainer's gender. Deenie was about as far from a viable dating prospect as she could get, but his mother would hear *female*, and hearts would explode in her eyes.

She'd been incredibly understanding when Monica left, giving him "time to heal," but somewhere around six months ago she'd decided he'd healed enough and started on the "when am I going to get some grandbabies?" refrain.

Thankfully, she didn't immediately start trying to get him to marry his dog trainer.

"I guess we'd better hurry up, then," she said—with just enough drama to lather on the guilt that he'd made other plans on *her* night. "Come on through. Mitch is making his tacos."

"Taco Tuesday!" her husband bellowed from the kitchen.

The house was small enough that no one was ever out of the conversation. Connor knew that—but he still had to shove down the familiar flare of irritation as he followed his mother into the kitchen he still thought of as *his*.

He'd put in more hours at that stove than Mitch ever would, teaching himself to cook from recipe books and cooking shows, and later from websites. His mom had worked full time—first as a receptionist in a law office, and then later as a paralegal when her bosses figured out her brain was wasted answering phones and making copies. Connor had been in charge of meals even when he had to stand on a stool to reach the top of the stove. And he'd loved it.

He still cooked nearly every night. But cooking for one wasn't the same. His mom had been his first fan, and his first critic. He'd always been trying to impress her with some new flavor. Some new technique. She used to gush over *his* tacos.

Though he had to admit, Mitch's were pretty fantastic. The smells that hit him as soon as he ducked through the archway into the kitchen had his mouth instantly watering.

"Hey, Mitch."

"Connor." Mitch saluted with the tongs he was wielding. "You two relax. Dinner will be ready in a jiffy."

Heavyset and almost entirely bald with white-blond stubble sticking out from the sides of his head, Mitch had skin of near-translucent white that turned cherry red in the heat of the kitchen—like it was right now—and round, genial features that made him the obvious choice for the Pine Hollow Santa every Christmas. Though there'd been a bit of a scandal this year, since his mom and Mitch had gone on a health kick and started running over the summer, both of them slimming down—until Mitch no longer filled out the costume. But luckily some stuffing had been found and the crisis had been averted.

He wore a red apron with KISS THE CHEF splashed across it in swirling letters over his standard uniform of khakis and a polo shirt, like he was always prepared for a game of golf to break out at any moment.

"So?" His mother tugged him down at the kitchen table, one of the few items in the kitchen that wasn't a holdover from his childhood. "How was your week? Tell me everything."

Mitch didn't even glance up from the stove. He was always careful to give them space, even when he was in the same room, but that wasn't why Connor bit his tongue.

His mother had been a paralegal with all the brains of a

lawyer and a fraction of the income. He'd decided when he was nine years old that he was going to become a lawyer—and not just any lawyer, but a partner in his own firm. His mother knew all his dreams—get married, have kids, make partner. He could joke with his friends, make cracks about never wanting kids, loving his single life—but his mom would never let him get away with such a bald-faced lie. She knew him too well.

He could tell his mother anything. But he couldn't tell her that he might not make partner.

So he offered something he knew she'd be excited about instead. "I joined some dating apps."

His mother's face was incandescent. "You did? Which ones? Ella at my gym said her son liked the one that's named after a bee."

"Bumble. I think that was one of them."

He'd joined four. Even though the profiles had taken hours last night. It was an investment in his future, and it paid to be thorough.

"Are you sure you don't have a date tonight?" she asked, her eyes sparkling.

"It takes a little longer than that." Though he had been getting matches all day. He'd had to mute the notifications to get any work done.

He was actually a little nervous about checking the matches. He'd met Monica on a dating site, six years ago. It had been one that touted itself as a marriage maker, with dozens of in-depth questions designed to align you with your perfect partner.

"Be sure you use a good picture," his mother urged. "Ella said it's all about the picture."

"I'm hoping for a slightly deeper connection than one just

based on looks. Not much," he teased. "Just deep enough that I know she's after me for my money too."

His mother swatted at him. "You joke, but love isn't blind. I don't care how many of those shows they put on Netflix claiming otherwise. People fall first with their eyes and *then* with their hearts. You have an advantage, because you aren't just brilliant and kind and successful, you're also *handsome*. I made the prettiest baby in Vermont, and this is the time to flaunt it. Just try not to let on right away what a workaholic you are."

"I'll take that under consideration," Connor promised.

"What did you say you were looking for?" she asked, leaning forward on her chair. "Smart, obviously. Funny. You're much too much of a smart-ass to ever date someone who didn't have a sense of humor."

"Thank you."

"Pretty, so I can have pretty grandbabies."

"Mom."

"And *fun*." She wagged a finger at him. "You need more fun in your life. Work hard, play hard is one thing, but you've forgotten the second half. You need someone who knows how to play."

Connor bit down on the urge to argue. *Play* was the last thing he needed. His father had left when things got too hard. Monica had run off when things felt too real. He didn't need *fun*. He needed stable. Reliable. Someone who would stick with him no matter what.

Like the woman across the table, who covered his hand with hers.

His mother must have sensed his nerves because she smiled, squeezing his hand. "Those women are going to love you. How could they not?"

He didn't remind her she was biased. He knew he wasn't going to win that argument.

Mitch, with his usual impeccable timing, announced that dinner was ready, and thankfully the conversation moved away from his love life. The topic wasn't resurrected until nearly an hour later, when his mother sighed happily. "I'm so glad you're getting back out there."

"And on that note…" Connor rose, picking up his plate, but Mitch took it out of his hands.

"Go on," he urged. "I've seen you looking at your watch. I've got cleanup duty."

Connor thought he'd been subtle, but he didn't argue, thanking Mitch. He'd be lucky if he made it home before Deenie got there.

Mitch gave his mother a meaningful look, and she tucked her arm though his, walking with him toward the door. She only released him so he could shrug into the luxurious warmth of his dark cashmere-blend peacoat. It had been a splurge when he bought it after landing the job at STK, but he loved the feeling it gave him every time he slipped it on.

His mom stroked his lapel, and he couldn't tell whether she was admiring the fabric or reassuring herself that he was still there. "I just want you to be happy," she murmured, not meeting his eyes, her gaze on her hand where she was still petting his coat.

He folded his hand over hers, stilling the motion. "I am."

She looked up then, her arched brow speaking volumes about how much she believed him.

"I will be," he promised. Then he winked. "I have a plan."

"Well then, I guess there's nothing for me to worry about." Though worry still filled her eyes. "Just don't let Monica—"

"Mom." He didn't talk about that. Not even with her.

She sighed. "All right. Go meet your dog trainer. And when you're done, get on those dating apps. You don't want to keep a lady waiting."

"That isn't how it works. None of them are waiting on me. I haven't communicated with anyone yet."

"Who said I meant those girls? I meant me. I want my grandbabies while I'm still the young, fun grandma. I want to take them waterskiing without worrying about breaking a hip, so you need to get to work, young man."

"Yes, ma'am."

She hugged him one last time before he ducked out the front door—past the godawful groundhog. He didn't dare ask if the thing had seen its shadow. His lips were curved with the residual contentment of a meal with his mom when he turned on his car—and cursed at the clock that lit on the console.

He was going to be late. And he had a strong hunch Deenie Mitchell would never let him hear the end of it.

Pine Hollow was a small town that prided itself on being pedestrian friendly—which meant slow speed limits and *millions* of stop signs between his mother's house and his own. As soon as he made it to the winding country road that led out to the ski resort and his house with its vast mountain views, he pushed his SUV to the limit, hugging the familiar curves.

There was no powder-blue VW Bug sitting in his driveway, and he silently thanked Deenie for being even later than he was—until he pulled into the garage and irritation kicked in that she was late, probably on purpose, since he'd made such a point of asking her to schedule a time.

Connor climbed out of the car, closing the garage door

and moving quickly into the house—fully intending to make it look like he and Max had been waiting by the door, watching the minutes tick by—

But as soon as he stepped into the mudroom that connected the garage to the rest of the house, he knew something was wrong.

The door hung open.

And Max was missing.

The door that led to the rest of the house didn't look damaged, but the frame warped slightly where it looked like it had been shoved until the latch gave way.

And on the other side of the door... silence.

With dogs and children, silence is always a bad sign.

Connor moved toward that ominous silence, bracing himself for another couch explosion, but the living room was pristine. It flowed seamlessly into the kitchen—by far his favorite room in the entire house—but that too was undisturbed—

Except for the pantry door that hung open.

Connor approached cautiously, prepared to find Maximus passed out in a mountain of kibble, but when he stepped into the doorway, the bins where he stored the dog food were undisturbed.

Instead Maximus lay on the floor, growling something into submission as he whipped his head back and forth. Liquid sprayed in every direction. It was the yeasty smell that alerted Connor as to what, exactly, the wolfhound had gotten into, even before he saw the six-pack clutched in the dog's jaws.

Beer.

Connor was more of a wine man, but he drank beer during poker nights and always kept a few six-packs on hand for when the guys were over. He'd restocked a few days ago, carelessly setting the cans on the floor of the pantry.

Where Max had found them.

He was staring at his dog, completely at a loss as to what he was supposed to do with a drunk wolfhound, when the doorbell rang.

Chapter Six

Connor's house was obnoxious.

Deenie stood on the front step of the several-thousand-square-foot showplace and glared at the ostentatiously gorgeous door. It wasn't a normal-sized door. Of course not. Connor had to have one of those oversized wooden doors that had probably been hewn from a century-old tree, stained near-black to match the gleaming glass-chalet vibe of the rest of the house, and polished to a blinding shine.

She shoved her hands into her pockets, already annoyed—and a little surprised he hadn't whisked the door open before she could ring the bell. She'd expected him to be waiting on the porch because she was late, pointedly frowning at the massive watch he always wore.

She should have known he'd be petty. He was probably going to make her wait a minute for every minute she'd kept him waiting.

She'd honestly meant to be on time. She'd set an alarm on her phone and everything—though she had taken a particularly mature moment to stick her tongue out at it while she did.

She would have been on time. But she'd been out at the Estates this afternoon, visiting Bitty in the memory care assisted living and ... it hadn't been a good day.

That was how the nurses put it, their voices so soothing and gentle. *I'm sorry, hon. It isn't one of the good days.*

Deenie had wanted to see her anyway, had wanted to read her one of her favorite poems. And yes, part of her had believed Bitty would recognize her, that she would perk up like magic and they would talk like they used to. Laughing until their sides hurt. It happened, sometimes. Even now, when it seemed like the bad days were starting to outnumber the good ones.

But there hadn't been magic. Not today. It hadn't been a good day.

Deenie had tried to read to her great-aunt, and Bitty had gotten frustrated. She tried to talk to her about Groundhog Day, and she'd gotten confused. Eventually they'd just sat together, watching the sunset, until Bitty had turned to her suddenly and declared, "I know you, don't I? I don't think I like you."

Deenie knew those words weren't Bitty. Her great-aunt was the one person in her family she'd always been certain, down to her core, loved her exactly the way she was.

But even understanding that the words were just the whisperings of Alzheimer's, she'd still broken inside. Even as she kept her smile firmly in place and told Bitty, "That's okay. I like you a lot."

Bitty had frowned at her, struggling to place where she knew Deenie from, and Deenie had held perfectly still, trying not to interfere with any magical synapses that might be firing in her great-aunt's brain—even when the reminder on her phone had gone off. She'd stayed motionless until Bitty finally huffed and looked away—and only then had she said her goodbyes.

So, yes, she was a little late—the Estates was on the opposite side of town from the ski resort and Connor's grotesquely showy mountain chalet—but was that really any excuse for leaving her standing here on his front porch?

"Come on, Connor! You've made your point," she called, leaning on the doorbell again.

The door flew open while the chimes were still ringing through the house. Connor stood in the entrance, wearing his designer winter coat, gleaming designer shoes, and a flustered expression she'd never seen before.

Max was nowhere to be seen.

"Going somewhere?" Deenie asked, eyeing the coat. It looked incredibly soft, and her fingers itched to test that softness.

"Come in." Connor yanked the door open wider, glancing behind him. "There's a situation."

Deenie stepped across the threshold warily—half expecting Max to leap out at her like a jack-in-the-box—but the house echoed with eerie silence. Connor took her coat, only noticing he still wore his own when she gave it a pointed look. He grimaced, shrugging out of the peacoat quickly, and hanging it up before she could see if it was as soft as it looked.

"I don't want you to think this is representative. This has never happened before," Connor insisted.

"I bet you say that to all the girls."

He shot her a look—and okay, it hadn't been her best quip ever, but she was inexplicably nervous about being inside his house. The money that saturated every surface felt like a thousand eyes watching her, judging her. She'd been in places like this before. She'd grown up in places like this.

She'd never been intimidated when she went to a massive showplace house for a princess party gig or a dress fitting— for the little girls whose parents wanted them to get the full seamstress pampering experience—but something about Connor's place, or maybe just the fact that it was Connor's, made her uncomfortable.

The vaulted ceilings soared high overhead, marked by exposed beams and dark, gleaming wood paneling. Hardwood floors stretched from the towering windows in the foyer through the rooms her mother had always called the "receiving" rooms—formal dining room, formal living room complete with a wet bar—and past that in an open-concept sprawl to the kitchen and a more casual sitting area beyond.

It was open and airy, a wealth of space.

Black wrought-iron railings curved around the stairs toward the second floor. There were more doors at the back of the house, leading to untold swaths of luxury, but what really drew the eye were the windows. Jaw-dropping floor-to-ceiling windows dominated the sunken living room at the back of the house, looking out toward the mountains.

The house had all the trimmings of luxury—multiple fireplaces, including one in that back living room with a stone chimney stretching all the way to the ceiling, and a state-of-the-art chef's kitchen with an oversized range that probably cost more than she made in a year.

But Connor didn't seem to see any of it as he made a beeline toward the kitchen and the door there that hung ajar.

"I had dinner at my mother's," he explained as he walked.

"I left Max in the mudroom, because that's what I always do when I have to leave him alone, and it's never been a problem in the past. He has a bed in there. Some chew toys."

"I'm assuming that wasn't enough to keep him occupied."

"No," he admitted. "He forced the door, found his way into the pantry, and..." Connor waved her through the open pantry door—and Deenie couldn't quite contain her startled squeak of laughter at the sight that greeted them.

Max lolled on the floor in a pool of beer, surrounded by the mangled aluminum cans that had been crushed in his jaws. Alcohol matted his fur and dripped in foamy trails from his mouth when he looked up at them, his furry face wet, jaws hanging open in a happy canine grin.

"He really did throw a rager," Deenie marveled, laughter in her voice.

"This isn't funny."

"It kind of is."

Connor's full lips didn't even twitch. "Can't this stuff hurt him? I didn't have time to try to get it away from him before you arrived."

He stepped gingerly into the pantry—and Deenie had to resist the urge to yank him back to save his expensive leather shoes and designer wardrobe from the spray. One of the cans sat abandoned in the corner, sending a narrow beam of beer jetting into the air like a busted sprinkler.

"We should probably get some towels. And he's going to need a bath if you don't want him smelling like a brewery for the next week. Why don't you get that stuff ready, and I'll gather up the cans, make sure they're all intact and he didn't swallow any aluminum pieces."

Connor paled. "That could shred his insides."

"He probably didn't swallow any. And if he did, we'll

take him right to the vet. There's an emergency place in Burlington that's open all night."

"That's almost an hour—"

"Relax," she soothed. "No panicking until we know if there are actually aluminum pieces missing—and even if there are, no panicking. You'd be amazed what dogs get into. Most of it just goes right through them, no problem. Deep breaths. If it comes to a choice between taking Max to the vet to check his gut and taking you to the hospital because you had a panic attack and passed out and hit your head and are bleeding from the skull, I think we both know I'm choosing Max."

Her gory vision of his untimely head injury seemed to snap Connor out of his panic and he glared at her. "I'll get the towels."

He left, and Deenie toed off her boots before venturing into the pantry. Her purple Target leggings and Rainbow Brite socks would wash, but her favorite boots weren't quite as likely to survive unscathed. She shoved up the sleeves of her favorite white sweater—the one she'd worn for Bitty with the sparkly silver thread woven into the knit so she felt like she was wearing glitter. She'd even put glitter on her cheeks, because her aunt loved stuff like that, but it hadn't done any good. Not today.

Shoving the thought away, she focused on the now. She knelt beside Max, ruffling his damp ears.

At closer range, the yeasty beer smell mixed strongly with eau de wet dog and had her eyes watering.

"Okay, buddy, let's see what the damage is."

She was a little more worried than she'd let on to Connor—aluminum really could be dangerous—but after a quick check of Max's mouth and gums, she didn't find any cuts or signs of blood. Though she did find her hands and face thoroughly licked for her efforts. She turned her attention to the cans, moving Max's big head away when he tried to reclaim the one he'd been lapping at.

There were eight partially chewed cans total—along with four more that had somehow, miraculously, remained unmarked, though they'd broken off from the original six-pack and rolled around the pantry.

Deenie gathered up the eight, carefully checking each one for signs that hazardous pieces might be in Max's digestive tract, but all she found were neat teeth holes and bent cans. Even the plastic rings that had held the two six-packs together seemed to have escaped consumption.

"Are we going to Burlington?"

When she looked up, Connor was looming in the doorway, both arms full of towels, face pale with nervousness.

He really did love this dog.

When he'd first expressed interest in adopting Maximus, she'd tried to talk him out of it. Connor was so rigid. So emotionally repressed. She hadn't been able to picture him as having the patience for a hundred-plus-pound beast who thought he was a lap dog. She'd been sure Connor would bring him back to the shelter inside a week.

But his worry was genuine.

Deenie spoke quickly to reassure him. "I don't think he swallowed anything except beer. You might want to call your vet to see if they want you to have him checked out, but I think he probably just needs a bath. And to sleep it off."

Relief flashed through Connor—doubly potent because not only was Max okay, but because Connor's failure as an owner hadn't hurt him. He'd never even considered that Max might be able to break out of the mudroom. Or that he would go straight for the alcohol.

Connor frowned down at the wolfhound lounging in his beer puddle. "Can dogs get drunk?"

"Yes?" Deenie answered—though it sounded more like a question. "I assume alcohol affects them, but given how much is on the floor and on his fur, I don't think he probably drank more than one or two cans' worth, and he's huge, so his blood alcohol content should be relatively low."

"I have a friend who can get hammered on two beers." But Mac was an anomaly. Maximus should be fine. Maybe Connor could call Levi. Get him to come give his dog a Breathalyzer. Not exactly how he'd planned to spend his Tuesday.

Deenie came to her feet, the knees of her leggings soaked through. There was glitter on her cheekbones, and his eyes kept going back to those sparkles across her milky pale skin.

"We should get him cleaned up," she said. "And you can call his vet. See if they want us to bring him in."

Connor handed her the towels. "I've got more upstairs. The master bathtub is the biggest. I started the water running, but it takes forever to fill."

"Don't fill it more than a few inches—he'll just splash it out."

"Right." He nodded, leaving her with the towels and jogging back upstairs. He pulled his phone out of his pocket and googled "what to do if your dog gets drunk?" as soon as he'd turned off the tap.

The advice wasn't particularly helpful. Lots of *it should be fine, but watch for these warning signs*. He had a feeling he wasn't going to sleep tonight, watching Max for depression, lethargy, vomiting, or hypothermia. How was he even supposed to tell if Max was hypothermic? He'd just have to keep him warm. He had a heated blanket lying around here somewhere—Monica had always been cold.

"Connor?" Deenie's voice drifted up from the bottom of the stairs.

He came down the steps to find her holding Max by the collar at the edge of the kitchen tiles.

"I don't think we're going to be able to get his paws completely dried off. Your floors—"

"Don't worry about the floors. I can wipe up wherever he drips. We should get him into the bath. I was reading online and apparently alcohol on his skin can be bad for him—"

"He's going to be fine—he's not even weaving," Deenie assured him, guiding Max toward the stairs.

The dog bounded up them—he really did seem totally normal—and Connor and Deenie herded him into the master bathroom.

Connor had wrestled with him for nearly an hour to get him into the tub the one other time he'd given Maximus a bath, but Deenie just stripped off her sopping socks, pulled up her leggings, and stepped into the tub. Max gleefully leapt in after her.

"This thing is huge," Deenie marveled. She filled one hand with the dog shampoo Connor had left on the lip of the massive Jacuzzi tub, while he stood back feeling useless. Until she nudged the dog shampoo toward him with her elbow. "Dive in."

She was so matter-of-fact about everything, making it

look so easy. He hadn't realized how much of an exercise in humility owning a dog was going to be.

Connor stripped off his watch, rolled up his sleeves, and filled his hands with soap. He started on Max's other side, leaning over the edge of the tub. It was big enough for all three of them, but he was still wearing his shoes—which, in retrospect, might have been a mistake. He probably should have changed into the clothes he used to work in the yard, but all he'd been thinking about was getting Max into the bath before the alcohol could soak into his skin.

"Did you ever see that movie *Turner and Hooch*?" Deenie asked out of the blue. "The one with Tom Hanks and the dog?"

"I don't think so. Is it new?"

"No, it's from like thirty years ago. I used to love that movie when I was a little kid. Tom Hanks and this dog solve crimes—but the dog is a total menace. Breaking through doors and drinking beer..."

"You think someone showed Max that movie? Gave him ideas?"

Deenie grinned, massaging suds onto Max's tail. "It's possible. We don't really know much about the first year of his life."

"I think it's more likely this was a crime of opportunity. Knowing Max, he probably bumbled into the door, knocking it open by sheer accident, and then tripped across the beer just lying there. I'm pretty sure I left the pantry door open." It hadn't occurred to him Max might get out. He'd thought the worst that would happen was he would destroy the mudroom.

"That sounds likely," Deenie agreed. "Do you have a cup? Something we can use to rinse him?"

"Rinsing. Right."

Connor straightened—on a mission to find something to pour water over Max—but the wolfhound took the movement as a sign he was done and lunged toward the edge of the tub.

Deenie yelped, "Whoa, Max! Stay!" and grabbed for him, but he was slippery and got one paw up on the edge of the tub—

Right on top of the button that started the jets.

"No!" Connor shouted.

But he was too late.

He saw it all happening in slow motion but was helpless to stop it. Max's paw slapped down on the button, the motor rumbled to life, and the jets fired on, full blast.

Fun fact: When a Jacuzzi is full, the jets provide a lovely massaging pressure. But when a tub has only a few inches of water, just enough to cover the mechanism that draws liquid in, but leaving the jets themselves above the waterline, it's like turning on a fire hose. Water sprays in whatever direction the jet is pointed, dousing anything in its path.

Max twisted sideways, leaping out of the tub in a single bound to get away from the spray.

Deenie wasn't so lucky.

The deluge from the main jet hit her full in the chest.

She shrieked as the water battered her. Max's barking echoed off the tiled walls. Connor nearly tripped over the dog in his lunge toward the tub. He smacked his palm on the button to stop the jets, but the damage was done.

Deenie was drenched, head to toe, pink-streaked hair plastered to her cheeks.

"Are you all right?" he asked.

She met his eyes, water dripping steadily from her chin

onto the sweater. "You give your dog a bath in a Jacuzzi. Of course you do."

He winced, forcing himself not to look at the curves outlined in clinging fabric. "I probably should have mentioned that."

"Probably," she agreed.

He held up a peace offering. "Towel?"

Chapter Seven

Twenty minutes later, Connor had cleaned up the lake of beer in his pantry, tidied the master bath, and spoken to Max's vet, who had taken his call, even though it was after hours.

Deenie's clothes were rumbling away in the washer, along with the most beer-soaked of the towels, and they'd managed to get Maximus as clean as he was likely to get. The smell of beer and wet dog had been replaced by the smell of wet dog and dog shampoo. Maximus was mostly dry and relaxing on the couch. Connor watched him for signs of lethargy and even threw a blanket over him to make sure he was warm enough, but Max just flung it off and rolled around, playing with it. He seemed completely unaffected by the entire episode.

The same could not be said for Deenie.

She was showering off beer and dog shampoo in one of his guest bathrooms.

Connor had left her a change of clothes—the best he could find considering she was at least six inches shorter than he was and built so slim even his sweatpants would probably slide right off her hips. Not that he was thinking about those hips. Or the lithe body that had been revealed when she'd been drenched. For someone who seemed to make a point of dressing like a child playing dress-up, her figure was very adult.

He'd known she had amazing legs. She was constantly running around in those neon-bright leggings, the eye-catching color begging people to stare. But on top it was all bulky sweaters, piles of scarves, and layers of funky fabric.

Until tonight.

Not that he'd been ogling her. Their relationship was purely professional, and it was going to stay that way.

Connor carefully restacked the papers he'd printed out this afternoon and left on the island for when Deenie arrived. Nothing had gone as he'd planned, but as soon as she came downstairs, they were going to get back on track.

Then he looked up and saw approximately eleven miles of bare leg walking down the stairs beneath his Yale sweatshirt.

His breath caught in his throat and he couldn't look away.

Deenie tugged nervously on the sweatshirt—not sure whether she should be tugging up or down. She was wearing a pair of Connor's workout shorts, but the sweatshirt was so long, the shorts weren't visible. She should have picked the pajama pants—though with the way they'd been sliding down, she wasn't sure she would have made it down the stairs without flashing a lot of leg either way.

He was staring.

Deenie forced her hands away from the hem of the sweatshirt and went on the attack, like she always did when she was uncomfortable. *Deflect. Distract.* "You planned all this just to force me to wear a Yale sweatshirt, didn't you?"

His eyebrows flew up—but at least he wasn't staring at her legs anymore. "You have a problem with my alma mater?"

"I have a problem with snobs."

His kitchen was pristine—which made sense. It was likely all for show anyway. The dangling copper pots had probably never been used. The only sign that the kitchen was lived in at all was the stack of campaign flyers proclaiming BENJAMIN WEST FOR MAYOR. THE RIGHT CHOICE FOR PINE HOLLOW.

"I'm automatically a snob just because I went to a good school?" Connor said with the first evidence of real irritation in his voice. "Even if I had to claw my way there with scholarships and financial aid?"

She was being a jerk, but she didn't like the way she always felt like she was on her back foot with him. He reminded her too much of the people who always dismissed her because she didn't have a job that came with stock options and a 401(k). The best defense was a good offense, so when she was around people like that, she tended to lash out—and throw what she knew they would think of as her failings in their faces. If she swung first, their hits could never land.

But it was probably best not to antagonize the man with the checkbook.

She nodded toward the neat pile of papers he was restlessly stacking and restacking, his long fingers constantly moving. "What's that?"

He looked down at the papers as if surprised to find them

in his hands. Connor shook himself, his spine straightening subtly, though she hadn't noticed him relaxing his rigid posture until all traces of relaxation were gone.

"I drew up a preliminary contract."

Deenie blinked. "A what now?"

She'd heard him clear as day, but he couldn't be serious, could he?

"Just the basics," he said, as if it were the most natural thing in the world to whip out a stack of legalese. He divided the papers into two piles, sliding one across the island while keeping a copy for himself. "Terms, payment structure, guarantees."

"You really don't believe in playing things by ear, do you?"

Connor pointedly ignored the question. "The last page is instructions—the door code and alarm code, if you could commit those to memory as soon as possible. Ben knows both codes, and he's authorized on the security account, so if you have any problems and I'm not available, you can call him."

"You aren't planning to be here? I thought you worked from home?"

"I do, mostly, but I may be in the office more in the coming months, and I often have to travel for business. I wasn't sure how long this training would take." He shuffled through the papers. "I kept the end date vague when I drew up the schedule, but if you can let me know when he'll be trained, I can fill that part in."

"It takes as long as it takes. Some dogs learn faster than others."

A frown flickered across Connor's face. "We should probably err on the longer end of the spectrum then. Max can be…challenging." His attention remained riveted on the pages in his hands. "I have the payment schedule as a percentage on signing and another upon completion, with specific metrics stipulated as to what completion represents, but if you'd prefer weekly installments, we can renegotiate. Any additional dog sitting, dog walking, or pet care duties above and beyond the training have been itemized in section C. I didn't know your specific rates, so I did a quick internet search to see what was typical in the region, but if you feel any of these numbers are unreasonable or if there are additional duties you think might come up in the course of your activities with Max, we can revisit that section as well."

Deenie paged through the stack of documents, the words blurring. "Are you kidding me? Is this a prank?"

Connor looked up from the contract in his hands then, meeting her eyes with a *very* serious frown. If she was honest, the hyper-focused uber-competent lawyer vibe was kind of sexy—but it also made her want to run as fast as she could in the other direction.

He tapped section C. "It's best if we're clear up front. I don't like misunderstandings—especially when they can be avoided with clear communication and a shared understanding of expectations."

She was standing barefoot in his kitchen, wearing his Yale sweatshirt with her hair still damp from the shower, and he still seemed to think everything in life could be planned for with a thorough-enough contract.

"I can't train Maximus if I have to be worrying about obeying every letter of your contract. Sometimes life throws you curveballs, and you have to react."

His gaze moved back to the contract. "I have a section on unforeseen circumstances—"

"The whole thing about unforeseen circumstances is that they're unforeseen. It's right there in the name."

"But we can still be prepared. I have categories of extenuating circumstances for missed training sessions, including natural disaster, illness, bereavement—"

"Connor." She stopped him with his name, shoving the scattered pages back toward him. "I'm not signing this."

"The schedule is fully negotiable. You said you didn't have any conflicts, but if you have preferred times and dates—"

"I said I didn't have a *calendar*. Not that I didn't have a life, or that you could schedule me at your whim."

"I'm not glued to these dates—"

"I don't want dates!" The words came out a little too loud, echoing off the ludicrously high ceilings. "At the moment I'm not sure I want to do this at all."

Panic flashed across Connor's face. "But you agreed..."

"To train Max. Not to sign a contract in blood with penalties and schedules."

Relief flashed across his face, chased by something so patronizingly indulgent she was surprised he didn't pat her on the head. "There's no blood involved, I assure you."

If there'd been anything close at hand on the pristine island, she probably would have thrown it at his face. Like a rotten tomato.

She'd done a tomato show at a Renaissance fair several years ago, overacting her way through Shakespeare to the delight of the audience and dodging the produce they gleefully threw at her. She still remembered the smell. And the wet slapping noise the mushy tomatoes made when they hit. It would be *so* satisfying to throw one in Connor's face...

"Deenie?"

"Just a second. I'm throwing tomatoes at your face in my mind."

That indulgent expression returned, redoubling the urge.

"Deenie." Ugh. He sounded so *patient*. "I'm sure we can come to an agreement."

"Except you aren't listening to me. I don't do all this." She waved a hand at the contracts—which he had gathered back into two tidy stacks. "Schedules and contracts and obligations." That had been her entire freaking childhood. Chore contracts. Grade contracts. Her parents were obsessed with living up to your word. They would *love* Connor.

But she didn't have to live by those rules anymore. She was an adult—no matter how much her siblings might scoff when she called herself one.

She was creeping up on thirty years old, thank you very much, and the only person in the world she owed anything to was Aunt Bitty. The great-aunt her parents always called crazy. The one woman who had encouraged her to walk to the beat of her own drum—and the woman who had decided she wanted to fund a "scholarship" for Deenie when her parents had balked at the impracticality of a major in Theater for the Very Young.

Deenie set her jaw. "I won't commit to a set schedule. I have an aunt at the Estates. She's in assisted living, and I'm her emergency contact. I need to be able to be with her when she needs me—and honestly, Connor, this is just unnecessary. I'll come by. I'll train Max. I'll stay out of your hair, but I don't want you giving me shit about being late or being early—"

"I can't have you just dropping by whenever it's convenient for you. I have meetings, social engagements—I might not be alone."

"Right. Of course."

Deenie felt her face heating at the reminder that even stuck-up snobs like Connor had social lives. He probably had women lining up to date him. Those cheekbones, the devastating dimples, the freaking *eyelashes*. Not to mention the granite jaw and the ridiculous shoulders, all musclebound and firm. The man was *gorgeous*. Even if he did have the personality of a rock. Though that wasn't entirely fair. He could be funny at times. Just...*rigid*.

"I'll text first," she offered, the picture of reason. "Make sure it's an okay time for me to come over."

"So whenever you want to come, I have to drop everything? To confirm whether it's an appropriate time, when you could just show up on a regular schedule so I can be prepared—"

"Two seconds to send a thumbs-up or a thumbs-down emoji won't kill you. It's called compromise."

Connor's square jaw worked. "Fine. But no coming by in the middle of the night."

"I think I can live with that. How about nothing before eight in the morning or after nine at night?"

"That's reasonable." He looked down at the contracts, visibly longing to delve into them again.

Deenie wanted to take her victory and run with it, but she sighed, relenting. "Let me see section C."

By the time Deenie's clothes were dry, they'd found a reasonable middle ground. Deenie rolled her eyes the entire time, making numerous comments about wasting time, but

Connor felt more centered the more notes he scratched into the margins of the contract.

It gave him something to focus on other than her legs.

"I'll amend these and leave two revised copies here for you to sign the next time you arrive," he said without looking up when he heard her return to the kitchen after changing back into her freshly dried clothes. "If I'm in a meeting, just be sure you sign both. I'll countersign, and then you can take your copy with you."

"Lucky me." Her tone dripped sarcasm.

Technically, they should be witnessed, but Connor knew when not to push his luck. He glanced up then, relieved on a cellular level to see her no longer wearing his clothes.

It had been entirely too intimate, watching her coming toward him in his threadbare college sweatshirt, standing across from her at the island with her long legs on full display—even if he hadn't actually been able to see them thanks to the island. He'd strategically stayed where he couldn't steal a glimpse.

Unfortunately, he hadn't been able to forget what they looked like. That was the curse of his memory. It had made tests a snap and given him an advantage memorizing stacks of legal texts and case files in law school, but when he *wanted* to forget something, it always seemed to be engraved in his brain.

Like the expression on his mother's face when she'd told him his father wasn't coming back. Or the exact words on the Post-it Monica had used to break off their wedding. The curly swoops of her handwriting.

Sometimes having an excellent memory sucked, haunting him with regrets he could never escape. He almost envied Maximus his apparent amnesia—the dog couldn't remember his training commands from one day to the next, but he always seemed to be enjoying himself. Maybe that was the secret to Max's live-in-the-moment joie de vivre. He didn't remember his mistakes, so he had no regrets.

Deenie was like that. Always in the moment.

While Connor couldn't seem to *stop* remembering. It was almost enough to make him envy her.

"Thank you for coming by tonight." The words were formal as he walked her to the door, watching her collect her boots and pull a pair of hot-pink earmuffs from the pocket of her coat.

There was still glitter on her face. He didn't know how it had survived the Jacuzzi drenching and the shower. The stuff had to be three parts superglue.

"No problem," Deenie muttered—though he had the feeling she still wanted to throw him off the nearest bridge. And there were a lot of bridges around here.

She wasn't in his clothes anymore, but that weirdly intimate feeling lingered as he opened the door for her. No one had worn his clothing since Monica—and now that he thought about it, he wasn't sure she ever had. Their relationship hadn't been like that.

Not that he wanted a relationship where a woman stole his clothes. He *liked* the kind of relationship he'd had with Monica—where she'd had her things and he'd had his, and the two had stayed neatly separate. He just needed to find a woman who wanted that kind of relationship, too.

Which was what the dating apps were for. *Not* what Deenie was for, he reminded himself as she lifted a hand in a wave and headed down his front walk toward her impractical little car. At least now that they'd hashed out the details of the contract, he wouldn't have to see her every time she came to the house.

Max would get trained. Connor would get his life back on track. And Deenie would go on her way. That was exactly how he wanted it. No matter how good her legs looked.

Chapter Eight

It was cold and clear the following Saturday afternoon when Deenie ducked into the warmth of the Cup, nearly running into Margaret Winter, who was exiting with her own takeout order.

"Deenie!" The mayor's wife beamed. "I had no idea you were still in town. How long are you staying this time?"

"Oh, you know, just until the wind changes. I'm terrible at staying in one place." Margaret was sweetness personified and an old friend of her great-aunt's, so Deenie slapped on her most cheerful persona, masking honesty with a cheeky smile.

"That's what Bitty always said—the only way to get you to stand still was to glue your feet to the floor. That's why I didn't believe it when I heard you were staying for good and going into business with Ally Gilmore."

"Oh no," Deenie assured her. "The shelter is Ally's thing. I'm just helping out until she can get all the new services at Furry Friends launched."

Margaret opened her mouth—and Deenie could see the wash of sympathy in her eyes, knew exactly what she was going to be asking next...*How's Bitty doing these days? How are you holding up?*

She was excruciatingly relieved when an irritable male voice rang across the restaurant, cutting Margaret off.

"That better not be a Magda's Bakery box in your hands."

Deenie hurriedly hid the box behind her back, but Mac was already glowering at her across the counter. The owner of the Cup was famously good-natured—except when it came to Magda's Bakery.

Deenie wasn't sure what had started the fight between the owners of the two most popular businesses in Pine Hollow—she only knew battle lines had been drawn, and the entire town had taken sides.

Her aunt had been firmly Team Magda in the ongoing feud—hopelessly addicted to Magda's decadent raspberry–cream cheese croissants. Deenie had only first come to the Cup a few weeks ago to pick up an order for Ally. And in the process she'd discovered that Mac did, indeed, make the best chai lattes in town.

But that didn't mean she was going to stop bringing her aunt her favorite pastries.

"They're for Bitty," Deenie explained, still hiding the pastry box behind her back. "And all I want is a large chai latte to go. Pretty please?" She fluttered her lashes at him.

Mac shook his head. "You're lucky I like you."

He turned away, grumbling something about defiling his place—and several of the patrons gave her dirty looks for putting the man cooking their food in a bad mood.

Deenie chose not to notice their negativity, blanketing the room in a glowing smile.

The small space was crowded, as always, each of the handful of tables full. The Cup had started life as an espresso bar, but over the years it had evolved as Mac expanded the kitchen and began adding semi-permanent "specials" to the menu. Come for the coffee, stay for the food.

Well. That and the gossip.

Nowhere in Pine Hollow did the gossip flow quite so freely—which Deenie adored, even as a speculative gleam lit Margaret's eyes. The mayor's wife was still standing beside her, holding her to-go order and smiling.

"So...you and Mac?"

Deenie barely resisted the urge to laugh out loud. She freaking loved this town. One flirty glance in the Cup and everyone would be talking. Completely ignoring the fact that Deenie thrived on meaningless flirty glances.

"We're madly in love," she deadpanned to Margaret. "He's going to leave all this behind and run away to Paris with me to study under the French chefs."

A flicker of alarm flashed in Margaret's eyes at the idea of losing Mac to the French, before she realized Deenie was joking and flushed at her gullibility. "You're horrible. I almost believed you."

"Well, there was your first mistake. Haven't you heard? I'm completely unreliable."

Margaret smiled, shaking her head fondly, and the two of them chatted for a couple of minutes about Margaret's recently adopted chihuahua, Peanut, and the improvements Deenie and Ally were making at Furry Friends. Deenie made sure to project her gushing about Ally's new pet photography studio in her onstage voice so other potential customers would be sure to hear. All those years of theater training finally put to good use.

By the time she accepted her chai from Mac, everyone in the restaurant was smiling again—including Mac, who, bless him, never seemed to hold a grudge against anyone but Magda.

"If you're going to be sticking around for a bit, you should talk to Gayle," Margaret commented as she held the door for Deenie. "I'm sure she'd love some help with the spring plays."

Deenie squashed the flicker of interest. She hadn't been involved in a play in years—months of rehearsals and weeks of shows were an awful lot of commitment. "I won't be here that long," Deenie assured Margaret. "Just until we get the new and improved Furry Friends off the ground."

And until she got Max trained. And until things with Bitty got to *that point*. The one she didn't want to think about.

"Adventurous Deenie." Margaret smiled. "I'll be curious to hear where you end up next."

"So will I." Deenie grinned and said her goodbyes before starting up the hill toward the Estates, moving quickly along the familiar sidewalks.

Normally she drove out to the Estates on the far edge of town, especially when the wind was brisk like this, but today her vintage Bug had wheezed in the cold when she'd tried to start it and she'd decided to let it rest instead.

The bright green tote bag she'd bought in Thailand bounced against her hip as she walked, filled with the glittery nail polish she always kept on hand for princess parties. Maybe, if it was a good day, she'd paint Bitty's nails, just like Bitty had done for her when she was a little girl and she'd come up to visit in the summers.

Those visits had always felt so magical. Ice cream for breakfast and dancing in the rain. That was Bitty.

Deenie knew those visits had only lasted a week, once a

summer for a handful of years, but they'd felt like forever. Like freedom without limits.

The driveway to the Estates was flanked by wide side-walks, smoothly maintained for the residents using walkers and scooters. But today the cold had driven all the elderly pedestrians inside save one, a tall, angular man moving slowly down the path with a bouncy little ball of fluff at the end of his leash—a familiar little ball of fluff, who gave an excited yip and scampered toward her.

"Hello, princess!" Deenie crouched to greet JoJo, the adorable little papillon she'd fallen head over heels in love with at Christmas. The miniature angel wore tiny purple bows at the base of each tufted ear and bounced up on her hind legs, bracing her tiny damp paws on Deenie's knee even as she wriggled with happiness. "I missed you," Deenie cooed, bringing their faces close together, before smiling up at the gentle octogenarian who had adopted JoJo. "Good afternoon, Mr. Burke."

"Hello, Nadine. Don't tell me you walked all the way up here in this nasty weather."

"It isn't so bad," Deenie argued as she straightened, and Mr. Burke turned around to fall into step beside her, heading back toward the main building of the Estates.

As senior facilities went, the Summerland Estates were on the posh end of the spectrum—and the price tag reflected that, especially in assisted living and memory care—but luckily Bitty could afford it.

"You here to see Elizabeth?" Mr. Burke asked softly after they'd walked a dozen yards.

"And you," Deenie insisted, linking their arms together companionably to mask the fact that she was steadying him over a patch of ice.

Aunt Bitty and Mr. Burke had known one another since well before they both moved into the Estates—Mr. Burke into one of the self-sufficient apartments and Bitty into memory care. They'd been friends a long time—and Deenie dreaded the question she knew was coming next.

A familiar wrinkle of sympathy pulled at Mr. Burke's brow. "How's she doing?"

"She's still really good. Lots of good days," Deenie lied with a bright smile, refusing to allow even a flicker of an eyelash to betray her thoughts.

Because Bitty hated the idea of anyone knowing she was slipping away. Because Bitty had taken her friends off her approved visitors list for just that reason. Because she wanted them to remember her as she was.

So Deenie got to be the one to deny she was sick. And Deenie got to be the one to watch her fade.

Mr. Burke squeezed her arm gently, letting her know she hadn't fooled him, but he didn't press her. "I don't suppose it's any secret to tell you that you were always her favorite," he said, the words light.

"That's convenient," Deenie said, matching his tone. "She's my favorite, too."

"She wouldn't want you to put your life on hold for her," he murmured softly.

Deenie sucked in a breath, but didn't let her smile falter. "I'm not. I'm just saving up for my next trip."

Mr. Burke looked at her out of the corner of his eye, but didn't argue with her.

They approached the portico to the main building, and Mr. Burke gathered JoJo's leash in his knobby, long-fingered hands. "Will you come by for tea when you're done visiting Elizabeth?"

"I wouldn't miss it," Deenie promised.

The doors opened automatically as they approached, and Deenie released Mr. Burke's arm.

"Say hello to your aunt for me," he requested, and Deenie saw sadness reflected in his eyes.

She forced a smile. "I will."

He gave her a regal nod in farewell. "Nadine."

She returned the gesture, adding a little bow just to make him chuckle. "Mr. Burke."

Mr. Burke headed out of the lobby, and Deenie beelined to the reception area. The woman at the sign-in desk was one of the longtime employees, and Deenie chatted with her for a few minutes, asking if her pregnant daughter down in Texas had had her baby yet. Then she headed down the wing opposite Mr. Burke's.

The rest of the property looked like a country club, with patio homes butting up to the golf course and multiple shallow swimming pools for water aerobics and aquatherapy, but when Deenie turned left at the elevators, the sterile smell in the air was more hospital than clubhouse. The assisted living wing stretched out in front of her, with its own elevator up to the secured memory care floor.

She stopped again at the nurses' station at the entrance to assisted living, complimenting Negin on her lovely coral hijab and asking Carmen if her sister had had any luck getting a work visa to come to the US yet. She tried to remember everything everyone told her whenever she came to the Estates—almost as if it was her job to keep up with it all, now that Bitty wasn't able to.

Then she arrived at Bitty's suite, her smile pinned in place, ready with a wall of good cheer, the pastry box from Magda's held up in front of her—but her aunt was fast asleep, propped up in bed, her head listing slightly to one side as her breath rose and fell.

Emotion pulled at Deenie's heart. She set the pastry box on the table and settled onto the chair beside the bed. Six months ago, Bitty would have told her she was being creepy for watching her sleep. But now...

She'd been so much better last August, before Deenie had gone to New Zealand for three months. Sure, she'd seemed confused sometimes, but the change had been drastic when she got back. Her great-aunt was less and less herself these days. The spark and fire and quickness of her wit kept slipping away faster and faster now.

She knew Bitty wouldn't want her to put her life on hold, but if Deenie left now, she might miss all the rest of the good days. She couldn't imagine that.

So of course she was staying. Ally would call it a sign from the universe—the way everything had lined up to keep her in Pine Hollow, but Deenie had never been much for signs. She hated the idea of the universe running the show. She wanted to be in control of her own life. Not some amorphous force.

But she wasn't in control here. There was nothing she could do to stop this. And she didn't know how much longer she could sit and watch the person who knew her best in the world slowly fade away.

But for now she sat. And she stayed.

Chapter Nine

I s this too much glitter?" Elinor Rodriguez held up nails painted a delicate coral with a dusting of pink glitter in the polish, angling them so the sparkles caught the light.

Deenie feigned shock from her position on the other side of Ally's kitchen table. "First off, I'm insulted that you would even speak the words *too much glitter* in my presence, because obviously there's no such thing. And second—no, it looks lovely."

"Thank you." Elinor grinned, holding out her other hand for Deenie to finish. Deenie grasped Elinor's wrist to steady it, wielding the nail polish wand.

It was Deenie's third Wednesday night living at Ally's and their first impromptu girls' night.

Wednesday was when Ben and Connor had a poker night with their buddies, apparently. According to Ally, Ben usually hosted in his basement so he didn't have to find a sitter for Astrid, but lately Astrid had been spending poker nights with her Aunt Elinor—who'd been her late mother's best friend—so Connor could host in his lap of luxury.

This week, Ally and Deenie had invited Astrid and Elinor

over to the farmhouse to make use of Deenie's stash of glitter nail polish.

Ally had had all sorts of reasons it was a good idea—it gave Astrid a chance to get used to sleeping at the farmhouse so it wouldn't feel so foreign when she and Ben had to retreat there during renovations in a couple of weeks, it gave them a chance to hang out with Elinor again outside of obedience class, it made the house feel more like hers rather than her grandparents'...

Ally rationalized. She had arguments.

Deenie just thought it sounded fun.

She and Ally had first clicked with Elinor at the shelter when she'd come to adopt Dory. The elementary school librarian wore giant glasses and always had her thick, dark hair pulled back in a low, no-nonsense ponytail. She reminded Deenie of one of those 1940s screen sirens trying to pretend she wasn't a bombshell by wearing glasses, but as Deenie had gotten to know her, she'd realized Elinor genuinely wasn't conscious of her physical appearance. She couldn't be bothered. Elinor was all brain and outward-pointing energy—fixing her laser beam focus on the people around her in a way that put them on their back foot and seemed to keep anyone from noticing she was actually a knockout.

Astrid had brought her drooly bulldog, Partridge, and Elinor had shown up with her Australian shepherd, Dory—who proceeded to literally run circles around the other dogs until she finally wore down. Colby had just watched the antics of the other dogs without lifting a paw, while Dolce's puppies yapped excitedly at Dory's heels.

Then the humans had gotten down to the serious business of mani-pedis. Astrid had picked the colors for everyone, and they'd taken turns pampering one another. Laughter had slowed them down—it was surprisingly hard to apply nail polish accurately when they were shaking from giggles—but it was worth the delays.

After a while, Astrid had headed off to bed—it was a school night, after all—and Ally headed straight for the kitchen to whip up some adult beverages.

"Doesn't this seem kind of sexist?" Elinor asked, nibbling her lower lip with her slight but incredibly adorable over-bite and watching Deenie stroke topcoat onto her nails in smooth, even strokes. "The menfolk go off to play poker, and the women sit around and do their nails?"

"Does that mean you don't want your fruity, girly drink?" Ally asked, emerging from the kitchen area to wave a mango-peach daiquiri under Elinor's nose.

"Of course not. Gimme that." She snatched it out of Ally's hand with her free hand, the one Deenie was working on not even twitching with the movement. "Thank you. But don't you worry we're reinforcing some patriarchal, antifeminist cliché for Astrid by being all girly?"

Ally set down Deenie's drink at a safe distance from her elbow and retreated to the kitchen to grab her own and the pitcher for refills. "Astrid doesn't get much girly time with Ben. We may as well load her up on it."

Deenie turned Elinor's hand to finish her thumbnail. "And I can't think of anything *less* feminist than making a woman feel guilty for liking things just because they're typically feminine. Like princess dresses. Or the color pink."

Elinor's eyes flicked to her pink hair. "I didn't mean..."

Deenie grinned a don't-worry-I-don't-take-it-seriously grin. "I know. We're good. And you're done." She released Elinor's hand.

She'd long since learned to let comments like that roll right off her. She'd been called childish and immature because she played with kids as a job, irresponsible because she didn't have a "real" career with benefits, antifeminist because she encouraged girls to want to be princesses, even though anyone who came to one of her parties could plainly see that her princesses—and her princes— were all about empowerment and owning what made you happy. Even if that was dressing up in floofy dresses and twirling.

"Deenie…" Elinor's eyes were worried. "I really didn't—"

"It's fine. Don't worry. And maybe next time we'll play poker. Or blackjack. We can work on Astrid's fast math skills. Though I should probably warn you I count cards."

Elinor grinned, reaching for her drink. "Somehow that doesn't surprise me."

"Actually, I had an idea about next time," Ally said, sinking down beside them at the table. "Or maybe time after next. The last Wednesday in February? Ben can save some money on the reno if he does the demolition himself, and I thought maybe we could all get together and make it a party. Rip out the kitchen. Free beer and pizza for anyone who helps."

"Sure, I'm in," Deenie promised. "At least this way if I have to spend more time around Connor, I'll be able to take out my frustration on some cupboards."

Ally eyed her over the rim of her daiquiri. "I take it the training isn't going how you'd hoped?"

"Training?" Elinor asked.

"Connor hired me to train Maximus," Deenie explained. "And he had an actual *contract* waiting for me the first time

I went over there. It's like he has this pathological need to make everything into rules."

Elinor's eyebrows arched above her eyeglass frames. "You don't like rules?"

"I don't like stupid, unnecessary rules. Stop signs are wonderful—they have a purpose. They give us a way to share the road. But the idea that you have to have a 401(k) to be a respectable adult is just bullshit."

Ally frowned. "Connor wanted to give you a 401(k) for training Max?"

"No, he just—he's one of *those*. The there-is-a-correct-way-to-live-your-life-and-you-aren't-doing-it people. The actual training is going fine. Max is a handful, but we'll get there. He just needs patience and repetition. He can't stay focused for very long, so I'm going over there a couple times a day for little practice sessions—and honestly, I hardly ever see Connor. He's always locked in his office—but when I do see him, it's like he's silently judging me with his eyes. He's definitely got a stick lodged somewhere unfortunate. It's quite sad, really, for someone so insanely hot to be wound so incredibly tight."

Elinor and Ally's eyebrows flew up in unison.

Ally cleared her throat delicately. "So you think he's *hot*…"

"I don't *think* he's hot," Deenie snapped. "He's empirically hot. It's objective truth." Those amber eyes. Those devastating dimples. His freaking *shoulders*. "It's also objectively true that his face has frozen into a disapproving frown that makes it virtually impossible to decipher the hotness."

"And yet decipher it you did," Elinor purred.

"It's not a thing," Deenie growled. "Don't make it a thing. I have zero interest in the tall, dark, and snobby type."

If possible, Ally's eyebrows climbed even higher. *"Tall, dark, and snobby?"*

"What? What are you grinning about?"

"Nothing. I just... when I first met Ben, I called him Tall, Dark, and Cranky in my head."

"No." Deenie held up one newly manicured finger, admiring the way the sparkly teal polish emphasized her point. "This is not remotely the same thing."

For one thing, Connor was taller, darker, and much more handsome—but there was no way she was making that argument, because he was also the last man she'd get involved with.

Ally's brown eyes glinted with humor as she lifted the pitcher to top off their glasses. "I just wasn't aware you and Connor had reached the intimate little nicknames phase of your relationship already."

"Okay, ew. There's no intimacy," Deenie insisted, forcibly ignoring the whole wearing-his-clothes thing, which she *definitely* had not mentioned to Ally. "I have never called him that or even thought of him as that before this moment, and I only did it now to make a point about how awful he is. Have you seen his house? What kind of man needs his ego massaged so badly that he lives by himself in a zillion-square-foot showplace?"

"In his defense," Elinor interjected, holding her glass steady for Ally, "he didn't want to live there alone."

Ally's ears practically pricked up. "Ooh, is this about Monica? Ben said something about her and then clammed up and made me swear I wouldn't say anything to Connor, even though he didn't really tell me anything."

Elinor sipped her daiquiri. "Connor's still pretty touchy about the whole thing. Not that you can blame him."

"Okay, now you have to tell us." Deenie grasped her glass between both hands, enjoying the chill against her palms. "Who's Monica?"

"Connor would hate me talking about this..." Elinor hedged. "But if it gets you to go a little easier on him, he might ultimately thank me...or at least not kill me..."

"I really didn't know you guys were that close," Ally commented—and Deenie nearly kicked her under the table for veering off topic.

Elinor shrugged. "He's a friend. We grew up on the same street. And then I dated Levi—which sucked me into their circle even more. They're some of my closest friends."

"And they don't invite you to poker night? No wonder you were pissed about the antifeminism." Deenie glowered, indignant on Elinor's behalf.

"Well, Levi and I broke up. So." Elinor shrugged again. "It's weird."

"And Monica?" Deenie prompted shamelessly.

Elinor bit her lip—the entirely too-cute overbite on full display. "Okay, you can never let on that I told you any of this," she whispered—and they all leaned forward. "They were engaged, and she ran off before the wedding— practically left him at the altar."

"That's it?" Deenie glanced toward Ally. "Is that what you were guessing? I figured she cheated on him at least. Maybe even had a kid she tried to pass off as his, or cleaned out his bank account to give the money to her drug cartel boyfriend."

"Trust me, jilting him two weeks before the wedding with absolutely no warning was cruel enough. She didn't even tell him in person." Elinor leaned forward, lowering her voice again. *"Post-it."*

The others gasped.

"Okay, that's cold," Deenie acknowledged.

"Are we sure she wasn't kidnapped? And the Post-it left behind as a decoy?"

Deenie and Elinor turned to look at Ally, disbelief written across both their faces.

"What?" Ally demanded. "She could be out there. Desperately trying to get back to him—"

"Okay, you're too in love. You're officially banished from this conversation," Deenie declared.

"I'm not too in love. I just think if there's a *chance*—"

"She wasn't kidnapped." Elinor's voice rang with certainty. "She didn't unfriend anyone on Facebook, so all of us who had followed her because of Connor got a play-by-play of her adventures through India to 'find herself' on her feed. Unless her kidnapper faked a lot of photos over the course of several months—including the huge party her parents threw her when she returned from her 'vision quest'—then she definitely wasn't kidnapped."

Ally winced. "Did Connor see all that?"

"I don't know." Elinor shook her head. "I hope not. He doesn't talk about it. *Ever.* Right after it happened, everyone in town wanted to tell him that we were on his side—but he would walk out of the room as soon as anyone even started to say her name."

"Oh God, the whole town," Ally groaned. "I hadn't even thought about that part."

"He was totally blindsided," Elinor explained, no longer bothering to whisper. "Monica was like the female Connor— all plans and organization and achievement. They were this golden couple, perfectly in sync, and then she just vanished one day. Connor already had that house. He bought it for the two of them to start a family in, and then he was alone."

Deenie sat silently, staring into the depths of her mango-peach daiquiri and weighing the likelihood that she was, in fact, a horrible person.

She'd been mentally throwing daggers at Connor since the day they met. Seeing in him all of her parents' dis-approval and her older brother's dismissal reflected back at her. She'd judged him by his clothes, by his lifestyle—by all the things she hated to be judged by.

Yep. Probably a horrible person.

"And that isn't even the worst part."

Deenie cringed, not sure she wanted to hear the worst part, but now that the seal had been broken, Elinor was spilling all the secrets.

"It was right around now when it happened. They were supposed to get married on Valentine's Day last year."

"Poor Connor," Ally murmured.

There were two people in every relationship, and rigid Connor probably wasn't the easiest to live with—he prob-ably had a contract for how often they would cuddle—but even as Deenie tried to mentally blame him and take the side of the free spirit who had toured India, it was hard to get behind the woman who hadn't even had the courtesy to dump him in person. A Post-it was harsh.

"Speaking of Valentine's," Elinor said in the most awkward transition possible. "Do you and Ben have any big plans this weekend?"

Ally blushed. "We just started dating. Neither of us really wants to put any pressure on things. We're just going to spend the weekend doing campaign stuff and getting things ready so Ben and Astrid can come over here once the renovation starts in a couple of weeks."

"You sure about that?" Deenie asked lightly. "Astrid

seemed awfully concerned about making sure your hands were photo-ready."

At Ally's blank look, she held up her own hands, waggling her left ring finger.

Shock flashed across Ally's face. "I'm sure she doesn't think...Ben and I haven't even *talked* about...I mean, we talk about that stuff, but it's always in the future. The someday. Next year or the year after. We haven't even been seeing each other two whole months. You don't think he's talking to Astrid about it already?"

"She's probably just hopeful," Elinor assured her. "Kimber Kwan's oldest sister got engaged at Christmas, and I'm sure she's shown Astrid all the photos. Two ten-year-olds might be planning your engagement, but I doubt Ben is ring shopping yet. He's too busy with the campaign and the house. You're probably safe."

"It's not about safe," Ally protested. "It's not like I don't want him to propose. I do. But it's so *soon*—"

"And Valentine's Day is horribly clichéd anyway," Deenie added, reassuring. "I'm sure he has better taste than that."

Elinor stared into her drink—and Deenie wondered for a moment if Elinor wanted to be proposed to on Valentine's Day. But Ally spoke before Deenie could remove her foot from her mouth.

"What about you two?" Ally asked. "Any Valentine's rituals to observe?"

Elinor was still buttoned up, so Deenie shrugged. "I'm almost never around for Valentine's, so I don't really have any rituals. That's the benefit of avoiding long-term relationships—no pressure about the big milestone holidays."

Elinor glanced at her, then murmured, "Yeah. No plans here."

"We should do Galentine's Day," Ally enthused. "An extra girls' night."

Elinor and Deenie exchanged a look of perfect under-standing. One that silently agreed that coupled-up friends were the absolute worst when they were trying to cheer you up about your lack of romantic prospects.

"I don't know," Deenie pretended concern. "Ben might be disappointed if he drops by to pop the question and you're out with us."

Ally rolled her eyes. "Stop. He's not proposing." But there was an extra flush on her cheeks that said if he did, she wouldn't say no.

Deenie felt a brief, unwelcome stab of envy.

Not that she wanted to couple off for a clichéd happily-ever-after, but no matter how much she pushed away the trappings of normal and the "usual" milestones of life, she did get lonely.

Ally and Ben fit together so well. They accepted each other. And she wasn't sure she was ever going to find that.

She didn't know where that person was, the one who would never try to change her, the one who would never make her feel like she was less-than or not good enough because she didn't always live her life the usual way. She'd never found anyone she felt just *got* her. Even the rebels she dated seemed to have their own sets of rules for rebellion.

Everyone wanted her to be a certain way, and whenever she hit that inevitable point where she felt like she was being shamed into changing, she ran. Ever since college. When she'd almost changed herself for a guy. When she *had* changed, only to realize she didn't recognize herself anymore.

She joked with Ally about being the worst at relationships. She joked about escaping the jaws of long-term relationships. Because it was easier if she said it—then it didn't hurt when other people said it. She could pretend it was intentional. That she didn't want someone to love her just the way she was.

She could smile and pretend her life was perfect. That it was the *exact* life she wanted. That she'd chosen to be a gypsy, and it wasn't just a way of making lemonade out of romantic lemons.

And most days, it was a choice. Most days, she *did* think her life was pretty damn perfect.

But days like Valentine's? Those were the worst. On those days it was *normal* to be coupled off. And Deenie had never quite been able to pull off normal.

Chapter Ten

Valentine's Day was the worst.

Connor punched the Stop button on his treadmill, ignoring the repetitive pings from his cell phone as he crossed his basement gym to the weight bench. Maximus sprawled on the floor, snoring his jowl-flapping snore. Connor had taken him on a massive winter hike this morning, but while Maximus was sleeping off the exertion, Connor's restless energy only seemed to keep climbing.

He freaking hated Valentine's Day.

He'd liked it, once upon a time. He'd been the guy who always showed up with roses and chocolates and made the other boyfriends look bad.

But then Monica had wanted to get married on Valentine's Day. She hadn't seemed to mind that it meant a Friday night wedding. Connor had been a little worried about the inconvenience to their friends and family—but they'd gotten a discount on the ballroom at a luxurious resort, so he'd told himself it was *romantic* rather than inconvenient.

Until Monica canceled the wedding after it was too late to get their deposits back. Then it was just inconvenient.

He'd gotten truly blackout drunk for the first time in his life on the day that would have been their wedding day. This year he'd decided he was going to take a healthier approach. He'd cooked himself an egg white omelet for breakfast and even tried a kale smoothie—which had been vaguely disgusting. He'd taken Maximus for a little two-hour nature walk, then come home determined to get a couple hours of work done.

But his phone would not stop making noise at him, and he hadn't been able to concentrate.

Friends checking to see how he was "holding up."

His mom "just touching base."

Grating pity in every character of every text.

And then there were all the messages from the dating apps.

He really should have known better than to join right before Valentine's Day. People had expectations on February fourteenth.

He'd had his first date last Thursday. Valentine's was on a Sunday this year, so the whole weekend was out for casual, get-to-know-you first dates, but he'd thought Thursday would be far enough away from V-Day to be safe.

He'd been wrong.

When he'd met his date at the Burlington restaurant they'd agreed on, he'd known instantly that he'd made a mistake. The lighting in the cheerful bistro had been lowered. A candle burned on every table, alongside a skinny vase with a single red rose that waved in his vision every time he looked across the table. Cherry-red heart appliqués filled the windows. And the only item on the menu was a "Lovers' Special for Two."

The waiter asking them how long they'd been together could have been funny—his date had tried to make light of the awkwardness—but Connor hadn't been able to laugh with her.

Instead, he'd found himself comparing every move she made to Monica.

She was allergic to shrimp—but was she? Monica used to claim to be allergic to things she didn't like so waiters would take her requests for substitutions seriously. If this woman was like Monica in that way, would *she* run off two weeks before their wedding?

The date...had not gone well.

And he'd been avoiding his matches all weekend.

What was he supposed to say? *Sorry. Bit of a weird day for me. I was supposed to get married a year ago today.*

He'd tried silencing his phone—but then he worried that his mother might actually need him, and he'd only lasted five minutes before he'd turned the sound back on. Telling himself she would call if it was urgent, he'd ignored the repeated buzzing of text notifications, but work simply wasn't happening, so he'd headed down to his basement gym.

Working out cleared his head. It made him feel calm and in control, like his body was a well-maintained machine. And yes, he may have become a little obsessive about his physical fitness when Monica left, but endorphins were cheap therapy.

The doorbell rang during his fifteenth biceps curl.

Connor set down his weights and swiped the sweat off his face and neck with a towel.

It had to be his mother. Or Levi. They tended to be the most determined when it came to checking up on him.

Connor jogged up the stairs—Maximus was so fast asleep, he didn't even lift his head.

He had a speech already prepared about how he was *fine*,

everything was *fine*, but when he yanked open the door, it wasn't his mother on the other side. And it definitely wasn't Levi.

He blinked. "Deenie."

Her leggings were yellow today—no pink, no hearts, thank God—and her pink hair stood up straight from the crown of her head in a spiky ponytail like Pebbles' from *The Flintstones*.

Her gaze dropped to his sweaty T-shirt and workout shorts. "Hey. Sorry. I tried to text, but you didn't answer, so I thought maybe I'd ring the bell? Is this a bad time?"

It's Valentine's Day, the worst freaking time of the year. He barely stopped the words from popping out of his mouth. "Uh, it's fine. I was just ignoring my phone. But Max is asleep. I took him on a long walk earlier, and he's been out cold since we got back."

"Oh. Right." Her gaze flicked down to his chest again. "Sorry. I shouldn't have just dropped by. I was just looking for an excuse to get out of the house. Ben and Ally are all gooey over there. I already spent all morning at the Estates—"

"Come on in."

She blinked, visibly startled by the offer, but when he stepped back and held the door wider, she barely hesitated before stepping across the threshold.

He didn't want to talk about Monica or Valentine's Day or feelings—but Deenie didn't know about any of that. She was safe.

And she was nothing if not distracting.

For nearly two weeks he'd been trying to avoid the distraction of her in his house. The sound of her voice cooing praise to Maximus. The little traces of glitter that seemed to crop up everywhere. The sight of her in those neon leggings. He'd hidden in his office, getting virtually nothing done whenever she was under his roof—but at least Max was getting better. He seemed to have a grasp on *sit* now, and *down* was definitely improving.

Connor could put up with glitter appearing in unexpected places around his house as long as the dog learned to behave.

He took Deenie's coat and hung it before leading the way to the kitchen. "You want something to drink? Or we can wake Max up if you want to work with him."

"He won't focus as well if he's groggy. And water would be great."

He grabbed a pair of glasses, filling them from the filter pitcher in the fridge, and handed her one. "So Ben edged you out at the farmhouse?"

"It's not like that. I like having him and Astrid there. I just feel like a third wheel. Or fourth, I guess, since Astrid's there. But it's just today. I'm sure it wouldn't be awkward if it weren't *Valentine's Day*."

She said Valentine's Day like others might say Root Canal Day, and Connor hid his smile behind a drink of water. In his pocket, his phone buzzed again, and he grimaced, pulling it out and setting it facedown on the counter.

Deenie eyed it curiously. "Why are you ignoring your phone, Connor Wyeth?"

"Valentine's Day," he explained. He was going to leave it at that, but then heard himself blurting out, "I'm on some dating apps."

She looked as surprised as he was that he'd admitted that. He hadn't talked to anyone but his mother about his plan to get back out there. Everyone else would assume it had something to do with Monica and their would-be anniversary. He was sick of everyone thinking everything he did was in reaction to her—even if he'd inadvertently trained the entire town to think that by overreacting since she left.

But Deenie didn't know any of that. And she made no secret of her dislike for him, so he didn't have to worry about her smothering him with sympathy.

"Everyone I've matched with seems to think today is the perfect day to strike up a conversation."

His phone buzzed again, and Deenie's blond eyebrows arched. "And you've matched with a lot of women?"

"I'm on a lot of apps," he said defensively. "I didn't know which ones were popular in the area right now. I haven't been doing this much over the last few years, so I wanted to cover my bases."

Deenie grinned, her bright blue eyes sparkling with eager interest. "Exactly how many online girlfriends are we talking about?"

"They aren't girlfriends. They're *matches*. Potential future romantic partners."

"Uh-huh. How many?"

"I don't know." He did some quick math in his head, tabulating the numbers from the various apps. "Seventy?"

Deenie choked on her water. "Okay. Wow. Though I guess I get it." She waved her glass at his body, the gesture making his cheeks heat. "Is that why you're working out? Getting fit for your harem?"

He shoved down the unwelcome pleasure, not wanting to be flattered by her matter-of-fact appreciation. "Exercise clears my head."

"And I'm sure it has nothing to do with your vanity."

His eyes narrowed. "I'm not vain." Yes, he liked looking

good. He liked when a woman gave him a double take or blushed just from meeting his eyes. It was satisfying, knowing he could have that effect. But he wasn't *vain*.

"Oh, come on. You love being a specimen. Admit it."

He raised his left eyebrow. "So I'm a specimen?"

Deenie rolled her eyes so hard her entire face moved in a circle. "You're obviously sexy. Don't get a big head. You're still a dick."

"Thank God. For a second there, I thought you'd been abducted by aliens and replaced with a clone."

"Ha-ha."

Her tone was dry as dust—and he had to fight a grin. He kind of liked exchanging barbs with her. It made him feel sharp, alive—and a million miles removed from the guy Monica had walked out on.

On impulse, he asked, "You wanna hide out here for a while? Maybe order a pizza and stream some super-gory horror movie?"

"You don't have big Valentine's plans with any of your harem?"

He groaned. "God, no. Valentine's is way too romantically loaded for a first date. Why do you think I'm ignoring my phone? Total communication blackout. That's my policy."

Deenie's brows pulled down into an angry *V* that looked out of place on her cute little pixie face. "Wait, so you're not going to respond to anyone? You're going to ignore all those single women who are just trying to give themselves the *hope* of a future connection on one of the most romantically obnoxious days of the year?"

"That's why I'm not responding. Everything is blown out of proportion on Valentine's Day. I need to manage expectations so no one reads too much into a simple hello."

"Because women are all bunny-boiling crazies who will latch on to you with our desperation tentacles if you come into range on February fourteenth?"

"Because I'm only going to be marrying *one* of them, and I want to minimize the emotional collateral damage with all the others."

Deenie's eyebrows flew out of their *V* into high arches. "You're getting married now?"

His cheeks burned. "Eventually. That's the goal." He couldn't believe he'd blurted that out. "The whole point of dating is so I never have to do it again. If I'd been thinking, I would have waited to set up my profile until after Valentine's, but I'm kind of on a deadline."

And if he was honest with himself, some of Ben's sappy romantic BS had rubbed off on him because he'd thought there was a chance one of the profiles would jump out at him and he'd *know* and he'd want to spend Valentine's with the One.

Only there hadn't been a One. There had been seventy maybes. And the more times he matched, the more overwhelming the idea of finding his One became.

"Do you have to marry by a certain date in order to inherit a massive estate from an eccentric uncle?"

Connor blinked, bringing himself back to the present with a frown. *"What?"*

Deenie grinned at Connor's startled expression. Poleaxed. That was such a good word. "I read a lot of romance novels, and that's pretty much my favorite trope. The whole forced marriage of convenience—only then they realize they're madly in love with one another, and the person they married in order to get the money actually means more to them than the money ever could, and they all live happily ever after—usually with the money."

Connor shook his head, baffled. "That doesn't really happen in real life. I'm not sure inheritance clauses like that are even legal."

"Technicalities. I choose to believe it could still happen. So what's the deadline?"

He grimaced—which made his dimple pop for a millisecond. "It's not really a deadline. I just…I'm trying to make partner, and it looks better from a work-life balance perspective if I can bring a girlfriend with me to some of my firm's events over the next couple months. To show that I'm more than a workhorse."

"You hired me to train your dog because you couldn't take fifteen minutes away from your computer to do it yourself, and now you're trying to find a wife to prove you aren't obsessed with your job?"

"It wasn't that I *couldn't* take the time. Hiring you was more efficient. You're an expert."

"I'm hardly an expert—"

"It's working. He's already improving. And it leaves me able to focus on my other goals. And I'm not just looking for a wife for work. I'd already decided it was time."

"How convenient for love to happen on your schedule."

"Love always happens on schedule," Connor insisted. "It's not a fairy tale. Real love, lasting love, is about finding someone you're compatible with and working every day to develop your bond. It's a choice—and it happens when we choose it. And if I need to choose it quickly so I have a plus-one for charity fundraisers and work events, that's my business."

"Wow, Connor, you're such a sappy romantic."

"I'm not saying there isn't romance—chemistry, attraction, that thunderbolt feeling the poets get so excited about—but that's lust, which is important, but doesn't sustain. Compatibility sustains."

Deenie grimaced. "You have a checklist, don't you? Characteristics you're looking for."

His expression was a flashing neon sign screaming YES. "Knowing what you want is important. Knowing what matters to you and what you're willing to compromise on can expedite the process by eliminating the obvious dealbreakers."

"You seriously found seventy women who check all your boxes?" With as long as his checklist probably was, she was amazed he'd found one.

"I haven't had a chance to discuss all the items on my list with each of them yet," he admitted. "And some things are easier to determine in person. Verbal chemistry. Communication style compatibility. Whether they spend the entire date checking their phone or actually engage with another human—"

"Maybe her best friend is nine months pregnant and she's waiting for the news that she needs to rush to the hospital."

"In which case, I would hope that my future wife would explain that to me. I don't think it's too much to ask to have dinner with a woman who actually believes in eye contact with something other than a device."

Deenie realized they'd been holding eye contact as they argued, both of them leaning across the island toward one another. She rocked back on her heels and forced her gaze away. It landed on his cell phone as it vibrated again.

She frowned, glaring at the offending device. "I still say you have to respond to some of those women. Not all of them. Just your top five. Don't be the dick who ghosts them on significant holidays only to pop up like nothing happened when there are lower emotional stakes. You owe your future wife that, don't you think?"

Connor pursed his lips. Then, reluctantly, "That might actually be good advice."

"See? I'm not totally useless."

"I'm aware of that. But I'm still not going out with any of them today." He caught her eye again. "Pizza?"

For some reason she wasn't ready to leave. "Yeah, okay. And the goriest slasher movie we can find."

Chapter Eleven

Maximus woke up before the pizza arrived.

Connor had jumped in the shower while she was ordering, and he reappeared at the same time as the dog, smelling entirely too good—Connor, not Maximus.

"Hello, puppy," Deenie cooed at Maximus, to keep from openly drooling over his owner.

Connor's grumpy scowl fell into place. "He's not a puppy. The vet thinks he's two."

"He'll always be a puppy. Won't you, baby?" Deenie gushed—which inevitably led to a pointless argument about what qualified as a puppy, but at least it distracted her from the desire to ogle Connor.

Since delivery took forever out by the resort, Deenie took the opportunity to run Max and Connor through their paces together—doing one of their agreed-upon supervised practice sessions. Connor complained that she was correcting him more than Maximus—and he wasn't wrong—but when she explained that *he* was the one in charge of the practice session, not Max, Connor snapped his mouth shut and actually listened.

It didn't go as badly as she'd thought it might. Tomorrow at class, they might not be nearly as disruptive.

When the pizza arrived, Deenie and Connor settled on the couch in his media room with a slice each. Max tried to jump up between them to share, but Deenie stopped him with a noise in the back of her throat and had him lie at their feet instead.

Connor stared at her like she'd just turned water into wine.

The movie they picked was moderately awful, but Deenie quickly learned a valuable fact about Connor.

He was a closet heckler.

At first it was just irritated grunts every time one of the characters said or did something particularly idiotic, but by the time they'd finished the pizza and Maximus had wheedled his way back up onto the couch in between them, his head on Deenie's lap and his hind legs sprawled across Connor's, Connor had graduated to grumpy editorial comments.

Deenie pressed her lips together, irrationally entertained by Connor's disgust. He seemed to take all the flaws in the film—and there were many—as a personal affront. And his irritation was kind of adorable.

"Why?" he snapped suddenly, loud enough to startle the snoring Maximus. "Why would you go *back inside* the house? The car is sitting right there. It's *right there*. Just drive away!"

Deenie couldn't quite suppress her snort of laughter.

Connor's burning gaze landed on her, as hot as if she herself had written the screenplay in question. "You think this is funny?"

Giggles rippled up from her chest. "Yes?"

Her laughter held a mirror up in front of him, and his

rage face fell away, replaced by self-awareness. His dimple flashed in a self-deprecating grimace. "I get annoyed when it doesn't make sense."

"I noticed."

"But seriously, why? Why would anyone go back into the house?"

"Because they need fifteen more minutes of movie and the bad guy hasn't been killed by the heroine yet? It's much less dramatic if she drives away and calls the cops to come handcuff him."

"It's *irrational*."

"Let me guess. 'Irrational' is one of your dealbreakers. On your romance checklist."

"It's not a romance checklist," he argued. "I just think it's important to know what you want. Oh, God, *seriously*?" he shouted at the screen. "Pick up the knife! The *knife*!"

"Have you been banned from many movie theaters?" Deenie asked.

"I don't go to the movies," Connor answered without taking his eyes off the screen. "It's a waste of money. I can see the same movie right here with my own popcorn and my own soda at a fraction of the price, and I don't have to wait in line or drive all the way to the nearest multiplex. Why would I do that?"

"Because it's fun? Because being in an entire theater full of people when we're all laughing and crying together reminds us that we're part of a larger shared human experience? Because by the time things come out on DVD, all the good parts have been spoiled?"

"I'm never on social media, so I don't have to worry about spoilers."

Deenie blinked and wondered if that had always been

true or if it had been in reaction to his ex posting pictures of her adventures.

"You don't have any vices, do you?" she asked. He was always so *controlled*. Though that wasn't necessarily a bad thing. The control he exhibited in his workouts evidently did a body good. Right now he was sprawled in sweats on the other end of the couch, and the man made it work. "Do you actually drink soda and eat popcorn?" He seemed more like the my-body-is-a-temple type.

"No, but I think I have some in the pantry if you'd like. Mac brings all sorts of random crap over for poker night."

"Ah, yes, the famous poker nights."

Connor glanced at her out of the corner of his eye. "Famous?"

"Ally was telling me about them. It sounded like a big deal. Heavy on the testosterone."

"It's just a tradition. One we're trying to resurrect. Part of my New Year's resolution plan." He reached out to rub Max's belly. "Along with adopting this guy, making partner, and finding my wife."

He said it so casually. As if everyone just sat down and decided one day that they were going to get married. How strange it must be to live in Connor's world.

"I've never really bought into the whole New Year's resolution thing," Deenie commented idly as the heroine attempted to sprint up a flight of stairs with a killer grasping at her ankles. "If you're actually resolved to do something, why do you need a specific day of the year to tell you to do it?"

"It gives you an excuse to take stock. Though if I'm honest, mine turned into more of a Groundhog Day resolution. I got busy in January and let myself forget about all my holiday plans. *Shoot him!*"

The actress on-screen stubbornly refused to comply.

"That's exactly what I'm talking about," Deenie argued. "People make all these big plans instead of actually *doing* things. You always promise yourself you're *going* to, but then you never do. It's like all the people who tell me how much they envy me because I was able to go to Paris or Thailand or whatever place was on their bucket list— most of whom could afford to go tomorrow if they really wanted to, but they'd rather stay home and make plans than *do* it."

"*Thank* you!" Connor shouted as the heroine finally emptied a gun into the villain and reached for a conveniently placed hatchet to finish the job. "You can't exactly say I'm just making plans. I'm being proactive now. I joined those dating apps. I've already had my first date."

"Oh?" Deenie felt her spine straightening and told herself she was just curious. She could never be jealous of Connor. "How'd it go?"

He paused, listening to the dialogue as the heroine stood over the decapitated baddie. He finally shook his head, grunting, "Not good." And it took her a moment to realize he meant the date, not the dialogue.

"No?" There was zero reason she should be perked up by that thought. She couldn't be less interested in dating him herself, and she no longer despised him enough to want him to wind up miserable and alone. She should be rooting for all his dates to succeed. "What happened?"

"It was just awkward."

"Some people are nervous on first dates—"

"It wasn't her. It was me. I just kept..." He huffed out a breath as the credits rolled and he could no longer pretend to be watching the movie. "I had a bad breakup, and now I feel like I'm braced for warning signs that these new matches might be like her. Anything they have in common feels like a red flag—but then if they don't have anything in common with her, it seems like they have nothing in common with me, and you can't make a life without common ground. My ex and I made sense, and our breakup made no sense, so now I feel like I can't trust myself."

Sympathy tightened her chest. "Give me your phone."

Connor's brow pulled into a frown. "What? No."

"Let me vet your matches. You don't trust yourself. So let me play matchmaker. At least if something goes wrong, you'll have someone to blame."

Connor paused for far longer than he probably should have, rolling the idea around in his head, before finally shaking it. "No. Hard pass."

Deenie shrugged, unoffended. "Suit yourself."

That was one of the things that made it so easy to be around her. Neither of them cared what the other thought of them, so they weren't sensitive. He didn't have to watch his words or pretend he wasn't the kind of guy who shouted his frustration at on-screen stupidity.

It had been surprisingly fun spending Valentine's Day with Deenie.

Of course, the alternative was having Max as his Valentine.

"Are you at least going to reply to a few of them? Trust me, being the guy who chats with them every day leading up to Valentine's Day and then mysteriously vanishes on the day is probably not the look you want."

"I know," he growled. "I just don't know what I'm supposed to say."

"Just say something. Silence is the worst. It lets our baggage fill in the gaps—I guarantee you at least five of them will be convinced you're on a date with someone else, and there will be one who thinks you're married."

He eyed her, from her pink Pebbles ponytail to her knowing blue eyes. "Do you date? I never see you with anyone."

"Happily single. Uncoupled by choice. My preferred method is expiration dating—only going out with someone when you know you have a firm expiration date, like a flight back to the States, to keep you from getting too attached. No disappointment, no unmet expectations. Just fun. But I have listened to all my friends in the looking-for-forever dating trenches, and, as I said, I read a ton of romance, which is all about relationships and the inside scoop on what's going on in the female mind. You should try it. Unlimited access behind enemy lines."

"I hardly think this is a war. And I don't have time to read."

Deenie gasped. "That is the saddest thing you've said to me yet. And you have said some mighty sad things, Princeton."

"Yale," he reminded her.

"Po-tay-to, po-tah-to."

Max groaned, stretching and descending from the couch to go flop on his bed, leaving Connor and Deenie to regain the feeling in their legs. Deenie instantly tucked her yellow-legging clad legs up on the couch and turned to face him.

"Okay, who are your favorites?"

"My favorites?"

"Your favorite matches. Come on. Work with me here. Who do you like?"

He held up a hand to stop her. "I don't need a coach."

"Clearly you do if you were going to just *ignore* your entire harem until Valentine's Day was over."

"It isn't a harem."

"Okay, your *matches*. Who are the front runners?"

He glared at her, but his glares had never intimidated Deenie, and she just smiled back at him, pink and glittery and impervious to his moods. "Fine," he growled, and began rattling off names. "Sarah, Ashley, Piper, Jennifer, Noor, Ashley—"

"Ooh, you must really like Ashley. You mentioned her twice."

"Actually, there are two Ashleys. Well, three, but the ones in my top tier are Ashley from Stowe and Ashley from New Hampshire."

Deenie's eyes widened delightedly. "You have three Ashleys. This is even better than *The Bachelor*. Okay. What do you like about the Ashleys in the top tier—I knew you would have tiers, by the way. Like Ashley from Stowe. Why do we like Ashley from Stowe?"

He grimaced, but played along. Only a fool refused help when he needed it, and Connor could admit he wasn't at the top of his game right now. "She's thirty-four, so not a child. That's important. Doesn't smoke or do drugs. Drinks socially, but not excessively—"

"Who's going to admit to drinking excessively in a dating profile?"

She had a point, but he continued as if she hadn't spoken. "Doesn't have children, but wants them. Never married, but wants to be. Similar income bracket—"

"So you don't have to worry that she's only after your money."

He frowned. "So I know we have similar goals and values."

"Cash is king?"

"Security and financial stability are important. And knowing I won't have to argue with my wife about money and reckless spending habits is important to me."

"Just because she makes a lot doesn't mean she never spends beyond her means. I barely make anything, but I'm one of the most fiscally responsible people you'll ever meet."

"I find that hard to believe."

Deenie smiled, all teeth. "I'm sure you do. I can't believe they actually tell you how much money she makes."

"Not all of the sites do. Do you want to hear about Ashley or not?"

She spread her hands. "By all means."

"She's a real estate agent, so moving to Pine Hollow wouldn't preclude her from having her own career—"

"Awfully presumptuous to assume she would move in with you."

"I'm not assuming anything. I'm just trying to anticipate future obstacles." When Deenie didn't keep arguing, he pressed on. "All of her profile photos are classy. Elegant. Charity events, sporting events, a family picnic with a cute baby nephew to show her maternal side—no bars, no cleavage shots. Professional. Polished."

"She sounds *great*."

He frowned. "I never know if you're being serious or not."

"No one does," she declared cheerfully. "It's part of my mystique. So what kind of Valentine's message did Polished, Classy Ashley send you?"

"No." Connor shook his head, rejecting on an instinctive level the idea of sharing his attempts at online flirtation with her. It felt too uncomfortable. Too inappropriate. "I'll send something—I promise—I won't ghost them on Valentine's, but I don't want you Cyrano-ing this. I've got it."

Deenie shrugged, unconcerned by his refusal. "Suit yourself."

"I am actually good at this, once I get my rhythm."

Deenie snorted. "That's what she said."

"Really?" He glowered. "Very mature."

"Maturity is overrated. Everyone acts like being grown-up is some badge of honor, but it's just another way of judging people. I know I look younger than I am, but I'm turning thirty this year, and everyone still treats me like a child."

"You don't have to dress like you raided a kindergartner's closet." He reached out, flicking a lock of pink hair that had escaped from the ponytail.

"So because I like bright colors and sparkly things, I must automatically be irresponsible? That's bullshit. Enjoy what you enjoy." She shifted on the couch—like she'd been doing all night, adjusting, fidgeting, the little movements constantly snagging his attention.

"You can't sit still, can you?"

"What's the fun in that?"

"Life isn't just about fun."

"It isn't all about work, either. Fun is a necessary component, and people who don't know how to have any should be more appreciative of those of us who bring the fun."

"I know how to have fun."

"I noticed. By heckling. *Very* mature."

"I don't heckle."

"Of course you don't." Deenie's smile was angelically patronizing.

Connor glared. "I just have a hard time ignoring irrational characterization."

"This may come as a shock to you, but *people* can actually be irrational. Especially when they're scared or stressed— and I have a feeling being chased by an ax murderer might be kind of stressful."

"I'd just like to watch one horror movie where the protagonist is good in a crisis."

"I think those are called 'action movies,'" she said, complete with air quotes. "Films where the protagonist is a badass fully equipped to deal with whatever the villain throws at them. Like *Die Hard*. Or *Alien*."

"You're saying incompetence is a tenet of the horror genre, and a movie stops being horror if the protagonist isn't an idiot?"

"I'm *saying*," she argued, "that being a person who doesn't have an arsenal in their basement and has to defend themselves against a supernatural horror using only the skills and tools everyday people would have is a common element of the horror genre. The reason you get so offended by the incompetence of the protagonist is because we are supposed to see *ourselves* in that character of the horror film—whereas I somehow doubt most people watch *Mission Impossible* looking for themselves. In an action movie, we're looking for a hero who is barely human, he's so cool and collected in a crisis— the sharpshooter and kung fu master with the coolest gadgets, who never breaks a sweat and banters with the girl—and who probably has major sociopathic tendencies because he's able to function no matter how many times a beautiful woman is murdered in front of him to raise the emotional stakes."

She made a good argument, but Connor wasn't about to concede defeat. "Relatability is one thing. But presenting the everyman like they have to be incompetent to be relatable is insulting to your audience."

"Or complimentary. Designed to remind us how much smarter we are. We want to believe *we* would survive the movie, so if we're smarter than the person who finally gets the killer, we like it. We're smug. That's why you keep watching horror movies, even though they drive you crazy, right? So you can feel smarter than everyone?"

He gave her his most over-the-top arrogant smirk. "I always feel smarter than everyone."

Deenie laughed. "Yeah. I've noticed that about you."

For a moment they just grinned at one another, and Connor realized how relaxed he was. How comfortable in his own skin.

He hadn't felt that way very often lately. He'd always had a rock-solid idea of who he was, but over the last year, when he wasn't looking, that had started to feel like it was slipping away. Like he was no longer the person he'd always thought he would be. He'd wanted to get that sense of self back— hence the plan to get his life back on track. But somehow, sitting here arguing with Deenie, a person he couldn't have less in common with, he'd found that feeling again.

Maybe it was having to defend himself to her that made him feel more present, but whatever it was, it felt good. And he wasn't ready for her to leave when she finally broke eye contact and stood up.

"I should probably get going. You have a lot of matches to reply to."

"I'm glad you came by," he said, standing as well. "This was fun."

"It was," she agreed, sounding moderately shocked. He would have been insulted, but he was as surprised as she was.

"Of course we'll never do it again."

"God, no," she assured him, with mock horror at the idea that made him grin.

Maximus stirred himself to walk to the door with them, and Connor snagged his collar to keep the dog in place as he opened the front door for Deenie, letting in a gust of cold air. The sun had set, and the night was still outside. A full moon hung low in the sky.

With anyone else it would have been romantic.

Deenie just shrugged on her coat and ruffled Max's ears. "See you soon, puppy," she promised the dog, not even glancing at Connor until she stepped out onto the front porch and the moonlight caught the pink highlights in her hair. The look she shot him was wry. "See ya round, Princeton."

"Yale."

"Uh-huh. Good luck with that harem."

He didn't watch her go, shutting the door and retreating to the kitchen to busy his hands tidying up the pizza boxes. He'd thought they would have leftovers when he'd seen how much she had ordered, but he'd underestimated exactly how many slices a woman as willowy and bird-boned as Deenie could put away. There were only ragged bits of crust left, which he tossed into Max's dish to be immediately scarfed up.

The kitchen was back to its usual immaculate state within minutes—and Connor had no more excuses to ignore his phone.

He scrolled quickly through the messages—like ripping off a Band-Aid. Most of them were perfectly innocuous.

Wishing him a good day, sending Valentine's greetings. Some with GIFs or emojis. Nothing worth hiding from all day. He'd been blowing the day out of proportion in his head.

But he still didn't know what he was supposed to say back. He didn't want to say too much. Didn't want to get sucked into a conversation. Not tonight. Maybe he could just say "Happy Valentine's Day" and leave it at that.

He was usually confident when it came to women, never worrying about saying or doing the wrong thing, but he seemed to have forgotten how to be carelessly charming.

His phone buzzed with a new text while he was still dithering.

Deenie.

He immediately opened the message when he saw her name. It was a GIF of candy hearts—like the kind he used to get in his Valentine's basket in first grade—spilling out of a box and doing a conga line. Connor grinned—and a second message popped up.

You could always send this to your harem.

Connor blinked. It was a good idea. Cute. Light. But still contact.

Safe.

He sent back a thank-you, copied the GIF, and opened the first dating app.

Chapter Twelve

Deenie's phone rang when she was climbing out of her car at the Estates the next morning. The weather had turned after the crisp, clear Valentine's night, and an icy drizzle brought the gray day to a new level of misery. She ducked back into her car to hide from the rain as she fumbled for her phone.

When she managed to fish it out of the depths of her bag and saw the caller ID, she hesitated.

She loved her sister. She really did. But nine times out of ten, Deenie came away from their conversations with an emotional hangover that lasted for hours, and she wanted to be at her best for Aunt Bitty.

But Kirsten almost never called her. It had to be something important. Their parents were getting older…

Deenie quickly tapped to connect the call. "Kirsten?"

"Deenie Baby!"

Deenie had long since stopped bothering to cringe at the old nickname. Her brother and sister, at eight and six years older than she was, respectively, had given her the nickname Deenie at birth—or Teenie Weenie Deenie, since she'd been so small—but when the Beanie Baby phenomenon hit, they'd latched on to the new version.

Her siblings had gone off to college when she was still so young their idea of who she was had gotten frozen at the Deenie Baby stage. And it didn't help that by their metrics of what it was to be an adult, she'd never actually grown up. No "real" career. No mortgage. No 401(k). No serious *adult* relationships. It didn't matter that she was pushing thirty. She was still Deenie Baby.

"You'll never guess what happened," Kirsten gushed, her voice that high-pitched talking-to-a-small-child voice she always seemed to get when she talked to Deenie. "Todd proposed!"

"Uh...wow. Congratulations!" Her sister had been dating Todd for a couple years now. She should have known this was coming. Especially since Valentine's Day was exactly the kind of clichéd proposal her sister would adore.

"You aren't even shocked, are you? Everyone I've told so far is all, 'About time!' Especially since I nearly broke it off when he didn't put a ring on it at Christmas, but can you blame me? Two *years* of dating? At our age? What was he waiting for? But it turns out it was Valentine's Day! How romantic is that? Now we'll always remember how it happened."

Because most people forget their proposals. Deenie forcibly swallowed down on the snark that wanted to come out. "That's so great."

"It won't be a long engagement. My biological clock waits for no man. We're thinking summer. June. July at the latest. And of course you'll be in the wedding. You have to promise you'll be here. None of that jetting off to swim with dolphins in Bora Bora or whatever it is you do."

"Oh. Wow. Are you sure you want me in the wedding?" It took all she had not to ask her sister if their mother had blackmailed her into making Deenie a bridesmaid. Or hell, maybe flower girl. At times it definitely felt like Kirsten thought Deenie was eligible for that role.

"Of course, silly! You're my only sister. You have to be in the wedding party."

Why? Because people will talk? "I wouldn't be offended if you didn't want me..."

"Do you not want to be one of my bridesmaids?" Kirsten asked in the same tone most people would use for *Do you really want to murder cute innocent little puppies, you monster?*

"Of course I do. I just...I want your day to be perfect."

And if there was one thing Deenie's family had always made clear to her, it was that she didn't fit inside their definition of perfection.

"Deenie Baby. Honey. It will be. But only if you're there."

She sounded sincere—and Deenie felt like even more of a brat for questioning her.

"We'll be having an engagement party on March sixth. Eight p.m. at the Lodge. Put it in your calendar right away." Kirsten's tone as she continued was brisk, businesslike. She probably had a checklist in front of her of topics to cover.

Announce engagement—check.

Make joke about nearly dumping Todd—check.

Summer wedding (biological clock, ha-ha)—check.

Member of the wedding party—check.

Engagement party save the date—check.

"I'll see if I can make it," Deenie hedged.

She'd been able to avoid invitations to most family events over the last few years—backpacking through New

Zealand for three months tended to be an excellent excuse to miss birthdays and anniversaries—but she'd made the mistake at Christmas of telling her family that she'd be staying in Vermont for the next few months. She was only an hour away.

"Deenie," Kirsten scolded.

"Okay, I'll be there. I'll make it work."

"Excellent!" Kirsten chirped. "I can't wait. Bye, honey!"

Deenie sat in her VW, staring at the sheen of drizzle on her windshield, the dismal day suddenly fitting her mood to perfection.

She wasn't upset Kirsten was getting married. Her sister sounded far too elated for Deenie to be anything but happy for her. Kirsten and Todd were well suited—almost too similar. Their relationship might be an echo chamber, but they would never argue.

She *wanted* Kirsten to get what she wanted. But seeing her family...that was complicated.

She loved them. And she knew they loved her. Which was why they were always trying to help her. To guide her. To show her how to be more like them.

She'd long since learned they were never going to see the world the way she did. But she could only keep a smile on her face and withstand their well-intentioned criticism for so long before she felt the need to run away to Iceland or Ireland or Indonesia to get back on an even keel.

But this time...March engagement party. June wedding. Bachelorette parties and bridal showers and dress fittings—would she be expected to do all of that? Would she be expected to stay the whole time?

There was plenty to do at Furry Friends, and she'd wanted to spend the extra time with Bitty while there were still any good days left to be had, but the idea of staying in Vermont until *June* made restlessness crawl up the back of her neck. She rubbed at it, shoving away the panic.

She was already late for visiting hours.

Deenie ran from her car to the portico in front of the main entrance, her head ducked against the chill of the rain. It slithered down her collar, and she shivered as she shook herself like a dog beneath the overhang.

Today, Suzie Keep, the Estates' volunteer dance instructor, was minding the sign-in desk, and Deenie paused to ask her how her grandmother was faring. They chatted for a few minutes before Deenie made her way to assisted living, stopping again to visit with the nurses.

When she arrived in Bitty's room, her great-aunt was staring out the window at the gray day. She seemed to spend most of her days weather watching lately. She'd never been much for television, and the nurses reported that lately she had trouble following the storylines. But she loved music, loved the radio, and the SiriusXM radio Deenie had brought her was playing hits from the forties and fifties as Bitty stared into the rain.

"Hi, Aunt Bitty," Deenie announced cheerfully as she entered. Her bag was stuffed, as always, with things to show her aunt, some that might spark her memory and others just to have something to talk about if it was one of the bad days when it felt like she was talking to herself.

But today, Bitty looked up, and a wide, familiar grin spread across her face. "Deenie!"

Relief flashed through Deenie so keenly that tears instantly filled her eyes, and she smiled even wider to conceal them.

"Can you believe this weather?" Deenie asked as she bent

to hug her aunt, the feeling of Bitty's arms closing around hers making the tears fight even harder against her efforts to keep them at bay.

"Pissing rain," Bitty declared with disgust. "Did I ever tell you about the first time I went to Paris? Rained like this the entire damn time. All those people gushing about how *magical* Paris is, and all I got was rain ruining my good shoes. What kind of magic is that? Now, *Rome*. That was the real magic."

Deenie settled into the chair beside her great-aunt to listen to her describe the light in the piazzas and riding around Rome on a moped, feeling just like Audrey Hepburn in *Roman Holiday*. She listened as the stories blended into memories of Monaco. Deenie had heard almost all the stories before—but the new details felt like treasures, and she hung on every word.

Bitty had been in the crowds on the streets of Monte Carlo the day Grace Kelly married Prince Rainier. That had been Deenie's favorite story when she was a little girl—and the beginning of her princess obsession. Deenie had even flown to England for the royal wedding when Will married Kate, skipping classes and missing an exam to be there, but some moments only happened once, and she'd been part of it. Just like Bitty had when she was nineteen.

Her great-aunt had grown up during the war, all of her earliest memories shaped by that time, and where it had made her sister, Deenie's grandmother, cautious and risk-averse, it had made Bitty want to leap into adventures with both feet, to take big bites to enjoy the flavor of life. She'd been the redheaded stepchild of her generation, just like Deenie was the odd duck in hers.

She'd never married. She'd seen the world. She'd learned to sail and to fly a plane before it was common for women to do any of that. She'd filled her brain to the brim with memories—and they were still there, even if she couldn't always reach them.

Deenie listened to her until she trailed off over an hour later, cocking her head.

"You didn't come here to listen to me yammer."

"That's exactly why I came here," Deenie assured her. "But I do also have news. Kirsten got engaged."

Bitty's pale blue eyes flared in shock. "No! Little Kirsten? She isn't old enough." Fog flickered across her expression. "Is she?"

She's older than I am, Bitty. Deenie kept the correction silent. She'd learned that they only made the confusion worse. She simply assured her great-aunt in her gentlest voice, "She's old enough. She's very excited."

"Oh good. She's such a dear little thing. I always figured she'd settle right down. Now, Deenie, on the other hand. Not my wild child." Bitty shook her head with a fond smile that held zero recognition that Deenie was sitting right next to her.

Tears clogged her throat, but Deenie just patted her great-aunt's hand. "I should be going. You must be getting tired."

Bitty nodded, her eyes rheumy. And Deenie hugged her again, holding on as long as she could.

It had been a good day. A *great* day. They'd had longer together—*really* together—than they usually got. But that didn't change the fact that Bitty was slowly becoming less and less herself. These might be the last good times.

So no matter how much it might chafe to grit her teeth and smile through an endless gauntlet of wedding events, Deenie would do it.

She had to stay. Because leaving would be letting go. And she wasn't ready to do that yet.

Chapter Thirteen

W hy did I think running for mayor was a good idea?"
Ben groaned, standing to one side of the stage
where he would soon be debating Tandy Watts for the honor
of governing Pine Hollow.

"Because you have a pathological need to solve every
problem you see, and it drives you crazy to think of four
years of watching someone else mess things up?" Connor
provided helpfully.

Townspeople cluttered the aisles of the theater, calling
greetings to one another and stopping to exchange gossip
before the town hall debate was set to start. The set for the
upcoming community theater production of *A Midsummer
Night's Dream* provided an unusual fairy forest backdrop
for the two lecterns set up downstage, but it certainly wasn't
the strangest setting for a Pine Hollow town event Connor
had ever seen.

Nearby, Astrid stood with Partridge, who was wearing a
bow tie and listing against Astrid's shin, while Ally wove
through the crowd, passing out BEN WEST FOR MAYOR
buttons like the one Connor had pinned to his chest.

Somewhere in the crowd, Deenie was doing the same thing, but Connor forced himself not to look for that telltale flash of pink.

In the week since Valentine's Day, things had shifted between them. He found himself drifting out of his office more and more when Deenie was training Max. Apparently all it took was sharing one awful slasher movie for him to be perfectly comfortable with the pink-haired trainer in his house.

They didn't always talk. Sometimes he just watched her work, oddly gratified when Max gave her fits—though she was infinitely patient with him. He'd realized as he watched her that she'd make a wonderful mother, calm and patient but firm. Not that he cared what kind of mom she'd be.

She was an object in motion, and she was going to stay in motion. He had no desire to try to catch her, but he'd found he liked the distraction she provided in his workday. He'd thought the breaks would negatively affect his productivity, but he was weirdly energized and more focused after her visits, getting more done this week in spite of them.

Maybe he *had* needed a little more work-life balance.

When they did talk, it was easy. Casual. He thanked her for the tip about the candy hearts—which had gone over surprisingly well and sparked a few fun conversations with his potential mates. She asked after his matches—whom she had taken to calling the Ashleys, regardless of what their names were. But mostly they talked about Max.

She'd encouraged him to bring Max to the debate tonight, as one of their contractual public events, but ultimately agreed that it would be too long to expect the dog to behave, and the result would be a little too bull-in-the-china-shop. Especially when they were both there to support the candidate.

Who was currently looking a little green.

"I always do this." Ben shook his head, staring but not seeing the crowd in front of him. "I overcommit, biting off more than I can chew. I was looking forward to being done with the council, and now what? I want to run it for another four years?"

Ally appeared at Ben's side, beaming and squeezing his arm encouragingly. "We're all out of buttons. Lots of supporters here tonight. You ready?"

"He's spiraling," Connor told her.

"The election is in just over two weeks, and we're ripping out my kitchen on Wednesday," Ben groaned. "We still haven't managed to empty everything out of the cupboards. Astrid has teacher conferences while we're living out of suitcases... Why did I think this was a good idea?"

Ally instantly sobered. "The contractor said they'd have the renovation done before you're sworn in, but that isn't what this is about, is it?"

"Everything okay?" Deenie joined them, glancing between them.

Ally didn't even look at her. "Ben, they're going to pick you. You saved the shelter and replaced the roof on the community center and did a thousand other things for this town. Everyone knows that."

Deenie hooked her arm through Connor's, gently tugging him toward the front row. "Come on, Mac and Astrid are saving seats." She waited until they'd moved out of earshot before adding softly, "He's been like this all weekend. I had no idea he wanted to be mayor so badly."

"He's always put a lot of pressure on himself," Connor said, counting the seats in the front row to make sure there was room for their whole group before moving toward one.

"He's not the only one, Mr. I Must Make Partner at All Costs."

He glared, folding himself onto the chair. "That's different."

"If you say so." She flopped onto the chair next to his, before immediately twisting to look around, waving to someone behind them.

She had glitter on her neck, a streak of it running from behind one ear down to her collarbone. A sparkling accent of the sleek length.

He jerked his eyes off it irritably. "Why are you always covered in glitter?"

"I had a princess party this afternoon." She met his eyes, absently touching her neck when he glanced down the sparkly streak. "It's like sand. It gets everywhere."

"Has it occurred to you that you might use too much?"

Her eyes flared with mock horror. *"Blasphemy."*

She glanced past him, nodding toward the edge of the stage. "Looks like the candidate has his game face on now."

Connor followed her gaze. Ben looked ready to storm the castle, Ally continuing to give him a pep talk. Still watching them, Connor lowered his voice. "How are things with the lovebirds? You know, you're always welcome to hide out and watch horror movies when they get too gushy."

"Be careful. I'll take you up on that. Though not so much to escape the gushing as to avoid being conscripted into helping again. We spent most of yesterday doing runs back and forth between the farmhouse and Ben's place, bringing over 'just the essentials' for him and Astrid."

"The offer's open. In fact, I've been meaning to ask you—I found out on Friday I have to go down to New York on business for a few days in March. Would you be willing to stay at the house and pet sit for me?"

"Yeah, of course."

"I'd pay you."

Her eyes sparkled as she grinned. "Good thing we have that section C."

"You joke, but you're grateful now, aren't you?"

"*Grateful* is a strong word."

He opened his mouth to argue, but the sound of a microphone crackling cut him off as Delia Winter, the current mayor, took the stage and called the meeting to order.

Connor had attended the debates before, but always in the back of the auditorium, ready to slip out when things got too ridiculous—but this was Ben, so he was stuck in the front row until the bitter end. He was braced to be annoyed, but when Tandy Watts started comparing the council's refusal to let her build a fifty-foot climbing wall in her backyard to communist Russia, he made a low sound of disgust in his throat, and Deenie started shaking.

He glanced over to see her studiously not looking at him, staring up at the stage and fighting a smile, though she whispered under her breath, "I should have known you'd even heckle a debate."

And suddenly he was fighting laughter himself.

For the rest of the debate, whenever any of the townspeople asked questions, or Tandy Watts herself said something completely ludicrous, he and Deenie would slide glances at one another. He barely got through it without laughing—and they both came to their feet, cheering for Ben when he made his closing statement.

As the candidates left the stage and the attendees began to shuffle toward the door, Connor stretched out his spine and checked his watch. "Only an hour and a half. That was almost reasonable."

Deenie's eyes gleamed up at him. "I thought you were going to break when Darren Wells asked which candidate would support his petition to stage a reenactment of a pirate invasion."

"We live in *Vermont*," Connor growled. "There are no pirates here. There have never been any pirates here."

"Yes, but it's his *dream*."

He glowered. "You're awful."

"Worse than Darren Wells?"

He opened his mouth to tell her that yes, she was, in fact, much worse than Darren Wells, because Darren was an innocent and she knew exactly what she was doing— but then a new voice entered the conversation, stopping his heart in his chest.

"Connor! Aren't you going to introduce me to your friend?"

His mother stood at his elbow, smiling delightedly at Deenie.

"Mom." The word came out choked. "I didn't know you were here."

Deenie's eyes widened at the word *Mom*.

"Of course I'm here. The whole town is here." She apparently decided she was done waiting for Connor to do the honors, because her next words were to Deenie. "I'm the mother. Mele Cooper. Call me Mele. I saw you two whispering up here all through the debate. I had no idea Connor was seeing anyone!"

Connor nearly choked on his own saliva. "Mom, no, it isn't like that—"

"We aren't together," Deenie chimed in. "This is purely professional."

"Deenie's my dog trainer. Remember? I told you I hired someone to help me with Max?"

"But you didn't tell me she was so pretty!" his mother gushed, utterly undeterred by their protests. She linked her arm with Deenie's, guiding her up the aisle toward the exits at the back of the theater. "So, Deenie, tell me all about yourself."

Connor had carefully avoided mentioning Deenie to his mother. There had been a chance, since he'd started dating via the apps, that his mother wouldn't see his dog trainer as a romantic prospect, but he hadn't wanted to risk it. His mother was a force of nature, and he didn't want her applying that force anywhere near Deenie. But now he could only watch as she set sail up the aisle, tugging Deenie along with her.

Mitch was already waiting outside, where the parking lot was a zoo. His mother continued whispering with Deenie as Mitch joined them. "Connor. Did your mom have a chance to talk to you?"

"About what?" he asked. "I think she got distracted grilling Deenie on her life story, even though *we aren't dating*." He raised his voice on the last words and his mother shot him a look—but she finally released Deenie's arm.

"I'm just getting to know Deenie," his mother protested. "There's no harm in being friendly."

"Uh-huh."

His mother swatted at him and tugged him down to her level for a hug. "I like her," she whispered in his ear while she squeezed his shoulders.

After five seconds? He stopped himself from scoffing, instead trying one last time to dissuade her. "We aren't together. She's an employee."

"Mm-hmm." She released him, stepping back with a Cheshire cat smile. "Good night, you two."

Connor watched his mother walk away with Mitch—and waited until they were out of earshot before curiosity got the better of him. He turned to Deenie. "Okay, what did she say to you?"

Deenie grinned, entirely too entertained for his peace of mind. "She said your genes were too good not to be passed on to another generation, and you'd make a wonderful father."

He groaned. "Subtlety isn't her strong suit."

"Subtlety's overrated."

It was a phrase he'd heard his mother say so many times he nearly did a double take. He'd never expected to see similarities between his mother—a woman he admired above all others—and Deenie—a woman he'd kind of dismissed as ridiculous. But they both went after what they wanted without an ounce of shame.

He cocked his head. "She didn't really say *good genes,* did she?"

Deenie grinned. "Technically, I think it was something about her making the prettiest baby in Vermont and you owing her adorable grandchildren as soon as possible."

"That sounds like her."

"But she did say you'd be a good dad. And she's not wrong."

"About the dad part? Or the pretty part?"

Deenie rolled her eyes. "You know you're pretty. Stop fishing." She fell into step beside him, heading across the parking lot to where their cars were parked side by side. "How are things going with the Ashleys?"

"Fine. Good."

Her eyebrows popped up. "*Fine?* Wow, Connor, don't get all sappy on me. Save the sonnets for your dates."

"It's just taking longer than I want it to." He shoved his hands into his pockets. "Lots of chatting. Setting up coffee dates and meeting for drinks, but so far..."

"No sign of the One?" She leaned against her car and he stood with her, waiting for Pine Hollow's version of rush hour to clear out. "Has it occurred to you that the stricter you are with what you think you want, the more likely you are to be disappointed? And to miss out on what life is throwing at you."

"I'm not being strict. And there are some promising prospects," he admitted. "Corinne from Burlington seems pretty great. She's been traveling for business, but we're going to meet up when she gets back. She really liked the candy hearts thing."

"See? I'm always right." Deenie preened, but it seemed exaggerated, like she was using the flash of her smile to hide something. "That's great, though, that you're hitting it off."

"It is. But I just found out about a fundraiser I have to attend next Saturday for work, and I don't know how I'm going to find my person before then. Unless I make it a first date, and that seems much too risky."

"There are always escorts."

Connor glowered. "Helpful."

She beamed. "I try." She shoved off the side of her VW she'd been leaning against, reaching for the door. "See you tomorrow?"

"Looking forward to it," he drawled, making her grin. But the strange thing was...he was.

Chapter Fourteen

The sledgehammer swung in a high arc, smooth and strong, and crashed into the kitchen island, shattering the ugly tile countertop into dozens of pieces. A cheer went up—and Deenie jerked herself out of her admiration of the muscles that had propelled the sledgehammer, adding her voice to the cheer.

Connor had shown up toting his own sledgehammer, gleaming so perfectly clean it looked like it had never been used. Ben and the other two members of their poker group—Levi, the chief of police, and Mac, who owned the Cup—immediately started teasing Connor about being too delicate for manual labor and not knowing which end of the sledgehammer to swing, which was laughable considering the way his shoulders stretched the fabric of his T-shirt and made him look like a walking power-tool commercial.

Connor had quickly proven he knew exactly how to use a sledgehammer. And the man looked *damn* fine swinging it. All those muscles bunching and straining...

"See something objectively attractive?" Elinor asked

sweetly—and Deenie yanked her gaze away from where it had fallen on Connor. Again.

"What? No. I was just lost in thought."

"Thoughts about someone empirically hot?"

Deenie rolled her eyes and grabbed a discarded cabinet door from the debris on the floor, shoving it at Elinor to shut her up. The cabinets were too old and worn to be donated, and were already in pieces, thanks to Levi and Mac ripping them off the walls.

Deenie, Ally, Elinor, and Astrid had all taken turns swinging the hammers—Elinor's blow actually took out the entire vent hood in a single swing—but ultimately they decided it was wiser to stay out of the line of fire. The kitchen wasn't big enough for all of them, and those who weren't wielding sledgehammers and crowbars had been toting the pieces between the kitchen and the dumpster temporarily parked out front.

A fine coating of dust hung in the air—and clung to the biceps revealed by Connor's snug black T-shirt. Deenie forced her eyes off the feast, grabbed an armful of debris, and headed out the front door.

"Hey!" Ally called cheerfully from her position chucking things into the dumpster. "There you are. I thought you got lost in there."

"She was busy ogling Connor," Elinor provided cheerfully.

Deenie shot her a death glare—grateful that it was just the three of them out on the front lawn at the moment, and that Mrs. Fincher, the next-door neighbor watching them work, had retreated inside. She did *not* need that rumor going around town. "I wasn't ogling anyone. I happen to have a lot on my mind right now."

"Princess party drama?" Elinor asked.

Deenie frowned, studying Elinor, unsure whether she was being mocked. Elinor never seemed judgy, but she was one of those people who checked all the boxes her parents loved—advanced degrees, retirement plans, home ownership.

"Is it your great-aunt?" Ally asked, pulling her attention away from Elinor.

Deenie had finally caved the night before and admitted to Ally she had an aunt out at the Estates. Ally had been worried that the chaos since Ben and Astrid had arrived was driving Deenie out of the house—which it was—and the only way Deenie had been able to reassure Ally without admitting how much time she'd been spending at Connor's had been to claim to be visiting Bitty all the time.

"She's always in the back of my mind," Deenie said, then tossed out the real reason she was distracted—at least the one she was willing to admit. "But it's actually my sister. She got engaged."

Kirsten had called again today to make sure Deenie was definitely going to be at her engagement party.

Ally's face creased with instant worry. "Do you not like the guy?"

"No, he seems fine. Honestly, I barely know him." Deenie grimaced. "I barely know her. We've never really been what you'd call close. She's the responsible one. The perfect one. If we had an easy out—like I was halfway around the world—I'm sure she'd jump at the excuse not to invite me to most of the wedding stuff, but I'm here, an hour away, and excluding your sister from the wedding party just *isn't done*, at least not in Kirsten's world, so I'm on the hook for all of it. Starting with the engagement party."

"If it's just a party…" Ally murmured, the *how bad can it be* implied.

Deenie shook her head. "It's never just a party. They're going to pick me apart. It's what they do. You think you're going to celebrate your nephew's third birthday, and then the next thing you know you're getting advice on how to get a real job and someone's shoving a card at you for a good therapist who can help you with your 'instability problems.' No. It's never just a party."

It was a thousand not-so-subtle jabs on how she'd chosen to live her life. A thousand little cuts.

"What you need is a date," Elinor suggested. "A meat shield. Someone to act as a buffer, so they have to be polite. They won't criticize you if they're distracted by the new guy."

"Even if I had someone I wanted to bring—which I don't—they would just criticize me about my taste in men," Deenie argued. "I've never dated someone they liked. And then I'll feel responsible for bringing someone else into the snake pit." She shook her head. "The only way it would work is if I somehow managed to find the kind of paragon of capitalism they approve of and convince him to come with me—"

Connor stepped out the front door, both arms wrapped around the stained ceramic sink he carried against his chest. Plaster dust clung to one high cheekbone.

"Aren't you cold out here?" he called, coming down the steps to chuck the sink into the dumpster. "We're nearly done inside. Just cleanup now."

Deenie barely heard him.

A paragon of capitalism.

Her parents would love him. He was *everything* they'd

ever wanted for her. Someone exactly like them. Straitlaced and rigid, with a five-year plan and stable, *normal* goals. She'd never wanted a guy like that, because if she fell for their idea of Mr. Perfect, they would win. And Mr. Perfect would undoubtedly make her feel like she wasn't good enough, like her life was *wrong*, just like her parents always did.

But if she wasn't falling for him...if she was just using him as a shield...if they had a deal...a *contract*...

"We'll be there in a minute," Ally assured Connor, shooing him back inside. Deenie barely noticed, her thoughts whirling fast now.

"I don't think I've ever seen Connor sweaty in public," Elinor marveled, staring after him as the door closed. "It's weird. Like hearing the Dalai Lama curse."

"Exactly," Deenie agreed, a slow smile spreading across her face. "He's *perfect*."

Of course, Elinor and Ally had misunderstood the "perfect" comment. And then they'd looked at her like she was a few bricks short of a load when she'd explained her plan, but the more Deenie talked it through, the more brilliant it seemed.

He needed someone to start going to his firm's charity events right away, but he couldn't spring that on the Ashleys until he knew them better. She could be a placeholder girlfriend at his charity fundraisers, buttering up his partners until he found the love of his life, and he could keep her family from picking at her like vultures every time she had to see them over the next few months. It was ideal.

Now she just had to convince Connor.

After Ben's kitchen had been stripped down to the floorboards, they retreated to Ally's farmhouse for beer and pizza. Connor disappeared for a while to check on Max, arriving freshly showered just after the food showed up. Deenie nibbled on cheese pizza and nursed a strawberry-kiwi craft cider as she watched for the opportune moment to spring her plan on Connor.

Now that she'd had the idea, she didn't want to wait to find out if it could work. It was the first glimmer of hope she'd had since she learned Kirsten wanted her to be part of *all* the wedding stuff.

Astrid had gone to bed, and everyone was sprawled around the living room chatting when Connor got up to get some water for Mac—who had somehow progressed to the belting-showtunes level of drunkenness on two beers.

Deenie saw her shot and trailed him into the kitchen.

"Hey." She leaned against the counter. "Do you have a second? I had an idea I wanted to run past you. A mutually beneficial thing."

Mutually beneficial thing. Smooth, Deenie.

Connor frowned, pausing with Mac's water in hand. "Is this about Max? I thought things were going pretty well."

"They are!" she quickly assured him, with a little too much enthusiasm, lowering her voice when Elinor glanced over from the living room. "This is something else. Totally separate. And if you think it's crazy, I won't be offended, but hear me out, okay? Because even if it is a little crazy, it might actually be brilliant."

He tilted his chin back. "Okay, now I'm nervous."

"Don't be. Nothing to be nervous about. All I'm proposing is a trade." He frowned, but since that was his standard expression around her, she forged on. "My sister just got engaged, and there's going to be a whole deluge of engagement parties and showers and family stuff I have to go to. My family... it's complicated. Just suffice it to say, it will be exponentially easier for me if I bring a date."

Connor's brows drew together as he frowned, but she ignored them, smiling as if he'd already agreed.

"*You* need someone to schmooze your bosses at company events until you find the One. I'm a classically trained actress. I can handle any role. I even have wigs I can wear so no one will think it's weird you're dating a girl with pink hair. I pretend to be Miss Pretentious Perfect Girlfriend for you—just until you find someone you really do want to show off at company shindigs—and you run the wedding gauntlet with me as my pretend boyfriend man shield. Everybody wins."

Connor's frown deepened. "Is this from one of those romance books you read?"

"Yes. But that doesn't mean it isn't brilliant. And yes, in the books, we would fall in love with each other, but that isn't going to happen here. I would never want to be with you, and I know I'm the last person on earth you would date—that's what makes it so perfect. We don't have to worry about mixed messages or feelings or any of that. This is purely a business transaction. Just a couple friends helping one another through a tricky time."

"And when I do find someone I want to date? How would I explain that?"

"You tell her the truth! That we were helping each other out, but there's nothing romantic between us. Less than nothing. You and I can 'break up,' as far as your bosses are concerned, and then you can start bringing your real girl around."

"Deenie..."

"Just think about it," she insisted. "Sleep on it. Mull it over. I know you're going to see how perfect this is."

Connor was pretty sure Deenie had lost her mind. Being her just-friends date to a wedding was one thing, but pretending they were actually dating was something else entirely.

Though it did solve a lot of his problems.

The first event he needed to attend to get in good with the partners was only a few days away. He'd only managed to meet three more of his online matches in person, and so far none had resulted in a second date—let alone the kind of relationship he would feel comfortable testing in front of his colleagues.

Deenie was hardly the kind of woman he would have chosen to bring, but she was an actress. He'd never actually seen her act, but could bringing her be any worse than bringing a first date? She had a vested interest in behaving herself, since she needed him to be her wedding shield.

It might not be a bad idea.

As he lay in bed that night, sleep eluding him, Deenie's plan started to sound more plausible.

While he tried to work through some contracts the next morning, it kept whispering in the back of his mind, tempting him.

By the time she arrived for her training session with Max at noon, he was waiting for her with a stack of papers in a neat pile on the island.

"We're going to need a contract," he informed her.

Deenie's smile covered her face, glowing. "I had a feeling you might say that."

Chapter Fifteen

Deenie descended the stairs at the sound of Connor's car pulling up on the gravel driveway and shoved her nerves down beneath an impenetrable layer of calm. She could do this. Piece of cake.

Ally looked up from the couch where she was relaxing with Colby and Partridge lying on her feet. It was late Saturday afternoon, creeping up on Saturday evening. Astrid had already left to spend the night at her best friend Kimber's house, and Ben was making his second trip of the day to "just look in on things" at the construction site that was his house. So it was only Ally whose eyes widened when Deenie entered—a relief, since she wasn't prepared for multiple people commenting on what she was about to do.

"Wow," Ally said, reclaiming her feet from the dogs so she could stand. "You look..."

"I know. I look like Corporate Cocktail Party Barbie. Or Corporate Cocktail Party Barbie's flat-chested sister. Corporate Cocktail Party Skipper," Deenie interrupted before Ally could decide how she looked.

She wasn't sure which would have been worse. Ally telling her she looked silly, or Ally telling her she looked good.

The dress had required some airing out after she'd gone to Bitty's storage unit to pick it up—along with the rest of the wardrobe she was going to need for this bizarre spring she'd signed herself up for. She'd gotten the storage unit for Bitty three years ago, when her aunt had sold her place and moved out to the Estates. Deenie occasionally stashed a few of her things in the extra space. Luckily, the slightly musty, damp smell no longer clung to the fabric, but it still itched—though she had a feeling that was psychosomatic rather than the satin's fault.

Her mother had bought her this dress. It was several years old, but the classic cut never went out of style—and neither did the designer label. The wide straps hit her right at the points of her shoulders, creating a deep *V*, and the built-in push-up in the boa-constrictor-tight bodice almost made it look like she had cleavage. She could barely breathe in the top, but she'd always kind of liked the skirt. It poufed out around her with ball gown fullness, even though it stopped at her knees—and there were even hidden pockets. A thin ivory belt tied snugly around her waist with a tidy bow at the small of her back. It was like a princess dress and a little black dress had a baby.

She even felt pretty, when she wasn't busy resenting the fact that she had to play a part to fit in.

"Your hair..." Ally marveled—and Deenie lifted a hand to the silky locks.

"Oh right. Meet Aurora."

The blond Sleeping Beauty wig was the most expensive one she owned—which meant it was also the most natural looking. The flowing blond waves curled over her shoulders, practically her natural color, and emphasized the Barbie doll effect.

The doorbell rang, and Deenie cursed internally. She'd planned to meet Connor at the car, but she'd stalled on the way to the door. She didn't want this to feel like a date. Yes, they were playing at being together, but when they weren't onstage, so to speak, she wanted to keep things as far from date-like as possible. So no picking up at the door. Except she'd dragged her feet, and now he was there, ringing the bell, and she couldn't exactly ignore him.

Her classic black heels—also a gift from her mother—clicked across the farmhouse's worn hardwood floors as she crossed to the entry, refusing to allow any of her hesitation to show. She plucked her coat off a hook and pulled the door open.

Connor blinked. "Wow."

His gaze dropped, taking her in from head to toe, and she couldn't really blame him because hers did the exact same thing.

He looked flawless. Crisp white shirt, dove-gray tie, a perfectly tailored black suit, and a tidy little flash of a pocket square. Connor Wyeth cleaned up *nice*. Not that he was ever anything less than impeccable—though he had looked pretty damn delectable the other day when he'd been sweaty and covered in construction dust.

His eyes were warm as they took her in. "You look—"

"No compliments!" Deenie practically yelped—but her frantic reminder did its job. His gaze shifted from appreciative to assessing as he nodded.

"Appropriate," he finished, as if that was what he'd been about to say all along. "Thank you."

Deenie inclined her head regally. "You're welcome."

He'd thought she was being silly when she'd insisted that "all compliments and mushy romantic stuff be restricted to necessary performance times." He'd argued that if they just got in the habit of being lover-like with one another, it would come off more naturally when they had to do it on command—such a freaking method actor—but she'd been adamant about the separation of church and state, so he'd finally written it into the contract they'd both signed.

She knew herself. She knew the last thing she needed was to start wondering if he really meant it or if he was just playing the part. Much better to keep the lines clearly drawn. No confusion. No worrying about feelings getting involved.

"Are you ready?" he asked.

"Absolutely," Deenie declared, ruthlessly squashing the last of her nerves. She had her clutch, her coat, and her dignity. She had this.

She called goodbye to Ally and stepped onto the porch, closing the door behind her. Connor offered his elbow at the steps, and she gave him a withering look.

"I can walk in heels," she informed him tartly—her haughty performance only slightly ruined by the fact that the driveway was gravel and her ankle wobbled on her second badass stride.

Connor's hand was instantly there, catching her elbow to steady her.

She muttered a galling "Thank you."

At least he refrained from saying "I told you so" as he opened her door for her and waited at her side until she was settled on the luxurious leather of his passenger seat.

The fundraiser wasn't due to start for nearly an hour and a half, but Connor had wanted to allow extra time for traffic and parking. The drive should take them nearly an hour, so

Deenie settled in, adjusting the temperature on her side and fiddling with the heated seats.

She waited until Connor had navigated through the slow starts and stops on the way out of Pine Hollow and was on the county road pointed toward Burlington, his sleek SUV hugging the road's curves, before she got down to business.

"Should we get started?" They'd agreed the drives to events would be spent prepping and the drives home deconstructing what had gone well and what they might need to troubleshoot later, both strategies designed to keep their memories fresh. It had been Connor's idea to put that in the contract, but Deenie had to admit it was a good strategy. "What do I need to know for tonight?"

"It's a silent auction and fundraising dinner for Easter Seals. My firm will have two tables."

"So who is it most important for us to impress?"

"The senior partners. Brent Sterling and Lila Karlson. My mentor, Davis, will be there. As well as some of the other associates vying for partner, I expect."

"The competition. Don't worry. We'll destroy them."

"Well, technically, I still have to work with them, so let's keep our destruction to a minimum."

"Right. Minimal destruction, but you still win." She nodded. "Who do you need me to be?"

Connor took his eyes off the road long enough to frown at her. "My girlfriend. Remember that contract we signed?"

"No, I mean like, am I an accountant? A financial analyst? A venture capitalist? I do a great venture capitalist."

Connor's eyebrows pulled together. "You can't just be yourself?"

Deenie shot him an incredulous look that he missed

entirely due to his focus on driving. "You want me to tell your bosses that you're dating a princess party planner and part-time dog walker?"

"Why not?" he asked, flicking a glance her way in time to catch her expression. "The idea is to show that I'm not uptight and work obsessed. Who better than a princess party girlfriend for that?"

"But you are uptight and work obsessed."

"I know," he snapped. "We just don't want them to know that. Or rather, they already know it, and we're trying to convince them I've changed. That I'm social and engaging, a leader and a mentor with a perfect work-life balance who will be an asset as a partner."

Deenie frowned. "Does it concern you at all that you have to pretend to be someone you aren't to get this job you think will be your dream job? How do you know it's what you really want if you have to be someone else to get it?"

"There are always aspects of any job that you have to adapt for. No job is a perfect fit. We do what's necessary to get what matters to us."

"And what matters to you? Status? Money?"

For a long moment he didn't answer, his hands tight at ten and two on the steering wheel.

"Connor?"

"Making partner."

"Yeah, but why this firm?"

"Because it's the best."

He spoke like that was the final word on the subject. And for Connor, it probably was. Why that job? Because it was the best. Why that house? Because it was the best.

But did the best actually make people happy? Did achieving the thing they'd always worked toward automatically flip a switch inside to satisfy them? Connor struck her as the kind of guy who didn't know how to be satisfied. How to just *be*. He had too much to prove.

Of course, she had a lot to prove, too. But her fight was more about proving she *didn't* have to be the best to be happy.

They really were the worst match imaginable.

"People have an unhealthy relationship with work," she declared, out of the blue, when the silence had stretched for too long.

Connor arched that one eloquent eyebrow that always had so much to say. "Care to elaborate on that?"

"The French take a *month* of vacation every year, but with Americans it's like it's a competition to see who can accrue the most vacation time that they never cash in because they're far too busy and important to take even a single day off. So I guess it's just Americans who have an unhealthy relationship with work. I amend my previous statement."

"Some people *need* to work."

"True. That's true for a lot of people—and I do recognize that I have an insane amount of privilege because I'm not buried in debt and, though I would never take a dime from my parents, I've always known in the back of my mind that they wouldn't let me starve if something went catastrophically wrong in my life. That psychological safety net is huge. But I'm not talking about people who are living paycheck to paycheck. I'm talking about people who have a pathological need to work themselves into the ground as if that somehow makes them better than everyone else."

"You can just say you're talking about me. You don't have to keep saying 'people' when we both know what you mean."

"It isn't just you," she argued. "You would be amazed how many people meet me and gush about how *liberating* my life must be and how much they *envy* my ability to travel and make my own schedule—but the second I say they can do it too, they start bragging to me about how they can't take time off because they are much too valuable to be spared for any length of time. People get their validation from their jobs, their entire sense of self-worth, and then when they retire or they get fired or they hit a point when they realize there's more to life than sitting in front of a computer for eighty hours a week—*crisis*."

Connor quashed his irritation that her words sounded entirely too true, keeping his tone sarcastic. "So you've figured out the meaning of life, is that it? And the rest of us are just too slow to catch on?"

"I'm not saying that. Everybody's got to find their own meaning of life. But I do think people should worry a little less about status and a little more about what truly makes them happy. My job isn't an ego trip. It's just a way to earn money I can use to buy time and freedom. I train your dog and plan princess parties and sew princess dresses so I can earn money to see the world—not because those things define me."

"Being a lawyer doesn't define me," he argued, but the words felt like a lie. He had built his identity around what he did—but was that really so wrong? Lots of people did.

"I know," Deenie agreed too quickly from the passenger seat. "I'm sorry. I got us off topic. We still have lots to cover before we get there. How long have we been dating?"

Connor frowned, annoyed with himself that he hadn't thought about this part before now. It couldn't be a first date. He didn't want Davis or the other partners to think he'd only started seeing someone to look good for making partner—even if that's exactly what he was doing.

Does it concern you at all that you have to pretend to be someone you aren't to get this job you think will be your dream job?

Connor shook away the thought. "Since Christmas?" That indicated a certain level of seriousness. Two months and counting. The kind of date he was likely to bring to an event. "We can keep it close to reality, since we met at Christmas."

"Technically, we met before Christmas."

He dismissed her correction. "Around Christmas. It was the Christmas *season*."

"Nope. Last summer."

She spoke so cheerfully, but when he looked over, there was something about her eyes that made his stomach knot. "I don't remember…"

"I guess we didn't *meet*. We didn't exchange names or anything. It was June, I think. We were both at Magda's— and I should totally tell Mac about your betrayal, but I won't rat you out. You had a Bluetooth thing in your ear, so I didn't realize you were on the phone, and I tried to strike up a conversation. I'm pretty sure it was a Saturday, and I was coming from a party I'd hosted, so I probably looked like I'd been dunked in pink glitter, but you just looked at me like I was something you'd scraped off the bottom of your shoe and said, *I'm working*."

Connor cringed. He could easily see himself doing that. "I'm sorry—"

"Water under the bridge," she declared, waving away his apology. "So we met at Christmas..."

"Right." He frowned, strangely unsettled by her first impression of him. "And we've been dating ever since?"

"Are we keeping the me-training-Max thing? Was that our meet-cute? You came to the shelter to get a dog, and then he was a handful, so you hired me and then fell madly in love with my wit and charm?"

"That sounds plausible," he admitted. *Entirely too plausible.*

"Who made the first move? It was me, wasn't it? I totally jumped you."

Connor's face heated. "I doubt that's going to come up."

"Okay, so things I need to know in case people ask...did you always live in Pine Hollow?"

"Except for college and law school."

"Right. So Pine Hollow, then Princeton—"

"Yale," he growled.

"I know." She grinned, unrepentant. "I just love winding you up. Did you do both undergrad and law school there?"

"Just undergrad. Georgetown for law school. Then I immediately came back here to start working for STK."

"Why Vermont?"

"It's home. My mother's here."

"Mama's boy. Check." She nodded cheerfully, while he growled, and continued blithely, "What do your parents do?"

"My mother was a paralegal and my father was an asshole."

"Professionally?"

He snorted, relieved she hadn't gone the sympathy route.

He hated the sympathy route. "I think he's in construction. I honestly don't know. My mom remarried a few years ago. What about your family?"

"Finance," Deenie declared. "*So much* finance. They were *not okay* with the liberal arts choice, though they try very hard to pretend to be supportive when we're in public. I'm pretty sure I'm a changeling. Somewhere in a fairy kingdom there's a financial analyst wondering why she's surrounded by glitter and rainbows all the time. You remind me of them sometimes."

He spared a sideways glance in her direction. "I'm pretty sure that's not a compliment."

"It isn't. But I try not to hold it against you."

"You didn't grow up in Pine Hollow…"

"Born in Connecticut," she filled in. "My parents bought a place on Lake Champlain when I was nine, and we moved up here. My sister still lives near my folks, but my brother decided to do the Wall Street thing. He lives in Westchester now."

"And you're the youngest?"

"Did I tell you that? Or did you guess? I'm six years younger than Kirsten and eight behind Peter. Not planned. I learned at a very early age that birth control is not foolproof. I am a walking object lesson."

Connor wasn't sure what to say to the mix of bitterness and humor in her voice when she talked about her family, so he asked, "Why did you move to Pine Hollow?"

"I didn't *move*. I don't really move anywhere. I just visit on a semi-regular basis. Stay long enough to replenish my travel funds, and then it's off to see the world again. My favorite aunt lives in Pine Hollow—technically great-aunt. She's up at the Estates now, but when she had her own place

I used to come live with her in between my trips, hang out, save up, plan my next adventure with her help. She's had the coolest life. She's seen *everything*."

"What's her name?"

"Elizabeth. But we all call her Bitty." Deenie wrinkled her nose. "You should probably know my real name—but I warn you, if you call me this, I will react violently and without mercy."

"I am duly warned."

He glanced over, and she took a deep breath, girding herself. Then, finally, dramatically, *"Nadine."*

Connor's eyebrows flew up. "That's a beautiful name."

"I know, but *Nadine*? Do I look like a Nadine?"

There was no right answer for that question, so Connor wisely kept his mouth shut.

They kept trading random biographical information—childhood pets (her: a Pomeranian named Pom Pom; him: none), favorite school subjects (her: theater; him: debate)—until he neared the hotel where the fundraiser would be held.

They were early, and Deenie refused to be early, so she directed him a few blocks over to an ice cream shop. He balked at the idea of ice cream before dinner, but Deenie insisted that it was the only way to ensure they had adequate room for dessert and that they would need fuel for the silent auction, so Connor gave in and found a place to park.

After much discussion of favorite flavors—and heated debate when Deenie insisted that Connor's lemon sherbet did *not*, in fact, count as ice cream—they grabbed their cones and wandered down Church Street on their way back to the car. He wasn't about to have ice cream dripping all over his leather seats, so Connor shed his peacoat and tucked it around Deenie's shoulders over her own jacket as they leaned against the SUV to finish their cones.

She was argumentative. Confrontational. He could never just say something without having it picked apart and debated—but she was also an excellent distraction. When they finally walked into the lobby of the fundraiser five minutes after the doors opened, he was too busy arguing with Deenie about whether they were still indecently early (her position) or bordering on late (his) to be nervous.

He'd been dreading this event all week. He'd built it up in his head as the make-or-break of his entire career, but as he handed their coats to the coat check attendant and Deenie ducked into the ladies' room to repair her ice-cream-ravaged lipstick, he was surprisingly relaxed.

Her crazy idea might just be the best thing that had ever happened to him.

Chapter Sixteen

This was, undoubtedly, the worst idea Deenie had ever had.

It had seemed so clever at first. She was good at playing parts—she'd thought it might even be fun to pretend to be Connor's arm candy for a few nights. But when she'd been cooking up the whole plan, she'd somehow failed to take into account that while this was fake for her, it was Connor's real life. It could have real consequences for him.

He really wanted this promotion. Even if she thought his priorities were seriously out of whack, she didn't want to screw this up for him. Making partner mattered to him. It was everything he wanted, and suddenly there was pressure—and that pressure was amplified by the fact that he wanted her to be herself.

She'd been perfectly prepared to play Ashley the Accountant, but as soon as he wanted her to be Deenie the Offbeat Princess Party Planner, her stomach twisted with nerves.

These were her parents' people. What if they didn't approve of her? And what if they took that disapproval out on Connor?

She wanted to run in the opposite direction, but she kept her mask in place, her smile perfectly poised as she took Connor's arm and entered the ballroom. A stage had been set up at the front of the room, with a giant screen displaying the Easter Seals logo. A stretch of banquet tables to her left displayed the silent auction wares, while the rest of the ballroom was filled with numbered, linen-covered tables.

The idea of fashionably late obviously hadn't occurred to the lawyers at Connor's firm. Their tables were already nearly full as Connor guided her toward them. When they were a few feet away, a circulating waiter offered them champagne, and Connor thanked him, accepting a glass for each of them.

Deenie took it, grateful for the prop, so at least she knew what to do with her hands.

She never had stage fright, so why was her stomach doing somersaults?

"Connor!" One of the men milling around the tables moved to greet them, a broad smile on his face. He was on the shorter side, with close-cropped black hair, and the kind of endearing, open smile that made Deenie instantly like him.

"Davis, good to see you," Connor said smoothly, nodding to the woman at his side. "Jodie, you look wonderful."

"And who's this?" Davis asked, his heavy black eyebrows bouncing up over a speculative grin as he studied Deenie's hand on Connor's arm.

"I've been meaning to introduce you two," Connor said— as if they'd been dating for months. "Deenie Mitchell, Davis Aquino and his wife, Jodie."

"Deenie." Davis beamed. "Aren't you a surprise! I had no idea Connor was seeing anyone."

"My fault," Deenie immediately claimed, hugging Connor's firmly muscled arm. "I've been keeping him all to myself."

Davis's grin got impossibly bigger.

And so it began.

A thousand names seemed to come at her, though it couldn't have been more than fifteen or sixteen. She tried to keep track of the partners and their spouses versus the associates in competition with Connor and theirs, but there were too many names—and she was too nervous. She could only focus on the moment in front of her, keeping her smile bright and her quips light and neutral enough to make whoever was standing across from her laugh.

It was like improv. The most important rule was the rule of yes—agree with whatever comes at you and build on it, lob it back. Keep the conversation rolling, think on your feet.

She lost track of the passage of time, until one of the partners—an older Black woman with sharp eyes and a name Deenie was ninety percent certain started with an *L*—suggested they all check out the silent auction offerings.

Connor placed his hand on her back as they broke into smaller groups, steering her toward one end of the long tables. They drifted away from the others, grabbing a few seconds to themselves, and Deenie's nerves swam up again now that she wasn't *on* anymore.

She pretended to study a silent auction description card without seeing it.

"You okay?" Connor's voice was low, pitched just for her.

Thankfully, this wasn't a big public-displays-of-affection kind of event, but she was still hyperaware of his hand resting on the small of her back. Deenie looked up into his

eyes—the distance shorter thanks to her three-inch heels—
and her fear that she was blowing it spiked when she saw
the concern there. "Did I say something wrong?"

"No, Deenie, you're perfect. Only... You seem a little
tense." As her stomach dropped, he quickly assured her,
"I'm sure no one else noticed anything."

But he had. He saw behind her mask. The thought was
mildly terrifying. Even her parents couldn't always tell what
she was really feeling when she decided to put on her
happy face.

Deenie redoubled her efforts to keep all traces of strain
out of her eyes, smoothing things over with a smile. "I'm
great. Don't worry. But we should work out some kind of
signal in case I put my foot in my mouth. Kick me under the
table or something."

Connor drew in a breath, but another voice spoke before
he could.

"What are you two bidding on, looking so cozy over
here?"

Connor's shoulders straightened so quickly Deenie knew
immediately that this new pair of couples included one of
the senior partners—the Sterlings?—and she flashed on her
brightest smile.

"Remember when we used to have things to whisper to
each other at these events, Brent? Before we descended into
old married coupledom?" the woman who had spoken la-
mented to her husband, leaning around them to see the silent
auction item Deenie and Connor had inadvertently paused
in front of. "Ooh, a weekend at a B&B on Lake Champlain.
That does sound romantic."

"I might have to fight you for that one, Wyeth," Brent
joked, and Connor grinned.

"Careful, sir. I'd go pretty high to make Deenie happy—and it is all for a good cause."

Mrs. Sterling practically melted at his words, patting Deenie on the arm. "Hold on to that one."

Deenie wound her arm tightly around Connor's. "I've got a good grip."

Mrs. Sterling smiled, her gaze fond.

"That went well," Connor whispered when the Sterlings eventually drifted away.

He was practically walking on air as they made their way back to the tables for the start of dinner.

Everything actually seemed to be going well. Which only made her more nervous. Waiting for the other shoe to drop. It was coming. She knew it was coming.

And it happened when they were seated for dinner.

One of the other women—she couldn't remember whether it was one of the lawyers or one of the wives—leaned toward her and asked, "So, Deenie, what do you do?"

Her stomach knotted—because of course that was what mattered to these people. Professional status.

She looked to Connor, giving him one last chance to come up with a socially appropriate made-up profession for her, but he must have misinterpreted her look because he leaned forward and started speaking as if he was proud of her.

"Deenie throws princess parties—you know the ones with the little girls in the dresses—"

"And little boys," Deenie interjected. "We're equal-opportunity royalty-friendly—though we do get more little princesses than princes."

"My goodness, that's adorable." The woman's eyes flared with delight. "And that's a full-time job?"

She flicked another look at Connor, waiting for him to

explain, *Oh, no, that's just her hobby. She's really a hedge fund manager.* But instead the words coming out of his mouth sounded a lot like "She also works at the animal shelter in the town where we live." His large hand closed over hers on the tablecloth. "That's where we met."

"Oh my goodness," the same woman—Allison? Abigail?—gushed. "You're a saint. That is so lovely of you to dedicate your time to something so important."

Deenie flushed, fighting to keep her mask in place. "Well, my friend Ally runs the shelter. I just help out."

"She's being too modest," Connor insisted. "She's a miracle worker with the dogs. She's the only one who's been able to teach my dog, Maximus, anything."

Thankfully, the conversation segued away from Deenie's professional achievements—or lack thereof—and on to pets. Connor told the story of Maximus and the beer and the Jacuzzi—somehow managing to make it an adorable anecdote from their early dating days. Others around the table shared their funny pet stories, generating so much laughter that Brent Sterling, who had been seated at another table, came over to inform them they were all having entirely too much fun without him. Connor's coworkers urged him to tell the Jacuzzi story again—and Deenie kept her smile pinned firmly in place as everyone laughed.

She watched Connor, his eyes alight, his devastating dimples flashing, casting intimate little looks her way, as if they shared a thousand secrets.

This was what it would be like if they were really together.

She hadn't expected that. She'd thought she would be playing a part. She'd thought all the stories they told would be lies. A convenient script. She'd been worried about keeping their stories straight—not about feeling like it could have been real.

Connor's casual touches—the small of her back when they looked at the silent auction, a brush against the nape of her neck as he whispered an explanation of who was who to her, his hand closing over hers when he told a story about the two of them—it was how he would be with a real girlfriend.

He was a much better actor than she'd given him credit for.

And he was in his element. Thriving. She'd given him a hard time in the car about chasing a job that made him pretend to be something he wasn't, but he was *shining*. And she felt completely off-kilter.

Luckily, she knew better than to let that show—though she was starting to feel the strain of holding her act for so long, when the dessert course finally arrived. Connor grinned at her, an intimate little grin reminding her that they'd already had dessert, and she focused on the delicate pavlova so she didn't have to face that smile.

Why was he treating this like it was so *real*?

"Thank God you're here," Jodie Aquino, seated on her left, leaned close and spoke under her breath. "You have to promise me you're coming to all of these from now on."

It took Deenie a moment to realize Jodie was talking to her. "I'm sorry?"

"You have no idea how boring these things usually are—everyone comparing stock tips and talking about work all the time. Don't think we haven't noticed where the change came from."

"Well, Connor…"

"Would be talking about legal precedent and stock tips, too, if you weren't here."

Deenie flushed. "If that's what they like talking about..."

"I think they sometimes even bore themselves. Occasionally I'll randomly interject something about art history just to watch the confusion on their faces. But pet stories, that was a stroke of genius. I'll have to remember that one."

Deenie didn't feel comfortable receiving credit for Connor's accomplishments—he'd been the one telling the funny stories—but before she could protest, another woman was standing between the two law firm tables, her eyes locked on Deenie.

"Do you really do princess parties?"

The volume at the table dimmed, all eyes turning back to Deenie and she flushed as she answered, "I do."

The woman's eyes flared excitedly. "I'm Serena—Brent's daughter-in-law. I'm at the other table, but I just heard about your parties. Do you do Elsa? My daughter is obsessed."

"Technically, I do Hans Christian Andersen's 'The Snow Queen.' Public domain."

The lawyers at the table all chuckled knowingly, making Deenie feel even more uncomfortably on display, but Serena just nodded eagerly. "Of course. Do you have your card? My daughter's birthday is the first week of April, and it would make her entire year if I could book you. You aren't already booked until the next decade, are you?"

Actually, she hadn't been scheduling very far in advance because she hadn't been planning to stick around, but now...

She caught Connor's eye, saw the pleading there, and smiled.

"I think we might be able to work something out."

"Thank you." He'd probably said it a dozen times since they collected his car from the valet and started back toward Pine Hollow, but he couldn't seem to stop saying it. "You were amazing tonight."

Deenie was quiet in the passenger seat. She'd been quiet ever since they left the banquet—and the silence was making him nervous. She wasn't a quiet person.

Maybe she was just tired. Tonight had been exhausting. Perfect, but exhausting.

She'd charmed everyone—and even landed a gig hosting a princess party for one of the senior partners' granddaughters. Which meant more face time with Brent—to whom he had graciously lost the romantic B&B getaway.

Connor couldn't have imagined it going any better. Deenie's crazy idea was officially crazy brilliant.

Though he shouldn't have been surprised. Especially not after some of the Deenie trivia he'd learned tonight.

He rested his wrist on the steering wheel. "You never told me you went to Brown."

"Didn't I?" Her heels lay discarded on the floor. She'd taken them off and tucked her feet up under the pouf of her skirt, making a little nest for herself in the passenger seat.

"I think I would have remembered that you went to an Ivy after all the shit you've given me about where I went to school."

"I don't give you shit because you went to Yale. I give you shit because you're an intellectual snob."

"I'm a snob? The guy who came from a working-class, single-parent household and had to earn every single thing that he got."

"Just because you're not an *entitled* snob who had everything handed to you doesn't mean you aren't an intellectual snob. If you measure people's worth by how educated they are or how financially successful they are, how is that not being a snob?"

"Levi is one of my best friends, and he never went to college."

"Would you ever date someone who didn't have at least a master's degree?"

He hesitated. And the words hung between them in the car, strangely stark.

Almost angry.

Connor gripped the steering wheel, focusing on the dark roads. "I'm not trying to pick a fight. I just wanted to say thank you for tonight, and I'm sorry if I underestimated you."

"So you only realize you underestimated me now that you know I went to an Ivy?"

He sighed. Apparently she *did* want to pick a fight. "That isn't what I meant." He'd thought everything had gone so well, and now she was as prickly as a cactus. "Are you mad at me? Did I do something?"

She huddled deeper into the nest of coats she'd made for herself in the passenger seat. When they'd first gotten into the car, it had been cold, and he'd given her his coat as a blanket. She still had it, though the heat was now blasting cheerfully and she had her seat heater turned up to maximum. He didn't know how she wasn't baking over there, but she just sat in her nest and glowered at him.

"You didn't do anything," she grumbled, the words steeped in irritation.

"Okay. So what's wrong?"

"Nothing," she snapped. "We're good. I'm just tired."

"You can sleep if you want. I'll wake you when we get home."

"Thanks," she muttered, burrowing into her nest and closing her eyes.

So she was cranky when she was tired.

Connor filed that information away for future reference. Because he had a feeling he might need it. He had every intention of taking her to any work event she was willing to attend over the next few months.

He still wanted to find the future Mrs. Wyeth, but until he did, Deenie was the perfect plus-one. He'd been so skeptical at first, but riding the success of tonight, he could see how genius her plan was. He didn't have to worry about her getting too attached—she had let him know repeatedly that he was the last person she would ever date—and he didn't have to worry about his own heart getting involved. He would never let himself develop feelings for someone like Deenie, someone who would happily run off to India the second the going got tough.

But she made a good date. Tonight had actually been *fun*. Something he never would have expected.

Now he just had to be the best damn engagement party date on the planet, because he wanted her to keep doing this. He needed her to need him, too.

Chapter Seventeen

On Sunday morning, Deenie woke up kicking herself.
Last night in the car on their way back to Pine Hollow, her mask had slipped. It was embarrassing, how unnerved she'd been, how much of her discomfort she'd let him see.

She'd snapped at him, wanting to remind herself that they weren't really a couple, that he didn't *really* accept her as she was, he was only playing a part—and then she'd taken the coward's option and pretended to sleep the whole way home, even as her thoughts had swirled in chaotic circles.

She'd freaked out. Over nothing. Making a mountain out of less than a molehill. Thank goodness she hadn't blurted out what had been on the tip of her tongue—that she didn't want to do this anymore.

Everything was perfectly fine in the light of day.

She wasn't going to apologize, she promised herself as she dressed and jogged down the stairs. Apologizing would only be acknowledging the behavior, and she'd much rather pretend she was always grouchy after events. She'd just go over to his place and train Max like nothing had changed. Because nothing had.

Ally and Astrid were in the kitchen when Deenie came downstairs—and Astrid immediately bounded over to her, enthusiasm bursting out of every pore. "We're taking in another dog!"

"We are?" Deenie asked, trying to match Astrid's enthusiasm. "That's awesome!"

Dolce's puppies were officially old enough to be adopted and had started going to their forever homes during the week—much to Astrid's disappointment. Most had already been claimed—except one little plug of a pup they called Tank—but all it had taken was Astrid taking him to show-and-tell at her school to solve that problem. The fifth-grade teacher had put in an application for him.

Now all traces of Astrid's disappointment over the depletion of the population at Furry Friends had vanished as she bounced around the kitchen. "His name is Lucky, and he's a tripod—which means he only has three legs. He's so cute!"

"Our vet in Burlington found him," Ally explained. "Hit and run, poor baby. I have a photo shoot this afternoon, but we're going to drive over to pick him up as soon as we're done with breakfast. You wanna ride along?"

It was tempting, just to have an excuse to avoid Connor for a little longer, but Deenie didn't want him to know she wanted to avoid him, so she shook her head. "No, I should go over and work with Max."

"I'm going to get my shoes so I'm ready to go!" Astrid catapulted herself off the breakfast stool she'd just sat on and thundered up the stairs, making an insane amount of noise for someone so small.

"Where's Ben?" Deenie asked when they were alone in the kitchen.

"Campaign breakfast at the Elks."

"He does realize no one is voting for Tandy Watts, doesn't he?"

Ally shrugged, slipping the crispy bits of bacon to Colby and Partridge, who were providing roadblocks on the floor. "He wants to earn it, I think. Even if it is a landslide. He got his town council position by default, and I think being picked by the town would mean a lot to him."

Deenie snagged a piece of bacon off the plate where it was cooling. "I can see that."

Ally got out plates, studiously casual. "So…how was last night?" she asked, the effort she put into making the question neutral betraying how much she'd been dying to ask. "You got in pretty late."

"It went really well," Deenie answered around a bite of bacon. "I even booked a party. Speaking of which, I should extend my website's booking calendar if I'm going to be hanging around until June."

"Really?" Ally's face lit, like the idea of Deenie staying was the highlight of her day.

"I've been hooked into Kirsten's wedding stuff. There's no escaping now." Her cell phone rang, and she flinched when she saw the name that popped up on the screen. "Speak of the devil…"

Deenie snagged one more piece of bacon and excused herself to take the call—though as soon as she'd reached the privacy of the porch, she seriously considered letting it go to voice mail.

Phone calls from her mother were rarely the high point of the day.

But there was no sense putting off the inevitable. May as well rip off the Band-Aid.

Deenie connected the call. "Hey, Mom."

"Nadine. Finally."

Her mother's superpower of making her feel guilty in five syllables or less was on full display. "Sorry," she said—her mother's favorite word from her. "I was in the middle of a conversation and had to excuse myself."

Her mother hated when people prioritized their phones over the people in front of them—provided she wasn't the one on the other end of the phone. "Kirsten just told me you agreed to be in the wedding party."

"Mm-hmm," Deenie confirmed, still unsure what she'd done wrong, but braced for impact.

Her mother made a small concerned noise. "Are you sure you're going to be there?"

"I told Kirsten I would."

"I know, darling, but you have to admit you don't have the best track record for reliability—"

Deenie's jaw clenched and she forced herself to relax it. "Not wanting to do everything you want me to do is not the same thing as being unreliable. I never promise to do anything I don't follow through on."

"Yes, but it's *how* you follow through. We all know you have a tendency to be dramatic, and I just don't want one of your scenes ruining your sister's wedding."

Deenie's breath caught as she realized her mother wasn't trying to badger her into attending the wedding, but rather trying to get her to back out. She rubbed absently at the new ache in her chest where the blow had landed. "I'm not going to ruin anything." *And I never make scenes that you don't provoke.*

"I know you never *intend* to, but sometimes you can make things about yourself, and your sister deserves to have a wedding day that's perfect for her."

"It was her choice to include me." To think Deenie had thought her mother coerced Kirsten into asking.

"You're her sister. How would it look if she didn't ask you? But I thought you'd make some excuse. You always have an excuse not to spend time with us."

Deenie gritted her teeth against the jab. "Not this time, I guess."

Her mother sighed. "Well, of course we're all delighted you're going to be at the engagement party. You are coming to the engagement party?"

"You bet. I'm even bringing a date. You'll love him."

"Sarcasm isn't called for, Nadine."

"I wasn't being sarcastic. You really are going to love him." So much so, it almost made her want to tell him not to come because she didn't want to give her mother the satisfaction.

Man shield, she reminded herself. Connor would be her vibranium shield, deflecting all sniper shots aimed her way by her oh-so-loving family.

"Just promise me you won't make a scene. Several of your father's clients are going to be there, as well as Kirsten's and Todd's work associates."

"No scenes," Deenie promised.

No matter how tempting they might be.

She really didn't want to ruin Kirsten's wedding, or any part of the run-up to it.

She'd never wanted to be the odd man out. She just hated that she had to obey all their rules to be accepted— and there were a *lot* of rules. Ridiculous rules that made no sense at all. Rules that felt like a straitjacket tightening around her.

But she had Connor. The engagement party would be fine. *Fine.*

Deenie looked gorgeous—and like she was about to throw up all over her hot-pink stilettos.

She was wearing the same black cocktail dress with the poufy skirt she'd worn last weekend at the fundraiser, but this time the sedate black heels had been traded for the pink stilettos and the wig was nowhere to be found. Instead, she'd curled her hair. Short pink and blond ringlets rioted in every direction on her head, and a hot pink choker rested at the base of her throat.

She looked like a rock star dressing up for the Oscars— wildness peeking out through a layer of elegance—and Connor was glad he'd opted for the black-on-black stylishness of his favorite suit to keep up with her, even if Deenie's glittery pink nails were digging into the expensive fabric.

"You okay?" he murmured as they strode into the ski resort's elegant ballroom, which had been set up in celebration of Kirsten and Todd.

Deenie flashed a smile that was bright and brittle and false. "Couldn't be better!"

He couldn't tell whether she was trying to be sarcastic or sincere. "It's gonna be fine," he soothed. "It's just an engagement dinner."

A string quartet played in one corner, in front of a small dance floor where no one was dancing. Waitstaff circulated with hors d'oeuvres and trays of champagne. Muted conversation rippled sedately through the room.

An older woman in a silver dress with her hair pulled into a sleek black knot separated herself from a group nearby and moved toward them, smiling serenely.

Deenie's grip tightened on his arm. "We need a strategy. In case we get separated."

He didn't have time before the woman arrived to reassure her that he wouldn't be leaving her side . "Nadine. There you are. I was beginning to wonder if you were going to make it."

"Traffic," Deenie offered with an apologetic grimace—as if she hadn't urged him to drive slower the entire way. "Hi, Mom."

Connor nearly did a double take. The two women looked nothing alike—dark and light, contained and wild—though now that he was looking for similarities, he noticed they had the same small ski-jump noses.

"May I present my date? Connor Wyeth, my mother, Joanne Mitchell."

"How do you do?" Deenie's mother extended her hand, her gaze frankly assessing, a whisper of a frown tugging her lips downward. There was something very firm about her. Unyielding.

"A pleasure," Connor said, taking her hand briefly. "And congratulations on your daughter's engagement."

"Thank you. We're so delighted to be welcoming Todd to the family. Aren't we, Deenie?"

"Absolutely."

Her mother's face flickered with the same uncertainty Connor had felt over whether Deenie was sarcastic or sincere—Deenie clearly hadn't gotten her excellent poker face from her mother. Then the elder Mitchell's expression cleared as she looked over Deenie's shoulder. A bright smile overtook her face, and she lifted a hand to wave. "I'd better go say hello to the Westons. You two be good!" she chirped, patting Deenie on the arm.

The admonishment sounded playful, but Deenie's hand tightened on his arm. He glanced down at her, his gaze catching on the platinum-and-pink curls. She couldn't be a natural blonde.

She caught him looking and arched her—very blond— eyebrows. "Changeling, remember? My sister is the spitting image of my mother, but if I didn't look like a carbon copy of my father's sister, we'd all be convinced I was switched at birth." Then she glanced past him and something hardened in her eyes. "Incoming."

"Deenie. It's been forever."

"Peter." Deenie greeted the new arrival with a distant nod—and then introduced him as her brother.

A month ago if someone had asked him where Deenie came from, Connor would have been sure her entire family was loud and affectionate and irreverent. She was so certain of herself, so overtly bright and free, that the idea of someone with her technicolor brilliance coming from a palette of sedate grays would never have occurred to him.

He'd found her aggravating, the way she always seemed to be jabbing at him, mocking his stiffness and his attachment to routine—but he also admired her spirit. A spirit that seemed distinctly muted as she made awkward small talk with her brother.

They spoke about his children. He thanked her for the Christmas presents she'd sent. And then Peter excused himself, and they moved on to the next family member—though the only distinction between family and near-strangers seemed to be the titles she used when making the introductions. It was all very civil. Very polite.

Very distant.

And no one, not one person, asked her anything about herself.

They gave her updates on their own lives. They occasionally made comments about events she'd missed or backhanded remarks about career planning not interesting her. But no one asked her how she was. Or even how long the two of them had been dating.

It was bizarre.

And then the bride rushed over.

"Deenie Baby!" The woman in the white cocktail dress did indeed look like a younger copy of Deenie's mother, with her sleek dark-brown chignon and chocolate eyes. She grabbed both of Deenie's hands, squeezing eagerly and beaming at her. "I'm so glad you came! Peter was taking bets earlier, can you believe it?"

"I hope you won a lot." Deenie smiled, but it was tight around the edges.

"Oh, I didn't bet. I knew you'd be here. I've been just dying waiting for you to arrive. There's someone you have to meet. One of Todd's friends is an investor, and she just *loves* your little princess party website. She's dying to talk to you about turning those darling little princess dresses into a real business. You could have your first location in Pine Hollow if you wanted—but Burlington does make so much more sense for a storefront."

"Kirsten, I don't want a storefront."

"I know it increases your overhead, and lots of businesses are internet-only now, but trust me, this could be so darling.

I had the idea when I was looking at wedding dresses last week. We walked in and there was champagne and these darling little cakes—it was a whole experience. And it got me thinking about how you said you go to your clients' houses to do fittings for their daughters, to make them feel like princesses, and I thought—what better than having a store where little girls can come in to get their princess dress fittings and have tea and adorable little cakes while you upsell their parents? Isn't it genius?"

"It's a great idea, but it's not me."

"But it could be!" Kirsten gushed. "You could make a living doing what you love! A *good* living. Even if it is just sewing."

Connor cringed, but Kirsten didn't even seem to notice that she might have insulted Deenie. Deenie's parents circled closer, their eyes on their youngest as if watching to ensure Deenie was going to behave herself.

"I'm doing fine," Deenie insisted, keeping her voice low. "And I like my life the way it is. I like being able to make my own schedule. If I want to go on a trip now, all I have to do is put a notice on my website and go. I don't have to worry about staffing a shop and making sure it keeps running without me."

"But this could be big for you. At least talk to Todd's friend—"

"Actually, I'm not even doing the princess dresses all that much anymore," Deenie blurted, cutting her sister off. "I'm a dog trainer now."

It was one of those moments that seemed choreographed by fate for maximum impact—the musicians finished their song, the silence somehow timed perfectly with a lull in the conversation around the room so Deenie's voice seemed to ring defiantly, echoing in the brief instant of quiet.

Heads turned. Her mother gasped.

Deenie flushed beet red. "So there's that. If you'll excuse me. I need to powder my nose."

She fled—and the musicians took that as their cue to strike up their next song. Conversation returned—the buzz a little louder than before. Connor almost started after Deenie, though he wasn't sure she would thank him for chasing her to the bathroom, but he froze when he heard a haughty voice from his left.

"She isn't serious."

Deenie's mother. Trying to smooth things over. Trying to erase the impact of her youngest daughter's presence.

Connor wasn't sure why, but anger sparked suddenly in his gut. "Yes, she is," he heard himself snap, the words crisp and clear. "And she's amazing at it."

Joanne Mitchell's gaze locked on him, a single thin eyebrow lifting. "And what do you do, Connor?"

Chapter Eighteen

Only in her parents' universe would admitting she was a dog trainer constitute causing a scene, but Deenie knew that was exactly how her mother would see it.

She hadn't meant to say it quite so loudly. She'd just wanted Kirsten to stop trying to turn her into Corporate Princess. She didn't want a store, and she was so unbelievably tired of having to hold her ground against their constant attempts to "improve" her, but she should have kept her mouth shut. Should have thrown Connor in the line of fire. That was why she'd brought him, wasn't it?

Another woman walked into the bathroom, where Deenie had been standing at the mirror for the last five minutes. She smiled and made a beeline for the sink beside Deenie, reaching into her purse for a compact.

"Deenie, right? Kirsten's little sister? I'm Katrina. One of the other bridesmaids."

Deenie smiled and turned on the water to wash her hands to justify why she'd been standing there. "Nice to meet you."

"Aren't Kirsten and Todd the cutest together? We're just

so thrilled for her. Though you caught yourself a good one, too, didn't you? That was your fella's Tesla Model X I saw you pull up in, wasn't it?"

Deenie fought to keep her face blank at yet another reminder of what mattered here. What you drove. How much you made.

"That's his car," she confirmed mildly.

"That isn't a car, sweetie. It's a *flex*." Katrina's smile practically purred as she reapplied her lipstick. "And kudos to you for landing a big one. Where did you find him?"

"Pine Hollow," Deenie said in that same bland tone.

Katrina laughed as if Deenie had told a marvelous joke. "You're kidding. If I'd known whales like that could be found in that little backwater pond, I'd have gone fishing up there years ago."

Deenie ignored the unwelcome flash of *something* that made her want to keep Katrina far away from Connor, not caring to examine the sudden possessive tightness in her chest as her hands clenched under the warm water. Connor *was* a catch. He was smart and funny, but all Katrina knew about him was what he drove, and here she was congratulating Deenie, as if his paycheck was all that mattered.

Silently reminding herself not to cause a new scene in the bathroom, Deenie flicked off the tap and dried her hands, turning toward the door with a carefully diplomatic "It's a great town." She left before Katrina could purr anymore.

Back in the dining room, she scanned the room, searching for Connor. She just wanted to grab him and get out of here. Away from these people.

When she locked eyes on him, he was already moving toward her through the crowd.

"You okay?" he murmured, gently cupping her elbow, his thumb rubbing absently over her skin.

"Peachy. Sorry for abandoning you. Did the jackals descend as soon as I left you unprotected?"

His lips quirked up at one side, those devastating amber eyes glinting at her. "I can handle your parents. Believe it or not, most people like me."

They'd probably loved him, but she still felt like she needed to apologize for bringing him here. Subjecting him to this. The fundraiser he'd taken her to had been fun. His coworkers were entertaining. But this...

"Do you think anyone will notice if we slip out quietly?"

"Come on," he urged. "Dinner's about to be served. We eat, we smile, we escape."

"Are you sure I can't interest you in my sneak-out-the-back plan?"

He shook his head. "No chance. You'll thank me later."

Somehow she doubted that.

Especially when the dinner began to drag on. There were toasts. So many toasts. Thankfully, that meant it limited the small talk with the other couples at their table—who she quickly learned were the other bridesmaids and their dates, all subtly comparing bank balances—but it made the dinner last forever.

When the father of the groom stood up for his *second* speech, Deenie leaned close to Connor and whispered, "I'm not going to make it. I need more chocolate to survive this." Or a lot more alcohol. The dessert course had been the world's tiniest cakes, and the waitstaff circulating to refill the champagne glasses seemed to be avoiding her—probably at her mother's request to prevent her from "making a scene," even though she had never *once* gotten drunk at a family event.

She was about to make another pitch for sneaking out a side door when Connor murmured, "I'll see what I can do," and slipped away from the table. She wanted to grab him back, beg him not to leave her alone with these people, but he was already moving away—on a quest for sugar.

She forced herself to focus on the unending purgatory of the toasts—until a body appeared in Connor's vacated seat. Her mother's shoulder brushed hers as she leaned close— and Deenie barely contained her surprise. "Aren't you supposed to be at the head table?" she whispered.

Her mother's frown radiated disapproval—and for once it wasn't aimed at Deenie. "I wanted one toast per family to keep things moving, but Kirsten didn't want to say no to her future in-laws. I only hope your father's clients aren't falling asleep in their chairs."

"So why aren't you talking to them?"

No one seemed to notice them whispering, but her mother lowered her voice even further, breathing the next words. "He's an actor, isn't he?"

"What?" She wasn't following.

"Connor. Your father thinks he really is a lawyer, and I haven't told him otherwise. We were speaking with him when you excused yourself, and your father was very taken, but then I remembered you have all those actor friends. That young man is very attractive, very successful—if he's telling the truth. Did you hire him to pretend to be your date?"

"Because the only way someone like Connor would date someone like me is if I paid him to pretend?"

It was insulting—and gallingly close to the truth.

Her mother tsked. "Don't be sensitive. I just want to

know so I can moderate your father's expectations. He's so pleased that you actually brought someone suitable."

"He isn't an actor," Deenie bit out. She carefully avoided mentioning that he wasn't her real date, either. Todd's father finished his speech, lifting his glass, and Deenie took the moment to stand. "Excuse me."

She quickly navigated the edge of the ballroom, keeping her head ducked down as if that would stop people from noticing her fleeing the room. The rest of the posh ski resort was quiet at this hour, the hallways dark, and she ducked down one, finding a little nook around a casement window, where she could press her back against the wood paneling and breathe.

So many people had it so much worse. She was such a brat with her first-world problems. None of this mattered. She was lucky. She got to live her life. See the world. What did it matter that she was constantly reminded that she would never be good enough in her family's eyes?

Unless she lived her life the way they understood. Started a successful business. Dated a successful lawyer.

"Cake?"

She hadn't even heard him approach. Connor stood at the edge of her nook, an uncertain expression on his face and a plate in his hands with *four* of the little chocolate cakes on it. Her heart leapt at the sight of him—and she had to forcibly remind herself that none of this was real.

"My hero," she murmured, making her tone dry enough that he wouldn't hear the sincerity in the words.

Connor's uncertainty cleared into a smile at the bite in her voice. He stepped into the little nook with her, extending the plate. "I come bearing chocolate."

"Thank you." He hadn't grabbed a fork—undoubtedly

expecting her to be waiting at the table—but she didn't let that stop her. She plucked one of the tiny cakes between her fingers and popped it into her mouth, groaning as dark chocolate landed on her taste buds. He didn't say anything as she reached for another cake.

"Are the toasts still going?" she asked when her shoulders had relaxed under the influence of cake and Connor.

"I think so. You okay?"

She grimaced. "Yeah. When the going gets tough, the tough run away, right?"

His eyes searched hers, inscrutable in the shadows. "You don't have to do that."

She cocked her head. "Do what?"

"Make fun of yourself. It's okay if you're struggling."

"It's not like I have anything worth struggling over. My mom thinks I hired you. Apparently you impressed my father while I was in the bathroom, and she knows me too well to believe I could ever land a guy like you. Smart woman."

"Hey." He stepped closer, cupping her chin with the hand that wasn't holding the cake plate. His hand was incredibly warm, his fingertips lightly calloused. "That's my friend Deenie you're talking about. Be nice."

She looked up into his eyes, not quite able to make out the color in the shadows of the vestibule, but she'd already memorized every line of his face. Every color. Every devastating expression, all the nuances of his perfect charm. She *knew* him. And her breath went short.

He didn't know why he did it—stepped closer to her, cupped her face. He'd hated the self-doubt in her eyes. He'd wanted to get rid of it. But he hadn't considered how it would feel, standing so close in the dark little nook.

It felt like he should kiss her.

All he had to do was lower his head. She was wearing another pair of sky-high heels, so he didn't even have to lower it that far. She'd worried off her lipstick—he didn't think she even realized how much she chewed at it when she didn't think anyone was looking. She was so good at keeping her smile in place, so good at deflecting attention away from herself and selling the story that everything was fine, but he'd seen behind the curtain now. He'd seen how hard she worked to make everything look light and easy. He'd seen the effort she expended to make everyone think she couldn't be bothered to try.

His heart ached for her and he just wanted to hold her, to let her know that he was here, that she wasn't alone, that she didn't have to paddle so furiously beneath the surface because he would help her. They were a team.

"Nadine?"

A feminine voice called down the darkened hallway, followed by the sound of retreating footsteps. Deenie flinched, her face shying away from his hand. He dropped his arm, his fingertips burning with the imprint of her skin.

She plucked another cake off the plate and mumbled, "You should eat the last one, before I steal them all."

The moment was gone.

Connor shuffled back a step, knowing he should be grateful they'd been interrupted before he did something stupid, but not entirely certain how he felt.

He lifted the plate between them. "I got them for you."

"Take it." She shoved the plate at him. "I've been greedy enough."

Even in the low light, he recognized the look on her face. It was the same one she got when she was training Max and she wasn't going to give up until she got him to do something. Mulish. Stubborn.

Adorable.

Not that he would ever tell her that. She'd probably deck him.

Connor popped the last mini cake into his mouth—the things really were addictively good—and linked his hand with Deenie's. "Come on. I have an idea."

He led her back toward the ballroom, relieved when he saw that the toasts had finally concluded and the musicians were back at their posts. A handful of couples swayed on the dance floor, and Connor smiled to himself. *Perfect.*

He set the empty cake plate on a tray and drew Deenie behind him onto the dance floor.

"I was really hoping your idea involved sneaking out the back," she muttered as he pulled her into a closed position and she rested her hand on his shoulder.

"Nonsense. We have something to prove."

The song was a waltz, and he guided her onto the beat. Her eyes narrowed with his first sure step. "Are you good at *everything*?"

Her expression was annoyed, but she was good, too, gliding naturally in his arms. So natural he had to remind himself not to focus on that feeling.

"My mom tricked me into lessons," he explained. "She said girls like boys who can dance. She failed to mention that ballroom would be useless in middle school."

Deenie's lips twitched. "I'll have to send her a thank-you note."

He adjusted his hold, drawing her a little closer than was

strictly ballroom. She cocked her head up at him. "What exactly are we trying to prove with this?"

"Is your mother watching?"

Deenie glanced over his shoulder, her lips pursing with irritation before her gaze lifted back to his. "She is."

"Good."

He bent his head and kissed her.

It was meant to be quick, a brush of the lips, but temptation caught him and he lingered.

She tasted of dark chocolate. Her hand tightened on his shoulder—and she was kissing him back, her lips soft and searching beneath his. The skin of her back was warm beneath his palm, his other hand cradling hers, still in the position to waltz, though he'd forgotten the steps, forgot to even sway as the net of Deenie's kiss tangled around him.

When she finally tucked her chin, breaking away to take in a breath, he straightened, embarrassed, even though this had been his plan all along.

He'd wanted to show her parents that this wasn't an act. That Deenie was perfect, just the way she was, but he hadn't expected to feel anything. He hadn't expected to get swept away.

"Ready to make our exit?" he asked, his voice inexplicably rough.

Composure fell over her face, the last traces of dazed heat wiped from her eyes. "Absolutely."

Chapter Nineteen

Connor was a *much* better actor than she'd given him credit for.

She hadn't expected to have to kiss him. Which, yes, she supposed sounded a little odd given the fact that they were supposedly dating, but public displays of affection weren't really a thing in her family.

Handholding? Yes. Escorting one another around a ballroom? Absolutely.

But she hadn't been prepared for the kiss.

That was why she was so affected by it. Shock. It had caught her off guard. That was the only explanation.

Deenie sat burrowed into his passenger seat again, though spring had made a surprise appearance in the last few days and the car wasn't nearly as cold as it had been when she pretended to sleep on the way home from the Easter Seals fundraiser. Rain drummed a steady beat against the windshield.

They hadn't spoken since they collected the car from the valet and started back toward Pine Hollow. Maybe she could pretend to sleep again. She knew they were supposed to discuss the night—they'd agreed on that in the contract—but she just wanted to hide.

She felt exposed in front of him. She never let people see that she struggled. That she had a hard time being the black sheep. She had long since perfected her strategies for deflection—but they'd all seemed to collapse in front of Connor.

"Thank you for coming with me tonight," she said finally, as the rainy night whipped past the windows outside.

As awkward as it had been, she knew it could have been much worse if he hadn't been there.

"Where did you come from?" he asked—the same question she'd been asking herself her entire life.

"I know, right?" she agreed. "They're all so perfect."

He shot her a quick, irritated look. "That is *not* what I meant. You're sunshine. How does someone from that family turn into Deenie Mitchell?"

She shivered when the words hit her, though she was far from cold. He made it sound like being Deenie Mitchell was a good thing.

"Remember I told you I have a great-aunt out at the Estates? The one I visit all the time?"

"Yeah."

"She was the black sheep of her generation. Didn't get married. Didn't have kids. Didn't become the perfect housewife everyone expected her to be. And my whole life she's been the one person who encouraged me to go a little wild when I need to." Deenie smiled at the memory. "She's the reason I went to Brown."

Connor glanced over, a quick look to tell her he was listening, to urge her to go on.

"My parents met at Princeton," she explained. "My

siblings both went there. It was the family school. That's where Mitchells went. And when I was in high school, I was still trying really hard to be what they wanted me to be. The only class I took that wasn't part of a strategically constructed academic resume was my theater elective. It was my escape. But I knew my parents would lose their minds if I told them I wanted to study theater—and honestly, I was really good at math. Finance and economics just made sense—maybe because I'd been hearing about them over the dinner table my entire life. So I figured I would apply as an econ major. Theoretical math if I was feeling *really* rebellious. But then we went on my college trip."

She shook her head, remembering that week.

"It was a formality. My parents were trying to use the trip to show me how much better Princeton was than all those other schools. 'Brown is so unstructured...Columbia is so crowded...New Haven is so dirty...'"

"Hey."

She grinned at his instinctive defense of Yale. "Then we got to Princeton." She groaned dramatically. "Have you ever been?"

"No," he admitted.

"It was so *stuffy*. The campus is gorgeous, and we were there on the most beautiful day. Sunshine and green grass. But everyone else on our prospective student tour was wearing sport coats and ties and fancy dresses like they were going to brunch at a country club. It was so formal. And I'd always just kind of assumed I would go there, but suddenly I couldn't breathe. I completely bombed my interview, but my parents kept telling me, don't worry, you're a legacy, you have good test scores, you'll get in. But I didn't want to get in. Every time they reassured me, I felt like I was going to have another panic attack. Then Aunt Bitty came to see me. She took me for ice cream. It was totally random—I'd always thought she was fun, and I loved spending summers with her when I was little, but my parents talked constantly about how kooky she was, so even though I loved being with her, I never really took her seriously when I was in high school. But then we're sitting there, eating rocky road, and suddenly I'm telling her about Brown and the theater program and how they let you create your own major so you can study the things you're most passionate about. And I knew. When I got home, I told my parents I wanted to go to Brown—and they were surprised, definitely disappointed, but it was still an Ivy, so they figured it was a reasonable compromise—until I told them that I wanted to take a gap year and go to Europe. That Aunt Bitty had offered to send me."

"I bet that went over well."

"A lot better than I would have guessed. They thought I needed to get it out of my system—whatever it was that made me push back against the prescribed order of the world. We compromised on a summer trip—six weeks backpacking across Europe by myself before I was due to start at Brown."

"Was that the first time you'd been abroad?"

"No, just the first time I'd ever been anywhere on my own. And I'm not going to pretend it wasn't terrifying. I think I cried more in the first week than I had in the previous two years. I was pickpocketed on a train and got lost in Madrid—I'd taken French in high school, but languages were never really my thing, and I spent most of my time with my little phrasebook in my hand begging people to speak English. I was so scared at first, but then I realized I could actually do it. I could live on a shoestring and survive on my own. I could see the world. And it was like something opened up inside me. I loved it. I made friends with other kids at the hostels where I stayed—we would always promise we were going to be friends for life and then never see one another again—but it was brilliant. I felt like for the first time I was allowed to be whoever I wanted to be and I started to figure out who that was. I came back in the fall for school, but I never really got it out of my system, that wanderlust. Even now I mostly just work so I can have the money to travel." *To remember who I am.* "And Aunt Bitty gave me that. She even helped me pay for college when my parents realized I wasn't going to get a 'useful' degree and cut me off. I wouldn't be who I am without her."

And now she barely remembers who I am…

Connor looked across the gearshift at her. "She sounds amazing."

"She is. Though my parents aren't her biggest fans. They blame her for my 'hobo lifestyle.' That's probably why my dad was so excited to see me with a lawyer. Finally a sign that I might actually grow up and get a real job. I'm pretty sure they all think Bitty is subsidizing my lifestyle. She isn't," Deenie added quickly—rushing to ensure he didn't think she was mooching off her aunt. "I haven't accepted a penny from her since college, and I've tried to pay her back for that, but she kept refusing. She wouldn't let me pay rent when I visited her before she moved out to the Estates, even if I stayed for a couple months, but I'd take care of the house. Take care of her. I always pull my weight. Even if my parents are convinced I'm irresponsible and immature."

"I know that."

"Sorry." She burrowed down deeper into the seat at his

simple words, tucking her bare feet beneath her. "I have such a complex about my family. I always feel like I have to prove I'm not what they think I am."

"Family's complicated," he commiserated.

"Even Connor Wyeth's?"

She didn't think he would answer. She was blatantly prying, but he looked over at her with a slight smile. "Even mine."

He shifted his grip on the steering wheel, and for a moment there was just the rhythmic swish of the windshield wipers.

Then he spoke, his voice deep and low in the hush of the car.

"I told you it was just my mom and me when I was growing up. My dad bailed when I was five. When I was a teenager, he got sober and tried to do the whole amends thing, but that didn't last long—and it didn't matter. I didn't need him. My mom was my everything. I'd tell her things I wouldn't even tell my friends. But then when I was twenty-four, she started dating *Mitch*."

There was a wealth of conflicting emotion in that single name, and Deenie twisted in the seat to face Connor, fascinated by these peeks into what made him tick. "You don't like Mitch?"

"Mitch is impossible not to like. He is an extremely likable guy," Connor said, bitterness tinging the words.

"That must make it even more annoying when you secretly want to drop him into the nearest pond."

Connor looked over at her, startled, then a laugh burst out of his mouth. "You know, it does. If he were a jerk, I would feel like much less of an ass for secretly resenting him."

"Of course you resent him. He took away your mom."

"But that's the thing. He didn't. From day one, he's been super understanding that my relationship with her will always trump his. He never tried to play at being the dad. He always just lets us keep him outside the circle. He never pushes."

"But it still changed your relationship to her. She has someone else to rely on now."

Connor looked over at Deenie so long, the tires edged onto the rumble strip at the side of the road, jerking him back to attention. How did she understand so easily? How did she instantly get what he'd been trying to wrap his head around for years?

He *liked* Mitch. But he'd felt less connected to his mother ever since his stepfather came into the picture. He'd thought it was because he was too possessive of her or because he relied on her too much—but the truth was he missed her relying on him.

His mom had told him over and over that he grew up too fast. That he shouldn't have had to be the most organized kid on the block. That he shouldn't have had to teach himself to cook. But he'd been so proud of being able to do that for her. He'd built his entire identity around being the guy who took care of his mom. It was why he'd wanted the high-paying job—so he could buy her a big house.

He'd spent the last several years trying not to resent Mitch and not always doing a good job.

And Deenie just *got* that, without having to be told.

"He's a good guy," Connor repeated, as much for himself

as for Deenie's benefit. "He makes her happy. And we're friends. Well. Maybe not *friends*, but we get along."

"Have you ever done anything with him without your mom there?"

"We've been alone together."

"On purpose?"

He could hear the skepticism in Deenie's voice and cracked a smile. "Okay, not on purpose."

Mitch had tried, back when he'd first started dating Connor's mom, but Connor had laid out the rules of engagement back then, and they'd all stuck to them. He liked Mitch. From a distance. But he didn't really know him.

"You do have something pretty major in common," Deenie added lightly. "You both love your mom."

He flicked a glance over at her as he slowed in the approach to Pine Hollow. "I thought this was my night to help you, not the other way around."

"You did. Believe me."

Connor focused on the road. He almost apologized for the kiss. It was on the tip of his tongue. But instead he murmured, "You're the toughest person I know."

He could feel her surprise pushing at him from the passenger seat. "What?"

"You made a crack earlier about not being tough. You are."

"Yeah. Running away to Europe is very tough."

He spared her a quick sideways glance. "You don't let anyone else tell you who you are or who you should be. That's tough." He cracked a grin. "And you're the only person I know hardheaded enough to train Max."

"Well, at least I have some skills."

He gave her a look. "You're going to have to stop doing that, Deenie."

"Doing what?"

"Making fun of yourself. I've figured out how awesome you are. You can't convince me otherwise."

When he looked over, her lips were pressed together and her eyes were on her lap, her cheeks rosy even in the dashboard light. Connor listened to the rhythm of the rain and turned toward the Furry Friends driveway.

Chapter Twenty

Deenie was a master at pretending nothing had changed, so the next day when she arrived to train Max, that was exactly what she did. *Nothing to see here, folks. Connor Wyeth didn't kiss me last night, and we certainly didn't get all intimate about personal family shit.*

It was just part of the contract, that was all. And they didn't have any more contractually obligated events to attend until the first week of April, when she would be throwing a princess party for his boss's granddaughter, so she could keep her emotional distance until then, rebuilding the walls that had somehow come down when she took him to the engagement party. Even as she flitted around his house, working with his dog.

It was all about distance.

It helped that the next few weeks were insanely busy.

Ben won the election on the second Tuesday in March—to absolutely no one's surprise. Connor threw a party to celebrate at his house, but Deenie managed to avoid him for most of the night, hanging close to Ally and Mac.

Ben was due to be sworn in on the first of April, by

which time he hoped the kitchen renovation would be done and he and Astrid would be able to move back to their own house. Though Astrid loudly protested that she was going to miss the dogs at the shelter too much every time the topic of them moving out came up.

More dogs were coming into the shelter all the time now. There were four new residents in the kennels who needed homes, including Lucky and a husky named Wolfgang, with nearly as much energy as Elinor's Dory.

Deenie helped out whenever she wasn't sewing princess dresses, hosting parties, or training Max. Her dress orders had spiked—likely due to Connor's colleagues placing orders for their kids—but she still made time to keep up the Furry Friends accounting ledger. For the first time, she was grateful for the business management courses she'd taken in college in an attempt to please her parents.

The supplies Ally and Deenie had ordered to turn the shelter into the Furry Friends Training Center and Agility Course had started to arrive. As soon as spring arrived in full force—rather than bouncing back and forth between snow and rain—they would set up the outdoor course. They'd already fenced off a section of what had once been the back pasture to use as a dog park, but the rest of the materials were piling up in Rita Gilmore's old art studio.

Deenie had expected to feel like a fifth wheel around the house, but it was fun, living amid all the chaos with Astrid and Ben and Ally's grandparents randomly dropping by. It was loud and busy and kind of perfect.

Not that she was thinking of hanging around. She was a nomad. Nomads didn't stay.

But for now she did.

It was hard to even think about leaving when she knew

these might be her last good times with Bitty. She spent more and more time out at the Estates, but it didn't seem to matter how much time she spent—there were still good days and bad days. She visited Mr. Burke and JoJo almost as often as Bitty, sitting on the floor of his apartment, playing with JoJo and Squeaky Mouse, listening to his stories and telling him about all the ongoing wedding drama.

The perfect venue had been secured for the first weekend in June—a luxurious resort in the southern part of the state with gorgeous mountain views for the multi-day event. The perfect dress had been rush ordered. Bridesmaid dresses had been selected—and when her mother had called to get her measurements, she'd repeatedly asked Deenie if she was *sure* she wanted to go to the expense of ordering one, if she was absolutely *positive* she was going to be there in June.

Deenie held her ground—Kirsten was the one who had asked her, and as long as Kirsten wanted her there, she was going to be there. Even if it meant gritting her teeth through all her mother's jabs.

With the wedding planner Kirsten had hired, there really wasn't all that much for the wedding party to do. Deenie had to make sure she had the dress fitted and wore the right shoes. Show up for the bridal shower and the bachelorette party, which Kirsten's co-matrons of honor were throwing in May. And then show up on the actual day. Kirsten had said she wanted Deenie to be involved in the planning—but that mostly meant she wanted to call Deenie once a week and tell her everything she'd already decided so Deenie could agree it was all brilliant.

So with everything on her plate, she barely had time to notice Connor. Or his dimples. Or his unfairly gorgeous eyes.

Or to remember the way he'd called her sunshine and told her she was awesome.

Who did that? Who just said things like that and left them dangling out there to haunt her?

She knew he was still dating the Ashleys. Not that they talked about it. They didn't talk about anything, really. She'd been avoiding the real topics. Keeping things light. Talking about Maximus and his progress.

And, miracle of miracles, Max was actually making progress. He'd figured out *sit* and *down* and *off*, even mastering *shake*—though *stay* and *come* were still works in progress. Even Connor was getting better about correcting him.

But it was still a relief when Connor left for his business trip in the middle of the month. She needed a break from the space he was occupying in her mind.

Though living in his house somehow didn't help her evict him from her thoughts.

Every room felt like him. It was odd, being in his space without him in it. Not that she *missed* him. Not that she found herself listening for the sound of his footsteps or his deep, slightly grumpy voice. It was just that the house was so big.

So she spent as little time there as possible.

Maximus barely fit in the back seat of her Bug, but she brought him with her every time the eerie quiet of Connor's house got to be too much for her and she drove over to Furry Friends, his massive head hanging out the window, jowls flapping in the breeze.

She took him on long walks through town to practice the Canine Good Citizen skills they'd been learning in the latest round of training courses. He was on his way to becoming a paragon of dogliness—or at least as close to one as the giant dopey mutt could get. He still climbed up on the couch every chance he got, flinging himself into her lap as if he were a terrier and not three-quarters wolfhound.

On the night before Connor was due back, Deenie was pinned beneath Max's bulk on the couch, watching an old horror movie on Connor's oversized television and telling herself that she definitely did *not* miss his color commentary, when her phone buzzed beside her.

She reached absently for the device, her attention snagging on the notification.

It was a travel alert. A discount flight to Sydney. She stared at it, poking her feelings, trying to figure out why for the first time in a long time, she didn't feel that itch that needed to be scratched at the back of her brain telling her to keep moving, keep searching.

It was probably just because she was so busy she didn't have time to daydream about Australia, but she hadn't been going stir-crazy, even though she'd been in Pine Hollow for months.

It had to be Bitty or Mr. Burke. Or Ally and Ben and Astrid. Or even the wedding.

It wasn't Connor, she rationalized. She wasn't *comfortable* here, she told herself, even as she nodded off on his couch, watching his television, trapped beneath his dog. Wearing his old Yale sweatshirt—but only because it was so soft and the smell comforted Maximus.

It had nothing to do with how devastating his dimples were.

Her eyelids heavy, she was only distantly aware of the sound of her phone buzzing again.

"Great work today. You really impressed Lila." Davis's voice piped through Connor's speakers as the car glided quietly through the night. "Any plans for your last night in the city?"

"Actually…" Connor cringed at Davis's perfectly innocent question and pulled into his driveway. "I decided to come back today, since we wrapped up early."

Davis released a knowing chuckle. "I should have known. You've got someone waiting for you."

Connor fought the urge to correct his mentor's assumption.

He'd failed to anticipate how many of his work conversations would become about Deenie after the fundraiser. How his colleagues would ask after her—how she was doing, whether she was there to wave to them when he was on video conferences.

She'd been a hit, which was exactly what he wanted, but he'd also come to the realization that this fake relationship wasn't going to be as easy to undo as they'd initially thought. It was good right now. They had a contract. Next weekend, she was throwing a princess party for Brent's granddaughter, and Connor had invited himself along to get more face time with the partners in a casual setting. People were starting to see him differently at work. It was working.

But it wasn't *real*. She wasn't the reason he'd come home.

"Max can be a handful. I didn't want Deenie to have to deal with him on her own any longer than necessary."

"Uh-huh," Davis agreed without an ounce of belief. "Say hi to Deenie for me."

Connor signed off noncommittally and pushed the button to raise the garage door. All three bays of the three-car garage sat empty. The powder-blue VW Bug was parked to one side of the driveway, getting wet in the steady rain. He'd told Deenie she could use the extra garage door opener, but apparently she hadn't taken him up on it. Stubborn.

He'd texted from the airport to let her know he'd caught an earlier flight—after realizing he didn't want to surprise her dancing in her underwear in his living room. She hadn't texted him back, which of course had caused the image of Deenie dancing in her underwear in his living room to live in his head for the entire drive home.

It was probably pink. Or polka-dotted. Or both.

Not that he had any business thinking about her underwear. That wasn't in the contract.

Connor climbed out of his car, retrieved his suitcase, and headed inside, making a lot of noise in the mudroom to warn Deenie to put her clothes back on. Neither Deenie nor Max rushed to greet him—and when he walked into the media room, he saw why.

It was only eight o'clock, but the only light in the room came from the ads flickering across the television Deenie must have been watching before she fell asleep. She lay on the couch in a pair of practically sedate navy leggings and his old Yale sweatshirt. Her pink-streaked hair was rumpled, smashed down on one side and frizzing up wildly on the other. And Maximus lay across her lower body, sprawled with her on the couch.

Something tightened in Connor's chest, and for a moment he just stared at her there. In his house, in his sweatshirt, her face relaxed in sleep, one hand draped over Max's shoulder.

Max lifted his head groggily.

"You are the world's worst guard dog," Connor scolded

him at a whisper—but Max's movement had already roused Deenie.

Her big blue eyes opened.

She blinked up at him, momentarily confused, and then a bright smile flashed over her face, hitting him like a mule kick to the chest. "Connor! Look, Maximus! Daddy's home early!"

The dog leapt toward him, and Connor braced for the greeting so Max wouldn't take his legs out from under him while Deenie scrambled off the couch and raked a hand through her rumpled hair.

"He missed you," she said breathlessly. "That's why I was wearing your shirt. So he could smell you."

"I didn't mean to surprise you—"

"No, I love surprises."

"I texted..."

"I must've fallen asleep before..." She scrubbed a hand over her face. "What time is it?"

"About eight? It's still early." Awkwardness hummed in the air between them as he straightened from petting Max.

Her face flushed. "I should go. It'll only take me a few minutes to gather up my stuff."

"You're welcome to stay here tonight," Connor said. "I'm not kicking you out."

"No, I should get back to the farmhouse," she said, the words fast. "Welcome home!"

She rushed up the stairs, practically running from him, and Connor silently smothered the weird mix of feelings in his chest.

It had felt like home, coming back to find her and Max sprawled on his couch.

Probably just the novelty of returning to a house that

wasn't empty for a change. He shouldn't get sucked in by that illusion of domesticity. He liked Deenie, but she clearly wanted to keep her distance, keep it professional. Which was good. It made sense. And Connor always did the logical thing.

So when Deenie hurried down the stairs three minutes later, he was waiting with his phone in hand. *Keep it professional.* "I was thinking I should pay you the final installment for Max's training when I send the money for pet sitting. Is the same account as before good?"

Deenie froze, visibly caught off guard for possibly the first time since he'd met her. "Um, yeah, that account's good, but we haven't—I mean, he hasn't hit all the benchmarks in the contract yet."

"No, of course you'll keep working with him, but I just figured we could get the financials out of the way."

"Right. Right, thanks. Yeah."

"So I'll go ahead..."

"Good. Yeah." She continued toward the door with her duffel, a bright green top where his sweatshirt had been. "Great. G'night, Connor."

"Good night, Deenie."

She pulled at the front door—which stayed firmly closed. "It's locked."

"What?" She didn't seem to hear him, pulling again at the door.

He came up behind her and reached over her shoulder to flick the dead bolt. She froze as his inner arm brushed her shoulder.

"I came in through the garage," he rumbled, close to her ear.

"Right. Of course." She didn't look at him, her spine

straight, pink climbing up the back of her neck. "Well, good night."

It was strange seeing her so flustered. Deenie, who always seemed to have a smart remark and a flashing smile cued up.

He watched her jog to the VW and drive away, telling himself he'd imagined the edge of heat to the awkwardness between them. The whisper of chemistry.

They had a contract. That was it.

And he didn't think about her after she was gone. Not for more than an hour or two.

Chapter Twenty-One

Deenie hesitated when she pulled into Connor's driveway and saw the cars already parked there. Poker night. She'd forgotten it was Wednesday.

The last couple of "poker nights," the guys had ended up at Ben's house, painting the new walls in the basement and demoing the upstairs bathroom so Ben could cut down on construction costs, but apparently they were actually playing tonight.

Deenie had scaled back the training sessions—in part because Max was doing so well, but also, if she was honest, because she needed to remind herself of the separation of church and state. Less time with Connor. More keeping things professional. But there were still benchmarks in the training contract that Max hadn't achieved, so she kept coming back.

She'd meant to come over earlier, but she'd lost track of time working on some dresses—which was exactly why she didn't believe in schedules. When she saw the cars, she considered skipping Max's session—but she hadn't been by in nearly two days, frantically rushing to finish some dress orders.

And maybe this was the perfect time. If Connor was distracted by his poker buddies in the game room, she could slip in, work with Max for fifteen minutes, and slip out. Her duty discharged, with no one the wiser.

Deenie punched in the door code and entered. She must've done this a hundred times in the last couple of months, but this was the first time since she'd started that it felt like she was somewhere she didn't belong. Creeping into his house while he was playing poker with his friends.

Max loped up to greet her, his tongue lolling out the side of his mouth.

"Hi, baby," Deenie greeted the big lummox.

She was whispering. Even though she had a perfectly good reason to be here. She'd even texted before she came and gotten a thumbs-up—though, admittedly, that had been almost an hour ago. She'd gotten sidetracked on the way.

A burst of laughter floated out of the game room, followed by groans.

She'd gotten to know Connor's friends a lot better over the last few months—mostly because she was living with Ben, and Ben's friends were Connor's friends. Levi, the chief of police, was tall and stern—definitely the strong, silent type. He didn't say much, but he always seemed to be in control of the situation.

On the other hand, Mac, who ran the Cup, was Levi's polar opposite. He was always smiling, always talking, and almost always putting his foot in his mouth. Deenie liked him enormously—especially when he'd had two beers and began demonstrating his encyclopedic knowledge of show tunes. They'd bonded over a shared love for *Hadestown* on the night they'd celebrated Ben's election.

She was comfortable around all the guys—but she still

hesitated to pop her head into the game room to let them know she was there. She'd never bothered Connor when she arrived before, just working with Maximus and slipping out again without disturbing him if he was busy. That was their routine. But it felt different with their voices reverberating into the room.

"You aren't expecting us to call you Mr. Mayor once you're sworn in, are you?" Her ears pricked up at the sound of Connor's voice.

"Absolutely." That must have been Ben.

"In that case, I'm going to insist you all call me Chief." Definitely Levi.

"I'm actually totally fine if you all want to call me Chef," Mac added cheerfully. "Especially if you snap to attention and say, 'Yes, Chef!' every time I tell you to do something."

There was a moment of silence and she could easily picture the looks they must be giving him.

Deenie wasn't *trying* to eavesdrop. She was just working with Max like she always did, and the sound of their conversation was carrying. It was the hardwood reflecting their voices. Weird acoustics. That was all.

If she could hear them, they must be able to hear her. Deenie made her voice clear and strong as she told Max to sit and shake, cooing at him in praise when he got it right. *Here I am, just training like normal, not eavesdropping at all.*

Ben's voice carried again.

"I just wish the contractor wouldn't keep adding another week," Ben complained, shuffling the poker deck with impatient motions. "I wanted the reno finished before I was sworn in and Astrid back into our normal routine before all the town stuff hit."

Connor stacked his winnings from the last hand as Levi rocked back in his chair, rolling a poker chip between his fingers. "You that eager to stop living with Ally?"

Ben shot him a glare, dealing the first card at Levi more aggressively than strictly necessary. "I just had an order I wanted to do things. We moved in out of necessity, and now we have to move out before our relationship can progress because otherwise it's not choice. It's inertia."

"You might be overthinking this," Mac commented.

"Exactly," Connor agreed, flicking his ante into the center of the table. "Stop worrying about the order things come in and trying to control everything."

"*You're* calling Ben a control freak? You?" Mac guffawed.

Connor reached for his cards. "I'm just saying he's wound a little tight."

"Oh yeah, he definitely is. It just seems like the pot calling the kettle obsidian there. All three of you are wound so tight you could snap."

Levi feigned innocence. "How did I get dragged into this?"

"I'm the only easygoing one in this room," Mac declared.

He wasn't wrong. Mac had always had an impressive capacity for Zen that the rest of them didn't possess.

"Though Connor does seem suspiciously relaxed," Mac commented.

Tension instantly knotted Connor's shoulders.

"I noticed that." Levi eyed him speculatively.

"Almost like he's met someone." A smug smile spread on Mac's face.

"No." Connor's voice was hard. "We're giving Ben a hard time. It isn't my turn."

"I really think it is." Ben grinned, relieved to be off the hot seat. "You can tell me I'm right anytime you like, by the way."

"Are you right about something?" Connor asked, making a show of searching his brain.

"Maximus? The dog you insisted you didn't need?"

"Where is Maximus?" Mac looked around the room as if the 140-pound dog might be hiding under the rug.

"Asleep somewhere." Connor didn't look up from his cards. Deenie had texted that she was coming by earlier to work with him, and he almost always napped after the training sessions.

"At least he's better than that menace of Elinor's," Levi growled. "I spend half my days tracking that damn dog all over town."

"I'm just relieved I don't have to worry about him whenever he's out of sight anymore. Deenie's been a miracle worker."

"Yeah…" Mac drawled. "We've noticed."

Connor narrowed his eyes at Mac. "What's that supposed to mean?"

"Just ask him," Levi commanded.

Connor frowned, looking between Levi and Mac. "Ask me what?"

Levi studied his cards with a flawless lack of expression, while Mac seemed to have forgotten they were playing, his hand facedown on the table. "Are you interested in Deenie?" Mac asked. "We all think you're sneaking around together."

"For the record, I don't think you're sneaking around together," Ben clarified. "I think she has better taste."

"She has been over here a lot," Levi commented, tapping his cards and watching Connor across the table.

"I'm not dating Deenie." Connor made his tone firm, un-equivocal. His work colleagues were already obsessed with Deenie. He didn't need his friends getting the wrong idea.

At Levi's skeptical stare, he admitted, "We have an arrangement."

"The dog training?" Mac asked.

"That, yes, but I also agreed to be her date for some family wedding stuff if she'll be mine for some work events."

Levi's eyebrows arched. "You sure that's a good idea?" When Connor challenged him with a look, he lazily shrugged one shoulder. "You're a serial monogamist. You get sucked into relationships and don't know how to let them go."

"That's bullshit."

Mac didn't quite meet his eyes. "You were engaged a long time…"

"Not as long as Levi," Connor snapped, earning a *piss-off* look across the table. "It's purely platonic," he assured them. "We're just friends."

"I didn't realize you two were friends," Levi drawled.

Connor hadn't really, either, but they were. Deenie had somehow become one of the people who probably knew him best. Obviously, they couldn't be worse suited for each other—she was always mentally planning her escape, and he could never let himself get seriously involved with someone who would pull a Monica on him—but he liked her. Liked spending time with her.

As friends, as strange as it seemed, they worked.

And yes, he may have had certain *thoughts* when he'd come home to find her sleeping in his clothes, but that was just a random aberration. Already forgotten.

A speculative look was all over Mac's face, and Connor spoke quickly to nip that shit in the bud. "I'm not going to get sucked in. I'm actively looking for the right kind of relationship on a number of dating apps."

"So you have met someone."

"No. I just have a plan."

Mac groaned. "You guys and your plans. Can't you ever just let things happen?"

"What's the plan?" Ben asked.

"To get married," Connor admitted. "To find my person. To just be done looking and know that my romantic future is settled."

Mac snorted, picking up his cards again. "How's that working out for you?"

"I've been on a few dates. Nothing really perfect yet, but it's a work in progress."

He'd been kind of bored on a couple of those dates, inadvertently comparing them to Deenie. Which was ridiculous. Of course Deenie would be more fun. She was flash and fire and wit. She argued with him, disagreeing with him with a smile on her face that always made him lean in.

But she was also unpredictable. And he never wanted to come home to another Post-it again. He *wanted* sedate and dependable. He just needed to keep reminding himself of that—which was why he'd given each of those women second dates. And been bored again.

It wasn't the women's fault. They just weren't a good fit. He needed someone who challenged him and was also settled. That was all. Someone fun and smart...

His memory snagged on a match that had popped onto one of his apps yesterday.

Connor's gaze flicked across the table, studying Levi's blank face as the cop studied his cards. "These apps are crazy. One of them even tried to match me up with Elinor."

He was watching for a reaction, but Levi didn't even flutter an eyelash. His eyes never left his cards. "Go for it."

Connor didn't bother to conceal his surprise. Levi had been head over heels for Elinor ever since middle school. The pair had called off their engagement a few years ago, but Connor had always assumed they would eventually get back together. Was it possible Levi was actually over her?

Even if he was, Connor didn't think he could change the way he thought of Elinor now.

But that didn't mean he wouldn't try to get a reaction out of Levi. "I might. We all know she's smart. Funny. Family oriented. Really, we're perfect for each other."

He expected a death glare. He expected Levi to lunge across the table and kill him with his bare hands.

The police chief didn't even blink. He lifted his beer bottle with two fingers, draining the last swallow. "Anyone else want another round?"

"Crap!" Deenie knew she didn't have time to make it out the front door before Levi emerged from the game room beside Connor's office. There was nowhere to hide in the open-concept sprawl of the main floor, so she hurried into the kitchen and pretended to be getting out the dog treats, as if she'd just arrived.

And as if she didn't bring them with her.

She had the door to the pantry open when Levi stepped into the kitchen and she feigned surprise. "Levi! Hi! Is it poker night?"

Levi made an affirmative noise and opened the fridge, pulling out four beers and holding them in one hand, dangling by the neck. His pale gray eyes traced her face—and she had the sinking feeling that he could tell just by looking at her that she'd overheard every word.

The man had an incredible poker face, but there was something oddly sympathetic about his lack of expression.

"I'm just here to work with Maximus. He's getting a lot better," she said, eagerly filling the silence. Levi was an incredible interrogator. All he had to do was grunt and she wanted to spill her guts.

His gaze flicked down to the dog, who was—thank God—sitting perfectly at her side. "Looks like it." He jerked his chin at her in farewell and ambled back toward the game room.

Her stomach clenched with indecision. Would he tell the others she was here? If he did, would Connor come out to talk to her? Would he know she'd been listening in? Would he know she'd heard him talk about how they were just friends, but he was three-quarters in love with Elinor already? Would he see the stupid jealousy she hadn't been able to control all over her face?

She didn't want to be with Connor. She *didn't*. So why did it bother her so much that he didn't want to be with her? Was it just vanity?

Levi paused, just before he came into view of the men through the open archway of the game room. He looked back at her, making eye contact, and jerked his head to the side. Toward the front door.

Deenie didn't need to be told twice.

She told Max he was a good boy, gave him one last treat, and practically ran for the exit.

When she burst out into the cool March night, she

flinched at the sight of the cars in the driveway. No wonder Levi hadn't bought her "oh, are you here?" act.

She was such an idiot.

For trying to hide that she'd been listening.

And for eavesdropping in the first place. She knew better. She *knew* you always heard things you didn't want to hear when you skulked around.

Like Connor repeatedly assuring his buddies that the two of them were just platonic. Not that she'd expected anything else, but after the kiss and telling her she was sunshine, telling her she was good enough, it kind of stung. Just like finding out he was secretly in love with Elinor.

Because of course he was. Elinor was organized. Prepared. No nonsense.

All the things Deenie wasn't.

Her friendship with Elinor had always been more distant than her friendship with Ally. Ally's energy was just chaotic enough to match up with hers, whereas Elinor was all order and discipline.

She was perfect for Connor.

And there was absolutely no reason for Deenie to be disappointed by that. She was never going to get involved with him anyway. He would only try to change her. Try to mold her into a better version of herself, like her parents always did.

No. Much better to keep her distance, emotionally. This was a good reminder. She was glad she'd overheard him. Glad she knew where they stood. At a safe distance. Clarity was priceless.

Or so she told herself as she climbed into her powder-blue VW Bug and drove home.

Chapter Twenty-Two

I t's the prince!"
Connor flinched as a dozen squealing five-year-olds in fluffy pastel dresses rushed him en masse.

When he'd told Deenie he planned to come with her to the princess party so he could get some more face time with the partners, she'd agreed it was a good idea. She'd just failed to tell him she was going to put him to work.

Though she'd made a good point when she handed him his costume. If he was going to come to a child's birthday party, he needed a reason to be there—and what better reason than to play a part?

Prince Charming had sounded like a pretty good role. Until he discovered the prince in this scenario was actually duplicitous, and Deenie was going to task the little girls with finding him and capturing him so he could be brought to justice.

He'd never expected to be the royal prey, hunted by a dozen pint-sized, princess-dressed vigilantes, but there he was.

And they'd found him.

He wanted kids. He liked kids. He'd just never been around this many at one time and didn't really know what to do with them. He generally treated them like small adults—which worked out pretty well—but he needed a new strategy as the screaming horde approached.

What would Deenie do?

The tide of little girls slammed into him, and he tumbled dramatically to the ground with a roar, all of them piling on top of him as he became the mountain in an impromptu game of king of the mountain. Or queen in this case. Or, really, princess.

"Freeze him!" Deenie called encouragement from a few feet away—as at least one of his colleagues captured the entire thing on a cell phone video. "Use your magic! Use your magic to capture him!"

The girls scrambled off him—letting him breathe again—so they could wave their arms to cast their magic. Connor sat up, surrounded on all sides by tiny faces, intently concentrating as they flared tiny hands at him.

"Don't let him escape!" Deenie coached breathlessly. "Do you have him?"

He pretended to freeze in place, one hand outstretched.

"We have him!" the birthday girl declared.

"Good! You keep working your magic! But now that we have him, do you think we can figure out why he tried to trick us? Do you think there's a reason? Look at him with your magic eyes!"

Tiny faces squinted at him.

"He's under a spell!" one little girl shouted.

"His heart was frozen!" another added.

Deenie gasped, shock suffusing her face. "Oh my goodness! A spell! Do you think we can save him?"

"Only love can save him!" the birthday girl practically screamed—and then rushed toward him so fast he flinched.

But she was just giving him a hug. Quickly followed by almost every other little girl at the party. He found himself in the middle of a squirming group hug with all of the little girls promising, "Don't worry! We'll save you!"

It was so freaking sweet his eyes got a little misty—and then he looked up, his gaze locking with Deenie's.

Deenie met Connor's eyes and something streaked through her. Something warm and unwelcome.

He was doing so much better than she'd expected.

She wouldn't have let him completely drown, but she'd sort of expected him to flail when she brought him along as her assistant. On some level she might have been trying to remind herself that they weren't suited. That he was stiff and rigid and everything she didn't need in her life.

But he wasn't stiff.

He certainly wasn't *comfortable*. She could see that in his eyes. But he had loosened his dignity straitjacket enough to be silly with the girls—and he was a hit.

He'd be a good dad.

As if in answer to the thought, thunder rolled in the distance.

The weather had been precarious all day. Ominous gray clouds roiled overhead—though the rain had held off long enough for them to chase Connor around the backyard. But now it looked like their weather luck was at an end.

Fortunately, the next portion of the party was set up inside.

Deenie gasped. "Do you hear that?" She cocked her head,

making a show of listening until the girls peeled away from Connor and quieted, straining their ears, too. "Are those the bells of the cake fairies? Do you think if we hurry we can catch them in the act of leaving the cake inside the house?"

The girls all screeched with delight—equal parts eagerness to catch the cake fairies and anticipation of the sugar infusion—and sprinted toward the doors, where the parents ushered them inside.

Deenie extended her hand to Connor, who was still kneeling on the ground. "Come on, Prince Charming. I think you've earned some cake."

His warm, calloused hand slid into hers. "Thank you for saving me," he said as she helped him to his feet.

Only love can save him.

No. No no no no no no. That was not at all what was going on here. She wasn't falling for Connor Wyeth.

Not the exact kind of man her parents had always wanted for her. A man with a five-year plan and a color-coded sock drawer who wanted a perfect wife at his side, when Deenie had always been far from perfect. Just *no*.

"Come on." She jerked her hand back. "It's going to rain any second."

Two hours later, rain pounded against the windshield in a drumming rhythm. Deenie didn't know how Connor could see, but he seemed perfectly relaxed behind the wheel, even smiling slightly to himself.

She supposed he had reason to be happy. The party had been a complete success—both from a kid perspective and from a networking one. While she had a cake and tea party with the girls, Connor had hung back with the parents and grandparents, chatting quietly with his boss. The two of them looked so chummy, Connor was practically a member of the family by the time they packed up and left.

"How much of that was planned?" Connor asked out of the blue when they'd been driving in the comfortable silence of the rain for several minutes. At first she thought he meant giving him extra time to butter up his boss by dawdling as she was packing up her gear, but then he clarified. "Did you know I was going to be the bad guy?"

"I don't like that term. Bad guy. It's too binary."

He didn't even have to look at her for her to feel the look he would have given her. *Answer the question, Deenie.* She was getting to know his argument glances all too well.

"I always have an idea, a sort of roadmap of where I think things will go," she explained, "but I like to let the kids guide the story as much as possible. I coach them and steer them when we're getting off the rails, but this is their chance to make the stories they read and watch in movies into *their* stories, so I want it to be as interactive as possible." She flicked a sideways look at his profile. He really was entirely too good-looking for his own good. "I figured there was a good chance they'd go the trickster prince route, since the birthday girl is obsessed with *Frozen*, and the prince in *Frozen* turns out to be not such a prince. I never want to exactly replicate the stories they know, but they make a good jumping-off point, and then we can take it in new directions—like saving the quote-unquote bad guy with love. Which I'm sure you're thinking is sappy and ridiculous—"

"Don't tell me what I'm thinking. I was actually thinking it's no wonder you're so popular. You're amazing with them."

She blushed, grateful to the storm snaring his attention so he didn't see her face.

"My bosses were really impressed."

"Good." That was what they were here for. His work. Nothing else.

Though she had gotten a massive tip on top of her usual fee, so she wasn't complaining.

"You did better than I thought you would," she admitted. "You were really good with the kids."

"I just kept thinking, 'What would Deenie do?'" He flicked a glance at her. "Do you think you'll ever have kids?"

The question hit her right in the ovaries, but she firmly reminded her girly parts that he wasn't asking because he wanted to have babies with her. He was only making conversation.

"I don't know," she hedged. "I want them—I love kids—but I'm not sure my life is compatible with parenting, you know?"

"I'm not sure that's true. But if you wanted them badly enough, you could make some changes."

"Maybe I'm just not cut out to be a mom," she said, the words a little too sharp, revealing a little too much vulnerability. She smoothed her voice over, making it light and joking. "My brother thinks I'd be a terrible parent. But then he has his children marching so perfectly in formation, I'm not sure his metrics of parenting are to be trusted."

"Did he actually say that to you?" Connor glanced over at her—more appalled than amused. She was off her game. She was usually so good at having people laughing at her failings.

"It was a long time ago," she assured him, as if she didn't remember those words every time she thought about settling down and having a family.

She'd been twenty when her brother's first child had been born. Recently back from running off to Europe to watch the royal wedding and rebelling against her family by studying theater instead of finance.

She'd held her tiny niece for the first time, in awe of her tiny little fingers and toes, and whispered, "I want one."

And Peter had heard her.

He'd given her a lecture about responsibility. About how she couldn't just *stop* being a parent whenever she wanted to run off to a foreign country. He'd told her not everyone was cut out for parenting.

And deep down she still believed him.

She loved working with kids. She'd love to have one of her own. Maybe even three or four. But just because she wanted it didn't make it realistic. Her life was a choice—the choice to be free. And raising children didn't exactly line up with unfettered freedom.

You could make another choice, a little voice whispered in the back of her mind.

But to do that, she had to find someone who wanted to make that choice with her. And she wasn't the kind of girl someone like Connor wanted to raise kids with.

"How are things going with the Ashleys?" she asked, to remind herself of that fact.

He shifted his grip on the steering wheel, taking a turn. "They're going well."

Well. That was simple. Bland. Telling her nothing.

"Though none of the ones I'm currently interacting with are named Ashley."

She almost asked him about Elinor, barely stopping herself before revealing she'd eavesdropped. "The Ashleys were duds?"

"One of them was always busy, and we never managed to find a time to meet up. The only time she was free was when I had to go to New York, so our conversations just sort of petered out. The other one . . . she had this really sharp way of speaking to waitstaff. My mom always said everyone should have to work in the service industry at least once in their life so they learn how to be kind to the people who serve them."

It was good advice. Deenie had been a barista and a bartender and held a dozen other short-term customer service jobs—each one showing her exactly how much variety there was in the way people chose to treat those who gave them their food and drink. But she had a hard time picturing Connor in a service role.

"You worked in the service industry?"

"College," he explained. "Waiting tables was good money. I could work around my school schedule, and my managers were understanding when I needed to trade shifts for extra study time around exams. I think they were pretty used to it around the university."

"They must have loved you. Mr. Responsibility. So hardworking. So punctual."

"I like being on time. Unlike some people."

Deenie glared at his profile—more because he expected her to than because she was actually offended. "There is a time and a place for punctuality and a time and a place for being judiciously tardy."

"Agree to disagree." Connor flicked a glance at her as his grin flashed in the dark cocoon of the car.

And suddenly something about that smile, about him, made her throat go tight.

Chapter Twenty-Three

Deenie held herself still, emotion swelling in her chest as they approached the Pine Hollow town limits. She never would have thought, two months ago, that she'd be driving through a thunderstorm with Connor, her heart pressing against the inner walls of her chest because it had expanded so much. But then, two months ago, she'd had a very different idea of who he was.

She knew him now. She'd known him for a while.

She understood why he was so determined to chase the vision of success he'd dreamed up for himself when he was the young son of a single mom. He hadn't had an organized life—so he'd given himself one. And now he worked harder than anyone she knew and spoiled his mother every chance he got. It was hard not to soften in the face of that.

Especially when he called her sunshine.

Those words continued to haunt her. Why would he say that? Why make her feel this way?

She'd been so sure he would be like her parents—that all the rules he had for himself would apply to her, and she

would never feel good enough around him, always feeling
like she had to change who she was, change her instincts
even, just to fit inside his life. But he never made her feel
that way. Not anymore.

He wasn't the one making her feel like she wasn't
enough. He was the one telling her that she *was*.

How was she supposed to defend herself against that?

Especially when she kept seeing him. When they kept
pretending they were together. When *he* kept pretending she
was exactly the kind of girl he was looking for, when she
knew she wasn't.

Did they really need each other anymore? Max was
nearly trained, and Connor knew how to work with him
now. He was on a good track with his bosses—they'd even
invited him for a dinner party. She hadn't had nearly as
many wedding events to attend as she'd anticipated. And
during the wedding, she'd be busy being a bridesmaid—too
busy to worry about having a date.

Maybe it was time they called this off. Before things got
even more confused. Before her heart got so tangled up in
him, she couldn't let go.

They pulled into the long driveway of Furry Friends, the
sound of the gravel crunching beneath the tires completely
drowned out by the heavy rain drumming on the roof.
Connor put the car into park after pulling as close as he
could get to the front porch of the farmhouse without driving on the grass. Deenie was still going to have to sprint
through the rain.

Connor turned toward her. "Thank you for today. You've
really saved me."

Only love can save him.

The echo of words from five-year-old mouths drove into

her gut, a sudden white-hot poker of aggravation. Angry futility.

"Maybe we should stop."

The words were out before she'd decided to speak.

Confusion pulled at Connor's brow in the dashboard light. "Stop what?"

"All of this." She waved around the car, as if their contract was somehow the SUV's fault. Her duffel bag with all the princess party gear sat in the back seat, her own dress and wig tucked safely inside. She was back in turquoise leggings and a funky denim coat she'd picked up at a market in Greece. She should have felt like herself, but she was crawling out of her skin. "We accomplished what we wanted to accomplish. Maybe we should just be done. You can bring one of the Ashleys to your things, and I'll do the wedding on my own."

The storm clouds outside had nothing on the ones gathering in Connor's eyes. "We just agreed to go to dinner with Brent and the other partners."

"I know."

"It was your idea. This whole thing was your idea."

"I know!" she snapped. "But I didn't expect it to feel—"

She slammed on the brakes, barely stopping the words from spilling out of her mouth. Where the hell were her filters? Where was her legendary composure? What was *wrong* with her?

Deenie catapulted out of the car. The deluge instantly soaked her, saturating her coat and chilling her skin, but she welcomed the shock.

"Deenie!" Connor shouted. But she was already slamming the passenger door.

She reached for the rear door, intending to jerk it open

and grab her princess bag, but the door was locked and she swore, yanking futilely at the handle.

"Deenie!" Connor was out of the car now, shouting over the rain. "What the hell?"

"It got too real!" she yelled at him over the roof of the car. "It's too much."

Screw it. Deenie spun on her heel, splashing toward the house through puddles that seemed to have instantly formed everywhere. She'd get the bag from him later. There was nothing in there that couldn't live in his back seat for a few days.

"Deenie!" Connor was suddenly in front of her. Blocking the way. Water streamed down his face, every inch of him as soaked as every inch of her. What kind of an idiot got out of the car in the middle of a freaking downpour? "What got too real?"

"Don't." She shook her head—not even sure what she was trying to stop from happening.

He stepped closer—still a foot away, but somehow that distance seemed to change everything. Instead of shouting across the rain, they were suddenly alone in it, a pocket of privacy, and she couldn't breathe.

"What got too real, Deenie?"

"You," she said, though the word made no sense—and yet it was the only thing that made sense. "I wasn't supposed to really like you. I hate that I like you!"

His face was granite and steel—all hard lines and hard edges—but his eyes were molten fire. She read the flare of heat in them a fraction of a second before he moved, fast and determined. His hands closed on her jaw, framing her face, and suddenly they were kissing.

This kiss couldn't have been less like the one on the dance floor at the engagement party.

That had been sweet and lingering and warm. This was a tornado. A hurricane. A natural disaster, a force of nature, it swept them up, swept her up, until she was in his arms, her feet off the ground, clinging to him, no longer feeling the cold or the wet because pure electricity was pumping through her veins.

She didn't want it to end. Not now. Not ever.

Her back hit something—a post holding up the front porch, holding her up, too, because her muscles and bones had completely lost their capacity to do so. She was heat and fire. She was a lit candle of pure want.

It was Connor who lifted his head, breaking the kiss—because of course it was. He could never just ride the tsunami, let it crash over the world and leave destruction in its wake, he had to control everything, plan everything.

"What are we—"

"Stop thinking." She grabbed his head and dragged him back into the gravitational force of the kiss. Both of them sucked back into the black hole of it, all their better judgment wiped away—until the obnoxious man broke away *again*, breathing hard, and fisted his hand in her hair.

"Stop." He growled, and the searing look in his eyes melted her girly parts into molten wax.

How did he make *not* kissing even sexier than kissing? Who was this man?

They were under the overhang of the porch—smart thinking. Trust Connor to maneuver them out of the rain even in the midst of the hurricane that raged between them. He really was quite useful. She could fling herself like a kite into the middle of a storm, knowing he would always keep her grounded—even if they both got struck by lightning.

"What are we doing?" he asked—the question she'd been trying to avoid.

"Kissing? Seemed like kissing. *Felt* like kissing." She moved against him and he squeezed her ribs to still her.

"Stop."

She froze, feeling the icy cling of her wet clothes again. "You don't want…?" She couldn't finish the question. Had she jumped an unwilling man?

But no. He'd grabbed her. Yes, she'd leapt on him like a puma, but he'd definitely started it, and he'd seemed like he was with her all the way. She was still pinned between his body and the porch post. She needed to send a thank-you note to his personal trainer, because the man was granite everywhere she touched.

"Deenie. I want you," he assured her, the roughness in his voice all the sincerity she needed. "But where are we going?"

"Does it have to go anywhere?" Why did they have to define everything? Why did everything have to have a plan? A freaking contract?

His gaze flicked past her toward the farmhouse and she realized he meant the question literally.

Her eyes widened. *"Oh."*

Ally and Ben and Astrid were in that house. If they walked in, soaking wet, and rushed up to her bedroom, there was *no way* they weren't having a discussion about their relationship status with the mayor and the shelter owner in the morning. Deenie cringed at the thought.

And then there was Maximus. They couldn't just leave him alone all night.

They could drag their soaking selves back into Connor's car and drive out to his place—but the reality of that made her shiver, her sense returning in an unwelcome rush.

Connor instantly sensed the change and stepped back, still beneath the overhang, but no longer pinning her to the post.

Deenie was grateful for the dark so he couldn't see the shades of burgundy her face must be turning. She took a slow breath.

"So. That happened."

He laughed softly, glancing back toward the car. "If you really want to stop being my plus-one—"

"No," she interrupted. "No, it's fine. I was overreacting. I'm sure we can keep that up and um…" She trailed off, a dozen dirty jokes about keeping other things up whispering in the back of her mind, begging her to relieve the tension. But for once she couldn't seem to find a way to hide. She'd shown him too much.

"So this…"

"Chemistry," Deenie said, making the word as dismissive as possible. "It was bound to happen. You're hot. I'm hot. We're pretending to be crazy about one another."

Connor snorted. "You never lack for confidence."

Wrong. He was so wrong, but she embraced the lie.

Deenie arched her eyebrows, even though she wasn't sure he could see them. She needed the *feel* of her face to get her mask back in place. "Are you implying I'm not hot?"

"No," Connor growled, with entirely too much feeling. "I'm not saying that."

Retreat, her instincts screamed. Deenie took a step up onto the porch. "I should go inside."

She hated the word *should*. If he knew her, he'd know that. He'd know that she would take the slightest excuse to rebel against what she *should* do and fling herself back into his arms. The back seat of his car was probably perfectly comfortable—and wouldn't have that awkward driving-to-his-house-for-the-express-purpose-of-making-a-reckless-choice delay. All he had to do was twitch a finger at her.

But he rocked back on his heels, shoving his hands into the pockets of his pants. "Right."

He'd left his fancy peacoat in the car when he leapt out after her, and his button-down shirt was clinging to *everything*. Seriously, how many abs did the man have? She knew he worked out, but that was just ridiculous. Why did he have to look so good? Why did she have to feel so stupid for walking away from him and also so scared to take the step that would bring her back into his arms?

"Good night, Deenie."

No, she wanted to scream. She was the queen of bad choices and even knowing getting involved with him would be a terrible choice, she desperately wanted to do it. Why couldn't he just be reckless and stupid with her?

He dipped his chin and turned, walking away—and looking just as good from the back. Seriously, the *shoulders*. She stood under the overhang, avidly objectifying him, but he didn't look back. He didn't even pause before climbing into the car and executing a tight turn in the driveway.

Not that she'd expected him to pause. It was pouring rain and she'd just sent him packing. But still.

She stood watching until the taillights were gone, shivering in her sopping clothing. It wasn't until she turned to go inside that she remembered her bag was still in the back of his car.

Chapter Twenty-Four

Connor forced himself not to look in the rearview mirror—either literally or metaphorically. He wasn't going to check to see if Deenie was watching him drive away. And he *definitely* wasn't going to think back to the moment he'd lost his mind and kissed her.

Except he couldn't seem to stop going back to that moment. When they'd been standing there in the rain, water clumping her eyelashes and plastering her hair to her head. The deluge had drowned out his sense and logic and every thinking part of his brain until he was only instinct and that instinct *needed* her.

He couldn't seem to shake that feeling.

He'd seen her now. The Deenie behind the curtain. The Deenie beneath the flashing smile and the brash confidence and smart-ass remarks. The Deenie beneath the glittery façade. Vulnerable Deenie. And the last thing he wanted to do was hurt her.

They were all wrong for each other. They both knew it.

He'd felt so helpless as a kid. He never wanted to feel that way again. And then when Monica had left, it had hit him again. That feeling that he was powerless. Out of control. He'd built his life back up by careful planning. He couldn't risk it all for someone who crashed through his neatly ordered plans like a wrecking ball.

Deenie made him feel out of control. That kiss...

What happened next? Her bag was still in his back seat. Was he supposed to bring it back? Would she still come back the next day to train Max?

Would they kiss again?

Connor tucked his car into the garage and put Maximus out onto the covered patio to pee before returning to the garage to wipe the water off the leather of the driver's seat. He stripped out of his waterlogged clothes, tossed them in the laundry, and climbed into a hot shower. Putting his life back in order. Erasing the evidence.

But her bag was still in his back seat. And the memory was still vivid, especially as he stood beneath the spray in the shower, the water mimicking the pounding rain, his body aching.

It was possible nothing would happen. Deenie was a master at pretending. She could pretend their mad kiss in the rain had never happened. But if she wanted it to happen again...

He didn't want to feel helpless again. He didn't want to be a victim to his emotions. But he could keep his emotions at a safe distance. He *knew* they were wrong for each other. He needed someone who would never run, someone he never had to doubt. That was the only kind of person he could give his whole self to. But until he found that person...

Maybe it could work if they were temporary. Expiration dating, she'd called it. Maybe if they *knew* it was only a crazy chemical thing, likely sprung from the fact that they sparked like fireworks. Opposites attracted. But they didn't make practical long-term partners.

Maybe he needed a fling. The rebound he'd never had after Monica. He and Deenie were friends now. So why not friends with benefits?

Or maybe the whole thing was a terrible idea. Maybe he should forget that damn unforgettable kiss.

He'd follow her lead, he decided. His own Pied Piper of bad ideas.

And he'd keep his heart safely locked away.

Deenie wasn't hiding from Connor, per se. Maximus really did need a day off from his training regimen every now and then. And she really had planned on visiting her great-aunt that Sunday. If she lingered and dawdled long after it had proven to be a bad day, in the hopes that Bitty would somehow magically surface from the fog she had fallen into and give Deenie the advice she needed, well...that was understandable.

She was just glad no one at the farmhouse had looked out the window last night and seen her making out with Connor in front of the porch.

Ally and Ben hadn't even commented on her drenched appearance beyond a casual "Wow, it's really coming down out there."

Deenie had snuck upstairs before anyone could get a good look at her. Convinced her lips were burning and a scarlet *C* was emblazoned across them. *C* for Connor, because it felt like they'd been branded with his mark. Which was ridiculous. Fanciful. But Deenie was allowed to be ridiculous and fanciful if she pleased, and she very much pleased.

She had *feelings* for Connor. Very inconvenient feelings.

It would be one thing if those feelings were strictly limited to lust. But combining lust and friendship and genuine affection...it was a dangerous cocktail. And she didn't know what to do.

Did she pretend nothing had happened? Did she take the bull by the horns and steer him firmly away from any kind of relationship? Or did she lean into the curve and ride this out until she got him out of her system?

The third option obviously sounded the best, but she wasn't exactly renowned for her good decision making.

Which was why she'd wanted to talk to Bitty.

Really, she'd wanted Bitty to talk to *her*, but today had gotten off to a rocky start. Bitty was confused and distressed before Deenie even arrived, and it had gone downhill from there.

Deenie slipped out of assisted living, making her way down the long hallway to the residents' tower. She hadn't called ahead, but Mr. Burke didn't often go out, so she took a chance, taking the elevator to the fifth floor.

She was approaching the door to apartment 5015 when it opened and a young nurse Deenie vaguely recognized stepped out. The girl said goodbye to Mr. Burke and gave Deenie a smile as she passed. Deenie smiled back, struggling to remember her name.

"Mr. Burke!" Deenie called before the door could shut all the way. "Is this a bad time?"

"Nadine!" Mr. Burke beamed at her with unmasked delight. She didn't know how, but somehow when he said her full name she loved it. JoJo yipped and scampered into the hallway, bouncing around Deenie's ankles with joy. "Here to see your girl?"

Deenie knelt to greet JoJo, scooping the sweet girl up for a cuddle and smoothing her cheek against JoJo's silky head as she straightened to smile at Mr. Burke. "Here to see you."

"Wonderful surprise. Come in."

Deenie entered his familiar apartment, hesitating when she saw the massive pill box on the coffee table, left behind by the nurse. "I should have called ahead."

"Nonsense. You come anytime. How's Bitty?"

The usual words, assurances that she was doing great and everything was okay, clogged in her throat. She followed him into the little galley kitchen as he fussed with a teakettle. They'd gotten into the habit, when she visited, of having tea and butter cookies, and he moved with slow, deliberate motions, preparing the tray.

"Can I help?"

"You can get out the cookies," he allowed, his pale gaze taking in every detail of her expression. "Extra cookies today, I think."

Deenie opened the cupboard, laying out the cookies on the little decorative plate he provided. Mr. Burke's late husband had been British and very particular about his tea and "biscuits," as Deenie had learned on a previous visit.

She'd been coming by the Estates more and more often, visiting with Mr. Burke and JoJo nearly as often as she had Bitty. Especially after she learned Mr. Burke wasn't in touch with any of his family.

Mr. Burke waited until they were settled on his couch, JoJo curled in a little fluff ball in his lap, before he eyed her over his tea. "Are you going to tell me what's wrong?"

Deenie flushed. "What makes you think something's wrong?" She tossed Squeaky Mouse, and JoJo leapt off the couch in pursuit, but Mr. Burke didn't take his eyes off her.

"Nadine, you're an excellent actress, but you don't have to act with me."

She met his eyes, and the weight of the last few months all seemed to crash down at once. She'd thought she wanted to talk about Connor. About kissing him and having far too many feelings for him and being certain she was about to make a huge mistake with him—but the words that spilled out of her mouth were much more raw. "She isn't good."

Her voice broke. Mr. Burke didn't have to ask who.

At the crack in her voice, JoJo abandoned Squeaky Mouse and jumped up on the couch, climbing onto Deenie's lap— her tiny paws and barely-there weight a sweet comfort. Deenie set down her teacup, rhythmically stroking the dog.

"I thought that might be the case," Mr. Burke said gently.

Deenie swallowed, fighting the tears that wanted to slip past her defenses. "She doesn't want people to know."

"I can understand that." Mr. Burke glanced at the coffee table. At the medication box and the slim envelope beside it.

It was a nursing bill. She recognized them. As Bitty's designated next of kin, she'd seen her fair share. The company name of the home-care assistants caught her eye, reminding her where she'd seen the young nurse before.

It wasn't from assisted living.

Deenie stared, realization swallowing her tangled emotions for Bitty and turning them in a new direction. She looked up, meeting Mr. Burke's eyes. His smile shifted, turning soft and accepting. "It's all right," he murmured.

Tears swam in her eyes. "How long have you been on hospice care?"

He seemed so healthy. So fit. For a man in his upper eighties, yes, but still. His mind was sharp.

"Not long. They think I probably have a few more months. Prostate cancer. When I was diagnosed, they said it would take ten years to kill me. The doctors said something else would probably get me before then. That was twelve years ago. Turns out nothing else got me." His smile was so calm. How could he be so calm?

Her chin trembled, and Mr. Burke narrowed his eyes. "Hey. None of that. I'm one of the lucky ones. I'm taking the best memories with me. No regrets. Though I do wish I had time for a few more adventures." His hand closed gently over hers. "Always go after the adventures, Nadine. You can put more money in the bank, but you can never put more life in the bank."

Her lips curled. "Bitty used to say that."

"Well, she got it from David," he said, speaking of his late husband. "He was very carpe diem."

"I wish I'd met him."

Mr. Burke's smile was fond. "Me too. He would have loved you. And this little girl." He stroked JoJo's silky head. "You'll look after her for me, won't you? I already got her all her shots and a veterinary certificate, so she's ready for you to take her anywhere in the world."

She pressed her lips together. The only thing she could do was nod.

His smile was so gentle. "You always think you'll have more time. It's amazing how fast it goes by."

Chapter Twenty-Five

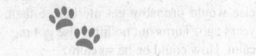

The doorbell rang.

Deenie never rang the bell anymore. That was Connor's first clue that something was different.

The second was the way she burst into the house, words flying like shrapnel in every direction.

"I don't want to regret anything." She moved past him, heading straight for the kitchen. Maximus bounded eagerly at her side.

Connor stared after her, moving slowly in her wake. "I don't want that, either."

The last thing he wanted was for either of them to do anything they would regret. All day today he'd been telling himself he was grateful things hadn't gone any further than they had last night. Good sense had returned while he slept, thank God.

"Life's too short."

She yanked open his refrigerator, pulling out a can of the hot-pink strawberry-kiwi craft cider he'd started keeping in there for her, for the nights when she'd stay late and they'd watch a bad movie together. It was too sweet for him, but Deenie loved it.

She spun to face him. "Bitty used to always say this thing to me about how the one thing you never get more of is time. Take the chances you're given, because you never know if they'll come along again. Look at *everything* like a once-in-a-lifetime opportunity. 'You can put more money in the bank, but you can't put more life in the bank.'"

Agitated, she popped the top on the can, but didn't raise it to her lips, gripping it tight in one hand.

"I always thought she was talking about travel—about valuing experiences more than a pile of numbers in a bank account—but now I'm not sure I understood what she meant at all." She paced the kitchen as Max danced around, trying to figure out the game. "She's dying."

The words were stark—and Connor took an involuntary step toward her, a hand out for comfort, but she didn't see him, pacing again.

"She's vanishing right in front of my eyes, and now Mr. Burke..." She shook her head. "Bitty was the only one who understood me. I wanted to be her. I wanted to take big bites out of life, but what if I'm so busy chasing those things, running around the world trying to see it all, that I miss out on all the adventures here? What if it isn't about always running off to the next thing, but about making sure I don't miss the moment I'm in, even if I'm here." She turned to face him. "With you."

Her gaze hit him. "Deenie..." He was no longer sure he knew why she was here.

"I know I'm not your forever—I know this has an expiration date—but doesn't it feel like we're here now for a reason?"

Connor gripped the edge of the island. "Ally's been rubbing off on you." She was constantly talking about signs. About the will of the universe.

Deenie set her untouched drink down on the counter with a clink.

"I want you." The words hung, stark and simple, in between them. "I know it's a bad decision," she said, in that same unvarnished way. "I'm the queen of bad decisions. But if you want me too, and we're both adults, and we both know what we're getting into—and what we're not— then…why not?"

Because it's reckless, his logic whispered.

Because I'll get addicted to you, his caution added.

Because I can't risk feeling powerless again when this all blows up in my face, his fear concluded.

But then she bit her lip, looking up at him, her big blue eyes so vulnerable and raw—and his heart kicked all those other voices to the curb.

He lifted a hand, brushing this thumb across the pad of her lower lip where she'd bitten it.

Why not? So many reasons.

But he still lowered his head. He still cradled her head between his hands. He still breathed in the sparkle and heat of her.

It was just a rebound. Just a fling. Just a fire that would burn fast and hot and then be done.

"No regrets," he murmured against her lips, hoping he wasn't making a huge mistake.

Her hands latched on to his shirt, pulling him into insanity. And the best bad idea of his life.

Chapter Twenty-Six

"When are you going to bring Deenie by for dinner?"
Connor groaned under his breath. He probably
should have anticipated this.

The scent of flowers filled the air. Spring had fully
sprung in Pine Hollow, and the weekly farmers market had
reclaimed its fair-weather location, filling the town square
with the brightly colored awnings of the local businesses on
the sunny May Saturday morning.

Ally was around here somewhere, luring people toward
her photography booth with the most adorable new residents
at the shelter, but Connor couldn't see her in the maze, and
luckily Max hadn't caught their scent yet. The wolfhound
looked around alertly, but stayed at Connor's side, not lunging or pulling toward the stands around them as Connor and
his mother strolled from booth to booth.

The labyrinthine Pine Hollow farmers market was better
than a Vegas casino at funneling people toward the center
and disguising the escape routes. They'd been circling the
fresh produce section—limited though it was this early in
the year—for nearly an hour.

"We're just friends," he reminded his mother—which wasn't *entirely* a lie. They were friends. With benefits.

Lots of benefits.

The last few weeks had been madness. Wonderful madness, but he'd definitely taken a break from sensible decision making, and he wasn't about to admit that to his mother.

"You should invite her for dinner tonight," she insisted, undeterred.

He almost blurted out the truth. *She can't make it. She's at her sister's bridal shower in Burlington.* The last thing he needed was his mother figuring out he had Deenie's schedule—such as it was—memorized.

"So you can spend the entire time gushing about what a cute couple we would make? No, thank you. We aren't together." *Not like that.*

But they were good at pretending.

She'd gone to the partners' dinner with him and charmed everyone all over again. He was starting to feel like he was her plus-one rather than the other way around—and he actually loved it. He was more relaxed at the work events now, more comfortable chatting with his coworkers. She'd taken all the pressure off him to be witty and clever, because she always was.

He still had the dating apps, but he hadn't opened them in weeks. He knew this thing with Deenie was temporary and nonexclusive—they'd both been very clear about that—but he didn't want to date anyone else right now. Not that they were really *dating*, but he liked having her as his fake girlfriend and semi-regular hookup, even if she was pure chaos energy.

She was the perfect fling—fun and passionate and unexpected—and when it ended, which it inevitably would, he would go back to his search with the last of his wild oats sown. He'd never even realized he *had* wild oats before Deenie.

He couldn't imagine growing bored of her, but she would tire of him. She would run. They both knew it. It was just a question of when.

So he didn't want his mother getting attached.

"She's just training Max," Connor insisted.

"And she's doing a wonderful job, isn't she, Max?" his mother cooed at the dog, who behaved angelically.

The training excuse wasn't going to last much longer. Max was on his way to becoming the best-behaved dog in Pine Hollow. Deenie still worked with him occasionally— but more often than not when she came over now, it was to see Connor. Just last night...

Connor quickly purged the memory from his thoughts. He did *not* need his mother reading something on his face.

"I'm just saying I like her," his mom declared, bending to inspect some asparagus.

"You met her one time. For five seconds."

His mother looked up at him, her eyes locking on his. "She's *fun*. And you're happy. Happier than you ever were with Monica. I *like* her."

There was no comparison to Monica. Deenie made everything into a celebration. She was walking joy, turning all her attention on the people around her, making them feel special in her spotlight. But it wasn't just Deenie that made him feel lighter.

Max bumped against his hip and Connor adjusted the leash. "You know, my happiness might not have anything to do with her. I'm about to make partner."

Something flickered through his mother's eyes. "I'm proud of you no matter what. You know that."

"Of course. But I still want to make partner." He'd always known he didn't have to be the best for his mother to be proud of him. But that didn't stop him from wanting to be the best for her.

"Just don't work too hard. You put your head down and forget anything else exists. You've always been like that."

"I'm not working too hard," he assured her. And for once he wasn't lying.

And that *was* Deenie's doing. It wasn't even just the sex—though that was a *very* welcome distraction. They streamed movies and ate popcorn—spending nearly as much time debating the films as they did watching them. Everything was an argument with Deenie—and he kind of loved it. Ben was his best friend in part because he was the only person who enjoyed bickering as much as Connor did—but if possible, Deenie liked it even more. And they had plenty to argue about. They seemed to be on opposite sides of nearly every possible subject, but he'd never felt more alive than when he was trying to mentally outmaneuver her. She was always a challenge. And their verbal sparring had become foreplay.

"Just take care of yourself. We have a history of heart disease, you know."

Connor's attention sharpened on his mother. "We do? Are you okay?"

"I'm fine," his mother insisted, threading her arm through his and wandering toward the next booth. "Mitch talked me into changing doctors a few months ago—that other one was not listening to me. The new doctor had me do a bunch of tests and I'm okay. Turned out I didn't need any kind of surgery, thank goodness. I'm just on some new medications."

Connor's heart stuttered at the word *surgery*. "What kind of medications? What kind of tests? When was this?"

"A couple months ago. Back in February. I didn't want to worry you."

"Worry me? *Mom.*" He no longer saw any of the booths around them. "If there's a problem, I want to know about it."

"We didn't know if there was a problem yet. And you're always so stressed. I couldn't add to that."

"So you talked to Mitch about this and not to me?" Maximus must have picked up on his distraction and chose that moment to lurch toward another dog. Connor corrected him with a low voice, frustration humming beneath his skin.

"Mitch told me I should tell you. But how could I put that on you?"

"It's not putting it on me. It's sharing it with me so you don't have to go through it alone." Except she hadn't been alone. She'd had Mitch. Jealousy spiked, irrational and blazing hot.

His mother was shaking her head. "I didn't always make the right choices when you were little. I relied on you too much. I let you grow up too fast."

"No, you didn't, Mom—"

"Let me finish."

He snapped his mouth shut.

"I put too much on you when you were little. I let you put too much on yourself. You don't have to take care of me, Connor—"

"I want to," he interrupted. She gave him a searing look, and his ears went hot as he swallowed the argument he wanted to make. "Sorry."

"You were so capable. So autonomous. You never gave me a moment's worry, and I know, now that I'm not just trying to get through every day, how hard you must have worked to do that, to put my mind at ease. You shouldn't have had to. You were the kid, and I was the adult. I know you're grown now, but I am always going to want to protect you however I can. Understand?"

He caught her hand. "I want to protect you, too. You are the most important person in my life, and if anything happened to you and I could have done something, but you didn't *tell* me because you didn't want me to worry—"

"Baby, nothing happened. I'm fine. I'm just on some new meds."

"But you didn't know it was going to turn out like that. Something was wrong. That's why they ran the tests. That's why you're on the medication. And you didn't tell me. Mom, you've gotta tell me."

She pursed her lips together, giving a tight nod.

Mitch appeared, grinning broadly, toting a bag from the bakery. "You guys are still looking at vegetables? I thought you'd be done ages ago."

Connor dropped the subject, the ache in his chest the only remnant of their argument as his mom smiled for Mitch.

His chest was still aching that night when he let himself into his house and heard the sound of Deenie clattering around in his kitchen. Maximus raced to greet her.

"You're back already?" he called, coming around the corner.

"Why do you not own any junk food?" she demanded, standing in his pantry doorway. "Do you have an aversion to tortilla chips that I should be aware of?"

She greeted Maximus—who had, thank God, gotten

past the leap-up-and-put-his-paws-on-your-chest form of greeting—and Connor leaned against the counter. "She who does none of the shopping has no room for complaint," he reminded her.

She made a face. "I probably owe you a case of organic popcorn kernels, don't I?"

"I think I can afford your popcorn habit." He reached around her, making sure to brush her shoulder as he did, and grabbed the organic popcorn kernels, moving next to pull the popper from a low cupboard.

The dog flopped on the floor—alertly watching for popcorn that might fly toward his face.

"You sure you don't want to draw up a popcorn contract?" Deenie boosted herself up on the island, watching Connor move around the kitchen. She was wearing little white shorts and she crossed her long bare legs at the ankle, swinging them idly. "I know you love your legalese."

"I'll accept a verbal contract. Just this once." He took out a small saucepan and began preparing the homemade caramel he knew she loved drizzled on her popcorn.

Her gaze lingered on his biceps as he stirred sugar, water, and salt in the saucepan. "We haven't been very good about sticking to the terms of the other contract."

The other contract, with its "all compliments and mushy romantic stuff be restricted to necessary performance times" clause, had been violated so many times they'd lost count.

"I could draw up an addendum."

She rolled her eyes, but sniffed the air appreciatively. "Is that going to be caramel?"

"You're going to destroy your teeth. This stuff is hell on fillings," he reminded her as he stirred. "So how was the party?"

"It was fine." Deenie pulled a face, but her tone lacked its usual acid when talking about the wedding stuff. "Very beige. But the faro salad was delicious. Apparently there was mint." She wrinkled her nose. "All anyone wanted to talk to me about was you. And they call themselves feminists."

Hearing something in her voice, he turned away from the stove. "Well, I am pretty incredible." He caught her by the knees and she unhooked her ankles, widening her legs and smiling as he drew her slowly toward him. She slid on the slick granite to the edge of the island, until her knees bracketed his hips.

"True," she agreed. She crossed her wrists behind his neck, her eyes—decorated by layers of glittery blue shadow—sparkling into his. "Though I don't dare tell you. Your ego is already out of control." She leaned into his kiss, though she only allowed him a few seconds before pulling away. "Don't burn my caramel."

He snorted. "Yes, ma'am." He turned back to the stove, resuming his caramel stirring as the kernels began to pop in the popper.

"How's your mom?"

Connor grimaced.

Deenie gasped dramatically. "Did you just *make a face* when I asked about your sainted mother? Connor Wyeth! I am shocked at you."

"She lied to me."

All the amusement dropped from Deenie's face. "What happened?"

"She didn't really lie," he clarified, staring into the caramel he was slowly stirring instead of into Deenie's keen gaze. "She was sick—or not sick, but having some tests done because something wasn't right with her heart—and she's on medication now, everything's fine, but she didn't tell me until it turned out to be nothing. She might have had to have surgery—she was probably scared, and she didn't even tell me. Mitch was the one who was there for her—and what if something had happened?"

"Hey." She slid off the counter, coming up behind him and resting her cheek on his back, her arms looped around his waist. "She's okay," she reminded him.

"I know. I'm just so mad at her for keeping me out of the loop."

"Don't stay mad long," she advised, her breath stirring the shirt on his back. "You never get more time."

He put one hand over hers where they were folded on his stomach. "I won't."

They'd talked about her aunt. About how her memories seemed to be slipping away more and more.

"Seize the day," he murmured, the words a promise. It had become their mantra. A reminder to one another to savor this moment, because they both knew it wouldn't last.

Connor had never been impulsive before. He was a planner, not a seizer of days, but he flicked off the stove now.

Deenie peered around his shoulder. "What are you doing?" He could hear the frown in her voice. It was never a good idea to get between Deenie and sweets—but he would make it worth her while.

He turned in her arms. "I'm seizing the day."

The kiss was soft, unhurried.

She pulled back, her brows a grumpy *V* above the glitter. "I had strong feeling about that caramel."

"I'll make you more caramel," he promised. "Later."

He pulled her close—and she fit perfectly into his arms.

Chapter Twenty-Seven

"Are you and Connor secretly dating?"

Deenie was carrying the wide plank of the canine teeter-totter and looked up so quickly at Ally's words that it slipped from her fingers and slammed down on her foot. She yelped, yanking her foot from beneath the plank and stumbling backward, tripping over a plastic tunnel and landing flat on her ass.

Ally's eyebrows lifted slowly, her lips pressed together to hold in her laughter. "I'm just going to take that as a yes."

Colby, the Saint Bernard who had been supervising their construction of the outdoor agility course, ambled over to push his giant face into Deenie's to make sure she was okay. She ruffled Colby's ears before nudging his massive shoulders out of her way so she could get up from the damp grass.

"I'm *not* dating Connor," Deenie insisted, before honesty forced her to add, "We're just sleeping together."

Ally's eyes flared wide. "I can't believe Ben was right. He's usually so oblivious to this stuff."

"He's not right," Deenie argued. "It isn't a thing. We're

just using each other for sex—and occasionally for decoy dates like we originally agreed."

"You're sure that's all it is?"

Deenie picked up the plank and maneuvered it into place. "It's a *fling*. With an expiration date."

"Because he's empirically hot."

Deenie narrowed her eyes. "Exactly."

Ally nodded, tipping the ramp they'd carried out earlier into position. This was the last step in their plan to revitalize Furry Friends. The dog park in the back pasture was already used daily by the local residents. Ally's pet photography was getting steady business—and she even had a few human customers. Enrollment in the training courses had been steady, and they'd had their first few doggie day care clients.

As of today, Furry Friends was officially updated. Deenie hadn't planned to stay after the new business was on its feet, but Bitty might still have some good days, and Kirsten's wedding was a month away. Normally she'd be looking at flights and mentally mapping her escape, even if she wasn't ready to take off yet, but her wanderlust seemed to have gone quiet.

Deenie stood back, surveying the course—with the Saint Bernard sprawled on his back in the middle of it. Colby was epically lazy, but dogs like Elinor's Australian shepherd were born for this. "Dory's going to love this."

Ally admired their work, fidgeting with the strings of her Furry Friends hoodie. "Are you going to Elinor's birthday on Wednesday?"

"Yeah. We'll be there." Deenie kicked herself, correcting quickly, "I'll be there."

Ally caught her eye. "It's okay if you guys are a *we*."

"We aren't," Deenie insisted. "We're just entertaining

each other while it lasts. I have to be here for my sister's wedding next month, and Connor is a pleasant distraction."

"It doesn't have to end, you know," Ally said tentatively. "You could stay here, adopt a dog…Maybe this is the universe telling you to stick around?"

It was tempting—far too tempting—but Deenie shook her head. "You can listen to the universe. I listen to my head and my heart, and they're both telling me that anything long-term with Connor would be a disaster."

Even if she wasn't ready for it to be over. Whatever it was they were doing.

"He's a good guy," Ally nudged.

"I know he is. But we're oil and water. Trust me. It's better this way."

Ally nodded—and something flashed between her fingers, catching the light. She wasn't fidgeting with her hoodie, Deenie realized, but with something on a chain she'd kept tucked beneath it.

"What is that?"

Ally's hand stilled as she met Deenie's eyes, suddenly seeming almost nervous. "We weren't going to tell anyone until after Elinor's birthday. We didn't want to step on her party, but it felt wrong not telling you."

Ally stepped closer, the item on the chain around her neck flat on her palm.

A diamond solitaire ring.

Deenie's jaw dropped. "You got engaged?"

Ally smiled sheepishly. "Surprise."

"How long…When did this happen? Ally! Congratulations!" Deenie shoved aside her shock and the complicated mix of emotions that were swirling through her, wrapping her friend in a hug.

"Thank you. It was last weekend. While you were at your sister's shower. He had Astrid help him. It was so cute. Apparently, they'd been planning it for weeks—I don't know how he kept Astrid from slipping up and saying something. He said he'd wanted to ask me for a while, but Ben being Ben, things had to happen in the right order. He thought we'd rushed into moving in together out of convenience because of his reno, and he didn't want to propose until we were each in our own space again, so I wouldn't accept just because it was the easiest thing to do." She shook her head, smiling. "He can be such an idiot sometimes."

Deenie grinned. "So I'm guessing you didn't just accept because it was easier than telling him no."

"We've both been dancing around the subject for months, talking about the future, and it was always assumed that in that future we'd be married, we'd have more kids, and he still didn't think I was going to say yes?" Ally rolled her eyes. *"Men."*

"Wow." A strange blend of emotion swirled inside her, too complicated to sort out what was what. "You're getting *married*. I mean, obviously I knew it was coming, but *wow*."

Uncertainty flashed across Ally's face. "You don't think it's too soon? The wedding won't be until Christmas, but we've only known each other for five months."

"Honestly, I'm amazed you've waited this long. You two were both born to commit. And you happen to be great together."

"Yeah?" Relief lit Ally's dark eyes.

"Yeah."

"Only our families know right now," Ally explained. "And Ben still wants to finish fixing up his house and put it on the market before we officially buy the farmhouse from my grandparents. He and Astrid wouldn't be moving in right away—and we all want you to stay. That's part of why I was scared to tell you. I don't want you to feel like we're edging you out."

"Of course not," Deenie assured Ally, even as a new set of deadlines shifted around in her thoughts.

Ally and Ben had claimed to be moving at sloth speed, but she'd known this was coming. She'd known that eventually they would be moving in together for good. And they wouldn't want Deenie hanging around when they did.

But now it was happening.

Deenie punched in the door code and let herself into Connor's house, saying hello to Max and tipping her head to listen to the familiar sound of Connor on a call.

She didn't know why she'd come here. Ally had gone over to Ben's place, and she'd had the farmhouse to herself, but something uneasy had been whispering through her thoughts ever since she'd heard about Ben and Ally's engagement.

She was happy for them. But she felt like the status quo of the last few weeks had tilted, and she was now sliding slowly toward the inevitable change. The moment when Bitty and Mr. Burke would be gone. When Ally and Ben would be living together, raising dogs and adorable babies. When Connor would be married to someone else...

She'd always boomeranged back to Pine Hollow. It was the closest thing she had to a home base. But maybe this time when she left, she wouldn't come back. Cleaner that way.

The thoughts had driven her to Connor's place.

Seize the day, she reminded herself.

Because before long the day would be gone.

She wandered back toward the office, listening to him sign off from the call before stepping into the open doorway. "Hey."

Connor took one look at her, his gaze shifting over her face, and his eyes darkened. "Ally told you?"

She stroked Max's head where he leaned against her hip. "Ben told you?"

"I'm his best man."

"Oh. Right." There was something incredibly sobering about those words. Not that she wanted to be Ally's maid of honor. But there had been no mention of wedding parties. Connor as the best man made sense. He and Ben had been friends forever. And Deenie never stuck around.

"You okay?" he asked without getting up—that posture he had when half his brain was still on his work. "How was putting together the obstacle course?"

"Agility course. It was good. Exhausting. I'll probably be sore for a week. I had no idea how heavy a teeter-totter could be."

His gaze flicked back to his computer, lured by the siren song of work. "You should take a soak in the Jacuzzi. Loosen up your muscles."

"I still have PTSD from the last time I was near your Jacuzzi."

His smirk was filled with memory. "Just make sure the water line is above the jets. Trust me. You'll love it. It's half the reason I bought the house."

"You working late?" She shouldn't stay. She should go back to her own place. Forget about this.

"A little longer. A few more things to finish."

She nodded, starting to slip out of the room, but his voice stopped her.

"Deenie. You okay? You're not upset about the wedding stuff?"

"No, of course not. It just gets you thinking, right?" About how one day Connor would be proposing to someone else, too. Someone like Elinor. "I'm not cut out for that stuff," she said, as much to remind herself as him. *"Forever."*

Connor nodded, something shifting in his eyes before he glanced away. "You might want to avoid the bubble bath. Once you turn on the jets, the water pressure makes the bubbles go nuts. You'll fill the whole room."

"Good to know."

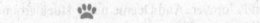

Connor tried to focus on his work. Tried not to think about the fact that Deenie was upstairs in his Jacuzzi right now. And the news Ben had sprung on him less than an hour ago.

It was good news. He was happy for Ben and Ally. So why did he feel this thick, sluggish wash of dread?

I'm not cut out for that stuff...

He pushed away the echo of Deenie's words, and away from his desk twenty minutes later. Maximus was sleeping on the couch again—Deenie had asked him if he wanted to train him not to get on the furniture, but he seemed so happy, sprawled out like a couch potato, that Connor hadn't had the heart to take it away from him—though he was *only* allowed on that couch. No more climbing into his office chair like a lap puppy.

They'd found a good balance. He and Max and Deenie.

He'd found himself thinking of that when Ben had told him about the engagement. Ben had looked so happy. So relaxed. He'd gotten a little sappy, asking Connor to be his best man—and Connor had gotten a little sappy himself.

He owed Ben.

His friend had never let him become a hermit. He'd never let him descend into self-pity. No matter how annoying it had been to have his friends breaking into his house to bother him, he was glad they'd never given up on him. The least he could do was be best man.

His thoughts still on the wedding, Connor climbed the stairs. The master bedroom was empty and quiet—no hum of the Jacuzzi jets—and the door to the bathroom hung open.

"Deenie?"

"In here!" she called through the open door.

Connor stepped through the doorway—and bit back a laugh.

He should have known Deenie would take his admonishment about the bubbles as a challenge rather than a warning.

She stretched out beneath a mountain of bubbles, only visible from the chin up, with her toes peeking through the mound of froth at the opposite end of the tub. It was like a scene out of a movie—one rated PG-13, where they wanted to keep the illusion of chastity.

"Care to join me?" she asked, scooping up a handful of bubbles.

He tugged off his tie—the one Deenie teased him for wearing in the house, even if he had an image to maintain on video calls. "You look like Julia Roberts. Am I Richard Gere in this scenario?"

"I am choosing not to be offended by the fact that you

just compared me to a famous on-screen prostitute, because I happen to love that movie."

Connor's face heated in the steamy air. "I didn't mean—"

"I know," she replied cheerfully. "Frankly, I'm stunned that you know *Pretty Woman* at all."

"I can watch rom-coms." He began on the buttons of his shirt.

Her eyebrows arched at the defensiveness in his tone. "You hate all things illogical. Rom-coms are an exercise in people abandoning logic for love."

Was that why he failed at love? Was he incapable of being foolish enough to be a fool for love?

Connor frowned, but Deenie didn't notice, drawing patterns in the bubbles.

"Thanks for the tip about the bubbles," she said. "I never pictured you as a bubble bath guy."

"It was Monica actually," he heard himself admitting, toeing off his shoes. "She was the one who discovered that bubble bath and Jacuzzi jets don't mix without a huge mess."

Deenie cocked her head, watching him. "I didn't realize you guys lived here together..."

Of course she didn't. He'd never told Deenie about Monica.

He'd told his online dates—always in a very factual way. Sharing history. The nuts-and-bolts business of getting to know one another. But with Deenie, he hadn't owed her his history. They'd only talked about what they wanted to talk about—and yet somehow she'd come to know him better than any of those digital dates. But this was still a hole. A gap he'd never wanted to discuss.

She eyed him. "Elinor said you guys were engaged."

He sat on the lip of the tub to take off his socks. "Did she tell you that she broke up with me with a Post-it two weeks before we were supposed to get married?"

Deenie cringed. "She might have mentioned that."

Connor nodded, but he didn't look at her, pretending to be absorbed in folding his socks. "I thought my life was so perfect back then. Perfect job, perfect fiancée, perfect house to raise our future perfect children. Monica and I planned every step of the way together. I was so sure we were on the same page—and then I come home to a Post-it note telling me she can't do this. She isn't *happy*, and she's going to India to find herself." He grimaced. "I burned her copy of *Eat, Pray, Love*. It didn't help."

He looked around the master bath, seeing it at a different time. When he'd still thought his life was right on track.

"This whole house became a giant reminder of how wrong I was. I hated it a little bit. Until..."

Until you.

He barely stopped himself from saying the words. Her comment from earlier echoed in his thoughts again. *I'm not cut out for that stuff. Forever.*

She'd been warning him. She knew he was getting too attached. She knew he was falling for her. Why else would she say it? She had to be reminding him that she wasn't the girl who stayed.

He'd promised himself he wouldn't fall in love with her.

He was such an idiot. What made him think he had any control over his stupid heart? He'd always tried to plan those things, but then the universe laughed at him.

"Did you have any warning?" Deenie asked. And for a moment he almost thought she was asking if he'd known he was going to fall for her.

Then he remembered. Monica.

"Looking back on it now, there were signs," he admitted. "But I didn't see them. I wasn't even looking. I guess I took it for granted that she would stay. When you commit to someone, you *commit* to them. I didn't think I had to question her."

And now he questioned everything.

"Connor..." Deenie's voice was soft from the mountain of bubbles, gentle. "All of that stuff...her running off like that...that was her. It wasn't you. You're amazing. And you're going to be an amazing husband and father."

Just not for you.

He arched one eyebrow, skepticism his best defense against the longing in his chest. "This from you? The woman who thinks I'm an insufferable snob?"

"You are an insufferable snob," she insisted. "But you're also a catch. I may not be the kind of girl who catches you, but trust me, you're one of the good ones, and anyone with half a brain can see that."

Yes, but can they love me enough to stay?

He kept that thought to himself. What was the point of wallowing in self-pity anyway?

The people who didn't want to love you were always so good at assuring you that you were worthy of love. If only practice didn't prove them wrong. She was so certain he would find the perfect love—it just wouldn't be *her*. And he needed to keep reminding his heart that.

Even as he climbed in the tub behind her. *Seize the day.*

Chapter Twenty-Eight

The Tipsy Moose Pub was one of only two bars within the Pine Hollow town limits—and the only one that allowed karaoke on the premises. Deenie had never been here for karaoke night before, so she had no idea if the cozy pub was always this crowded or if this many people had turned out just to celebrate Elinor's birthday—though if she'd had to guess, she would've said the latter.

She'd known Elinor could sing—the two of them had bonded over irreverent Christmas carols in December—but she hadn't expected the mild-mannered librarian to be so comfortable in the spotlight, crowding onto the tiny stage with Magda from the bakery and Kendall from the ski resort, their arms draped around one another as they shouted the opening lyrics of "I Will Survive" into the microphone.

Though the Birthday Girl shots may have had something to do with their enthusiasm.

Ben and Ally danced in the middle of the crowd with Connor and Mac—who was supposed to be grabbing the song book so he and Deenie could pick out a duet. The diner owner had already belted out "I Believe" from *The*

Book of Mormon to rave reviews and was determined to get Deenie up on stage with him. Not that she'd been hard to convince—but now Mac kept getting sidetracked as Elinor, Magda, and Kendall bellowed their independence at maximum volume.

Everyone in the bar was on their feet, laughing and yelling the words along with them—except for the still, broad-shouldered form of Levi, sitting on the barstool next to Deenie, staring fixedly at the stage, his jaw tight.

Deenie leaned against the bar beside him, folding her arms next to his as she watched Connor watching Elinor. "Did you know she could sing like that?"

Magda and Kendall had dissolved into laugher, but Elinor was crushing the song, belting the lyrics out with a power that belonged on one of those singing competition shows. Elinor was *good*.

Levi didn't take his attention off the stage, and at first she wasn't sure he'd heard her over the music. Then his mouth tightened slightly. "I knew."

Deenie studied Levi and his carefully blank face. "Do you always win when you guys play poker?" she asked.

A slight pause. "Usually. Why do you ask?"

"You have the best poker face I've ever seen." But she had the distinct feeling something was going on with Elinor. A man didn't stare at a woman like that if he was indifferent. "Why did you tell Connor to go for it with Elinor?"

Levi met her eyes and saw far too much. "Don't worry. He won't."

She flushed. "I'm not worried."

They hadn't told anyone they were together. They *weren't* really together. But Levi had seen it. Or Connor told his friends?

Deenie stared past Levi at the stage. Why did Elinor have to be good at everything? It was entirely too intimidating. She was smart and capable—the kind of person who matched perfectly with Connor, and now she had to be a freaking amazing singer, too? How was that even *fair*?

How was Deenie supposed to compete with that? Not that it was a competition. This thing with Connor was temporary. Elinor was forever.

The song ended to raucous applause. "Are you gonna sing?" she asked the man of stone at her side.

He tapped his ear. "Tone deaf. You should work on Connor, though. He's almost as good as Elinor."

"You're kidding."

Connor had flatly refused to sing, claiming he was awful.

Deenie twisted on her barstool, searching him out in the crowd—and watched as Elinor flung herself off the stage into his waiting arms.

Her heart dropped to her toes with a thud.

"That was amazing." Connor caught Elinor as she nearly tumbled off the stage, catching her foot on the uneven edge. Laughing, she clutched his arms until she had her balance. "Aimed at anyone in particular?"

Elinor shoved off his chest a little harder than necessary, but her smile was innocent. "I don't know what you're talking about."

"Uh-huh." They stepped to the side as one of the other teachers at Pine Hollow Elementary climbed onto the stage and began a rendition of "Eleanor Rigby" with a very loose relationship to the actual lyrics. "Having a good night, birthday girl?"

"The best," she declared, then gave him a nudge. "How about you? Did you bring anyone? I saw you on Match. It's good to see you getting back out there."

"Yeah." Except he hadn't been out there much in these last few weeks. Every time he considered going on an online date, he found some reason why she wasn't suitable...but the truth was he just liked being with Deenie. "I almost called you when we matched. That was..."

"Weird." Elinor nodded. "Clearly their algorithms are a little wonky."

"It's not that crazy. You're analytical. I'm analytical. Neither of us is insane. Honestly, I don't know why we never dated."

She laughed. "Because Levi would have murdered you and hid the body where no one would ever find it?"

"Yeah, before. But not now. When I told him we matched, he told me to go for it."

Emotion passed over Elinor's face so quickly he almost didn't see it, but it looked like hurt.

"That's ridiculous," she said, too brightly. "You're like my brother."

"I'm sure he knew I never would," Connor said, trying to repair the damage.

Elinor's baby sister, Charlotte, chose that moment to fling her arms around Elinor from behind. "Birthday girl! No hiding in the corner! You have to pick another song!"

Charlotte dragged a smiling Elinor away into the crowd, and Connor looked around for Deenie, but the space where she'd been at the bar was empty.

"What are you doing out here?"

The patio was microscopic, more of a dingy smoking nook than an actual outdoor space, but it was quiet and it was empty, and the cool night air felt amazing on her face. Deenie wasn't sure how long she stood out there, nursing a mojito and staring blindly up at the stars, before Ally found her.

She looked over at her friend, her emotions swooping unsteadily. "Connor and Elinor matched on one of those dating sites."

Ally's face took on that cautious pacify-the-drunk-person expression. "Okay..."

"I'm not drunk," Deenie snapped. "Well. Not very. But you have to see it. Elinor is the kind of person Connor should be with. Even a computer program thinks so."

Ally's eyebrows flew up. "Do you remember laughing at me because I was convinced Ben was engaged to Elinor?"

"Yes. But that was all in your head. This is a real thing. An actual thing. Connor even said they'd be perfect for each other. I heard him."

"Then why is he in there looking for you?" Ally asked. "Connor isn't interested in Elinor. He's interested in you."

"But for how long?" Deenie blurted—and flushed at how much those four words revealed. "I'm not what he wants."

"Is he what you want?" Ally asked gently.

"I don't know." Deenie had always been so sure of what she wanted. How could she not know anymore? When had everything gotten so confusing?

"Can I offer you a little advice, if he is what you want?" Ally's words were soft. Cautious. "You might have to actually tell him that." She settled herself next to Deenie, gently bumping their shoulders together. "You're so confident. I've always admired that about you. But you can be a little guarded."

"I don't mean to be," she said.

Except she did. She kept her walls up. And she wasn't confident. She never expected anyone to accept her the way she was. She threw her faults in their faces, challenging them to see the real her, but never really letting anyone in. Even Ally. Who had become one of her best friends.

"Even when you keep us at a distance, you're worth it." Ally linked their hands together. "And I know Connor thinks so, too."

"I'm not what he wants," she repeated.

"So what? Maybe you're better. *I* think you're pretty awesome. I'd ask you to be in my wedding right now if I wasn't trying my hardest not to pressure you to stay just because I want you here." She leaned her shoulder against Deenie's. "Does Connor make you happy?"

That was the easiest question. But it didn't negate all the others. "He wants someone like Elinor."

"What makes you so sure he knows what he wants? Weren't you the one who said men have to have their faces shoved in what they need? And seriously, what is it about Elinor that brings out all our insecurities?" Ally wondered.

"She's annoyingly perfect."

"Who's perfect?"

They both looked toward the door, where the birthday girl herself stood. "Are you guys okay? Mac is looking for you. He said you two were supposed to do a song."

"Right." Deenie nodded. "Sorry. Just having a little relationship drama out here."

Elinor's gaze immediately went to Ally. "Is everything okay with you and Ben?"

"It's me actually," Deenie said, throwing the words out like bombs and watching them land. "Are you dating Connor? I know you guys matched. And it's okay if you want to."

"Why is everyone giving me permission to date Connor? I'm not interested in him like that. I never have been."

"So you wouldn't mind if I was seeing him?"

Something flashed across Elinor's face, and Deenie felt her doubt like a knife between her ribs.

"You think I'm not good enough for him." She knew she was being too aggressive, but she flung the words out. *Say them first and they won't hurt as much.*

"It's not about good enough," Elinor argued.

"But you think we're wrong for each other." Of course she did. Deenie knew they were wrong for each other.

"I just don't want him getting hurt," Elinor explained gently. "He's a good guy. A good friend. And he was destroyed when Monica left. We all saw it, and you...you *leave*. That's your whole thing."

"Well, maybe I don't want that to be my thing anymore," she snapped.

They all froze, Deenie as shocked by the words as Ally and Elinor were.

Was that really what she wanted? To stay? To do the normal, stable, everyday routine?

And even if she wanted that, what if he didn't?

She shoved away from the patio table. "I should go find Mac."

Mac was the kind of guy she should be with. Easygoing. Sweet.

"Deenie…" Elinor's voice stopped her. "I didn't mean…
I don't know what I meant."

Deenie opened her mouth, not even certain of what she
was going to say, when her raw fear spilled out. "Even if I
stay, he might not want me."

"Then he's an idiot," Elinor said flatly.

Deenie snorted. "Spoken like a woman who's never had
to worry she isn't good enough."

"Deenie." Elinor braced her hands on Deenie's shoulders,
no nonsense. Firm. So certain of the world around her.
"You're good enough. Obviously. You're awesome. Now
own it."

"Yes!" Another voice burst into the conversation as Mac
stumbled onto the patio. "Own the awesomeness! What are
we singing?"

Deenie pulled Elinor close for a hug. "Thank you," she
whispered—a fraction of a second before Mac shouted,
"We're hugging!" and tackled them both.

"Why didn't you sing?"

Deenie stumbled slightly to the side and Connor caught
her elbow, steadying her on her heels—which earned him
a glower. Miss Sunshine and Glitter, he was learning, was
a belligerent drunk. Though she'd been hugging Elinor and
Ally and Mac all night. Apparently he was the only one she
was irrationally pissed at.

"Levi says you have a great voice," she challenged when
he didn't immediately answer.

"Levi should keep his mouth shut."

"*Elinor* certainly thinks so." The party had ended, rather

spectacularly, with the birthday girl going toe-to-toe with the chief of police and informing him that he had *no right* to comment on whom she dated or didn't date. Connor felt a little responsible for that—but since it was Elinor and Levi, it was probably bound to happen anyway.

"Are you afraid you'll look silly if you sing?" Deenie demanded, right when he started to hope she might have forgotten her question. "We all look silly. Karaoke is *about* the silly. But you and your stick up your empirically hot butt can't be *silly*. Nooooo."

Her toe caught on the sidewalk and he caught her before she could do a header into the pavement.

She had declared—with the firmness that only came with too many Birthday Girl shots—that she was going to walk home, and Connor had assigned himself the task of getting her there in one piece, since he hadn't been drinking. And because he was kind of entertained by this grumpy version of sunshine-and-light Deenie Mitchell.

"Why didn't you sing?" she demanded again, this time clinging to him from a distance of inches.

"I'm not a singer."

"No." She shoved off him, marching another few steps. "You're a *lawyer*. You're Mr. Perfect. You and your *dimples*."

"You have a problem with my dimples? I'm learning so much tonight."

"They aren't *fair*. You aren't allowed to be smart and nice and successful and perfect and have stupid devastating dimples, too. There are *rules*."

"I'll keep that in mind."

She nodded. "Good."

They walked on in silence until the farmhouse came into

view and curiosity got the better of him. "What was that song you sang with Mac tonight?"

"'Take Me or Leave Me.' *Rent*." The last word was explosive and it took him a moment to realize she meant the musical. "It's supposed to be for two women, but Mac killed it as Joanne."

"It seemed very pointed." He didn't remember all the lyrics, but there had been a lot of stuff about making lists in his sleep and being a control freak from Mac while Deenie was singing about being a tiger in a cage and needing to be free.

"It's a good song," Deenie said with exaggerated innocence.

"It's a breakup song."

She stopped suddenly on the edge of the gravel driveway, swinging toward him. "Is that what you want? You want to break up?"

"Is it what *you* want?"

She shook her head wildly, but her next words seemed to contradict the gesture. "We should have known this was never going to work."

"Deenie."

"I'm so stupid. Why am I so stupid? I can't believe I let myself fall in *love* with you."

"What?" The words slammed into his chest, knocking him out of commission.

She spun and stalked away, shouting into the night. "Who falls in love with the guy they're pretending to be in love with? Me. That's who."

She was five feet up the driveway before he realized she was getting away. "Deenie! *Stop*."

He caught up to her, catching her arm and spinning her around.

The words fell out. "I love you, too."

Her eyes flared in horror. "Don't say that."

"Not the reaction I'd hoped for. But I hadn't planned on telling you when you were drunk out of your mind, either." He studied her bleary eyes. "Are you going to remember this?"

She shook her head steadily, her eyes huge. "We're breaking up! It'll never work. We're oil and water."

"Does that mean we don't try? I thought you liked skydiving."

"With a parachute!" she yelled, pulling away. "This is...You're..." She stalked a few feet up the driveway before spinning back. "Why are you doing this?"

"Maybe I want to be with you. Not this halfway thing we have now. Maybe I want it to be real. And yeah, maybe it scares me to think that you might vanish on me someday, but maybe that's how I know I really want this. If I'm not afraid of losing you, how do I know this actually means anything?"

"I don't want you to be scared. But if we do this, you will be. You'll never trust that I'm going to stay, and I'll always feel like I'm trapped here. It'll eat away at us. It'll destroy us."

"What if it doesn't? What if it works?" He approached her, willing her to let him close. "You said yourself you've never had a real relationship. What if you love it? What if it's amazing?"

"You try to control everything—"

"And you don't? Isn't that what you're doing when you push people away? Trying to control your heart? Trying not to let anyone close enough to hurt you? You're just as much of a control freak as I am. You just hide it behind pink hair and a passport with a million stamps. But I don't want to try to control this. I don't want to *miss* it, Deenie. What if we're happy? Haven't you been happy?"

Tears glistened in her eyes. "What are you asking me?"

"*Stay.* That's all. Just...stay."

"Connor..."

"Just say you'll stay."

Her eyes held a swirling mix of hope and fear and vulnerability, but she stared up at him like she couldn't look away. Her teeth snagged her lower lip.

Her answer was a whisper. "Okay."

Chapter Twenty-Nine

Memorial Day weekend was insanely gorgeous—sun shining everywhere in idyllic perfection. And Deenie's mood couldn't have been less sunny.

Though she did a good job of faking it. They were at Connor's company picnic, after all, and she contractually owed him a smiling date...even if things were all muddy and messed up with where the contracts ended and *they* began.

She'd agreed to stay. She *wanted* to stay.

But what if she screwed it up? She wasn't good at staying put. She never had been.

"I come bearing hot dogs." Connor appeared at her side, holding two overloaded paper plates.

She flashed a bright, everything-is-great smile and accepted a plate. "My hero."

The law firm's Memorial Day weekend picnic was a surprisingly casual event, with a bouncy house and face painting for the kids and plenty of grilled meat for the adults. She and Connor found a spot at a crowded picnic table and devoured their hot dogs amid lively conversation.

The Sterlings joined them as they were finishing. "Can you believe this weather?"

Deenie smiled. "I think it's an apology from the weather gods for all the rain we've had this spring."

"I don't know. I like the rain." Connor slanted a glance at her as his forearm brushed hers where they rested side by side, and the memory of kissing him as the rain drenched them both filled her thoughts.

Deenie fought a blush as a pair of little girls she recognized from the party she'd hosted raced up to the table.

"Princess Deenie! You have to get your face painted! They have so much glitter!"

Deenie hesitated, glancing at Connor, but he grinned. "Go on," he urged. "I know better than to stand in the way of the Gospel of Glitter."

One little girl latched on to each arm, and Deenie let them pull her toward the face-painting station. Other kids from the party swarmed around, each wanting input on which design she was going to choose for her face. When the committee had finally settled on the *perfect* colors, Deenie sat in the face painter's chair. She felt Connor's gaze on her and glanced over at him, winking—until the artist asked her to look the other direction.

She chatted with the artist when she didn't need to hold her face still—the two of them agreeing they needed to exchange cards, since there was so much overlap in their business. And since Deenie was staying in the area indefinitely now.

Indefinite. It was such an intimidating word.

"Look to the left for me," the artist directed her, and Deenie turned her head, spotting Davis approaching Connor.

She watched the two of them speak, watched surprised

pleasure pass over Connor's face. A moment later, the two of them shook hands and Connor stood for a moment by himself, as if too stunned to move. But he regained his composure quickly. He was already moving toward her when the artist declared, "You're all set."

Deenie took the mirror, admiring the delicate fairy poised in flight across her cheekbone. The tiny fairy was looking over her shoulder, as if fleeing anyone who would catch her and pin her to one place—or maybe that was just Deenie projecting.

Thanking the artist, she slipped some money into the tip jar. The kids around her tugged on her arms, but she sent them on a mission to guard the bouncy castle from the incoming dragon army so she could intercept Connor without pint-sized helpers.

His eyes still looked dazed, like he wasn't quite seeing her, when she put a hand on his arm. "Is everything okay?"

"Everything is amazing," he said, keeping his voice low, just for her. "Davis just told me it's mine. The partner position. Not officially. I still have to wait two weeks until the all-partner meeting for the final decision, but he thinks I've got it in the bag." His gaze focused on hers. "And it's all thanks to you."

"That's ridiculous, and you know it. You've been working your butt off for years for this firm."

"But I wouldn't have made partner. Not without you."

She shook her head, dismissing his words, trying to dredge up the excitement she knew she should be feeling. "Congratulations. I'm so happy for you," she said, as if saying the words could make them true. She *wanted* to be happy for him. So why did she feel…*this*?

Like his victory was a nail in the coffin. Only she didn't

know which coffin or why. Just that it didn't feel like she wanted it to.

Luckily, a pack of kids raced over to her, needing her help defending against the imaginary dragon army, and she was able to escape before she had to look too closely at why everything felt wrong.

She went through the motions all afternoon, putting on her most glowingly happy face, then slept in the car on the way back to Pine Hollow—actually slept rather than feigning sleep, inexplicably exhausted by the afternoon.

By the time they got back to Pine Hollow, they barely had time to grab Max and the picnic basket before they were due to meet Ally and Ben and Astrid and Elinor and Mac in the town square for Movies in the Moonlight—a Pine Hollow summer tradition where they played old movies while the residents picnicked on the grass.

It was idyllic. Romantic.

And she had to fight not to squirm through the entire film, even though *The Philadelphia Story*, with Katharine Hepburn and Cary Grant, was one of her favorites.

Which, of course, Connor picked apart.

He kept his voice down, so as not to disturb the other people in the park, but he muttered all his complaints for Deenie to hear.

Normally, she would defend the film's honor, but tonight the battle felt pointless, and she could only wonder how she'd ever thought a relationship would work with a man who didn't like *The Philadelphia Story*.

"So the moral of the story is that she should go back to a relationship that made her miserable?" he grumbled as they walked Max home, their steps slow and lazy.

Deenie flicked him an irritated glance. "Did you miss all

that stuff about how he sobered up and she lightened up so they could come back together to find the love they'd had all along?"

"So they both had to change to live happily ever after?" he countered—and continued to argue, but she didn't hear any more of the words.

That was what happened in rom-coms, right? They both changed to live happily ever after? But that wasn't what was happening here. They hadn't compromised. She had.

Connor was getting exactly what he'd always wanted and Deenie was getting…

She'd changed everything she wanted, for him. She'd given in. And uneasiness whispered in her ear.

Connor was ninety percent sure he was being paranoid, but the other ten percent kept telling him that Deenie was pulling away.

He'd thought things would be settled when she agreed to stay, but he didn't feel settled. He'd said he loved her. She'd done the same. But he still felt like they were two boxers in the ring, feeling one another out, both waiting for the other to deliver the knockout blow.

The paranoia was a problem.

He *knew* he was looking for signs that she was about to run. He hadn't seen any of the early warnings with Monica, and he didn't want to make that mistake twice, so he was hypervigilant now—and seeing red flags everywhere.

Last night in the square, he'd been worried that she wasn't arguing with him as much as she used to. She wasn't calling him Princeton and poking at every little thing he said.

So when the movie started, he'd been absolutely merciless, harping on everything he could think of—and she'd been strangely subdued.

He was reading into every glance, every flicker of an eyelash. Braced for something to happen. After Monica—after his dad, if he was honest—he saw emotional black holes everywhere, just waiting to suck him in again. Deenie had said she would stay, and he wanted to trust that she would, but how did he make himself do that?

She wasn't even with him—spending the entire day at her sister's vineyard tour bachelorette party—but he couldn't seem to stop worrying.

"How did you trust Mitch not to leave?"

His mother looked at him in surprise. Not that he could blame her. He was a little surprised himself. They didn't really talk about Mitch.

The two of them—and Max—were strolling through the Pine Hollow Memorial Day Festival, which had closed all the streets on the town square, filling them with booths from local businesses. Furry Friends had a booth on the north side of the square, but when Connor had suggested Deenie might want to get one for her princess dress business, she'd looked at him like he was trying to poison her.

"I just did," his mother said simply, unhelpfully.

Connor grimaced. "After what happened before, weren't you...?" He didn't know how to finish the question. Luckily, she didn't make him.

"Mitch was nothing like Aaron." She'd stopped calling Aaron Wyeth "your father" the day he left. "But I know what you mean. It wasn't about him, it was about me. How do you let yourself let someone in?"

"Yeah."

She tucked her hand through his arm, moving around a little girl on a tricycle. "Is this about Deenie?"

He shrugged—and thankfully she didn't push.

"Well." She cleared her throat. "For me it was about knowing myself. About knowing I didn't need a man to feel complete. I'd raised a good son on my own. You were happy and healthy and doing very well in school, and I was perfectly content on my own. But my empty nest was awfully empty. I missed having someone to look after, and I realized that even if I didn't need someone, I wanted someone. Mitch made me laugh. He let me set the pace—and it wasn't always perfect. He's so easygoing that sometimes I just wanted to throw something at him and tell him to get upset about something. Anything. I accused him once of not caring about me enough because he wasn't pushing me to be more serious. And then he showed me the ring he'd been carrying around in his pocket since our third date, just in case I decided I was willing to marry him. I stopped giving him a hard time about not caring enough then."

"I'm not sure that strategy would work with Deenie." He couldn't think of a way to make her run faster than to propose.

"She doesn't seem anything like Monica."

"But that doesn't mean she won't leave." She was even more likely to run than Monica had been.

Except...that wasn't Deenie.

She wasn't unreliable. She didn't promise to do things and never do them. She didn't make schedules, because she knew she would feel obligated to keep them, and she didn't want to feel restricted by that *need* to follow through on her word. She wasn't irresponsible. She was *hyper* responsible.

She cared intensely about not letting people down, and for her to say she would stay...

She had to mean that.

Didn't she?

Mitch joined them before he could say anything, and Connor snapped his mouth shut. He didn't talk about real things with his mother's husband.

But a moment later, his mother darted away to say hello to someone, leaving Mitch and Connor standing awkwardly in silence—and Connor remembered Deenie needling him about not giving Mitch a chance.

This man who made his mother so happy. Who never pushed, but not because he didn't care.

"I think I'm going to make partner," he said, speaking the words out loud for the first time since he'd told Deenie. He didn't know why he told Mitch. He hadn't even told his mother.

"You don't sound happy about that," his mother's husband mused.

"I am. I just thought it would feel different."

Mitch nodded slowly. "Why did you want it?"

Connor opened his mouth...and didn't have an answer.

You've got it in the bag, Davis had said yesterday. *If that's what you want.*

And Connor had only been able to think, *Of course it's what I want. It's what I've always wanted.*

But the surge of victory had been quickly chased by something else. A vague disquiet.

Was it just that it was too good to be true? That he didn't trust how everything was falling into place? Or was it something else?

"You know your mother will be proud of you no matter

what you do. If you're a lawyer or a…" Mitch trailed off, at a loss, and Connor filled in the gap.

"A dog walker?"

"Exactly."

"I know," Connor admitted. "But I still wanted to be the best for her."

Mitch nodded again. "I've always admired your drive. Even when it can be a little intimidating."

"I didn't mean to intimidate—" He caught himself. "Actually, I probably did. I know it's stupid to be jealous of you—"

"Oh, don't worry, I was jealous of you, too," Mitch assured him with an easy smile. "But I do admire you, kid."

Connor looked at this man with his infinite reserves of calm. Who had never seemed to care about competition—which made it incredibly frustrating to feel like he was in competition with him. "I admire you, too," Connor admitted, realizing the truth as he said it.

His mother reappeared then. Mitch smiled, and his spine straightened a little, the slight shift in posture the only indication that he clearly thought their moment of bonding was over now that Mele was back.

But Connor looked over at him. "We should get a beer sometime. Just you and me."

Mitch's eyes held surprise, but his smile was ready. "I'd like that. I'd really like that."

Connor caught his mother's eye, seeing the tears in hers. "Don't."

"What?" she asked wetly. "I'm just happy. Can't I be happy?"

Chapter Thirty

"Y ou guys, I am *so happy!*"

Deenie had never seen her sister drunk. She'd never even seen Kirsten *tipsy*. She was always poised. Always elegant. Always in control.

And at the moment she was swaying drunkenly in the back of a party bus, drinking directly from an open bottle of rosé.

The bachelorette party had sounded as if it would be far from raucous based on the embossed invitation Deenie had received from the co-matrons of honor. An afternoon touring a selection of wineries on a luxurious bus, nibbling cheese, and celebrating the bride-to-be. There would be no strippers. No phallus-shaped necklaces. No hot-pink shots—which was probably for the best, since Deenie was still taking it easy after Elinor's birthday party two weeks ago.

Frankly, Deenie had expected to be bored. She had *not* expected the wine bus to rapidly turn into the drunk bus as Kirsten and all her bridesmaids quickly progressed from a sedate champagne toast to purchasing full bottles "for the road" at each vineyard and drinking directly from those bottles as they cruised toward the next idyllic location.

Deenie had a few sips, but she was currently the sole representative of sobriety—not counting the bus driver, who, thankfully, seemed deeply amused by his sloppy-drunk-ladies-who-lunch passengers.

"Seat belts!" He shouted a reminder as Kirsten lunged up from the seat where she'd been sitting and staggered across the aisle to fling herself into the spot beside Deenie.

"Whoops!" She giggled, the bottle in her hand sloshing before she raised it to her lips again.

"Classy," Deenie drawled.

"It's my bachelorette party. I'm *supposed* to be drunk," Kirsten declared. "It's *tradition*."

"Mission accomplished."

Kirsten toasted her with the bottle, then dropped her head onto Deenie's shoulder with a sigh. "Deenie Baby, I'm so glad you're here."

"Me too. Water?" She traded her sister a water bottle for the half-full bottle of rosé.

Kirsten straightened. "I'm serious," she insisted, as if Deenie had argued with her, struggling to focus her brown eyes. She had their mother's coloring, that dark hair and eyes that had somehow skipped Deenie entirely. "I can't believe you're actually here. You never come when I invite you."

"So you weren't secretly hoping I'd say no when you asked me to be in the wedding party?"

"Of course not! But I didn't think you'd say yes. You don't even like me."

"*Kirsten.* I love you."

"I know. I love you, too. But you don't actually *like* me. You never want to be around me."

"Kirsten." She twisted to face her sister, taking her hand. "I like you. Me not wanting to be around has nothing to do with not liking you. I just feel like I'm always defending who I am when I'm around you guys. It's exhausting." At Kirsten's blank look, she explained, "Mom and Dad have been badgering me to get a real major, a real degree, a real job, for as long as I can remember."

"But you know I don't care about that stuff."

Deenie arched an eyebrow. "The storefront?" she reminded her sister gently. Kirsten had cornered her before they got on the bus today to remind her again that Todd had a friend who wanted to take her business to the next level.

"I'm just trying to help you succeed—"

"On *your* terms."

"I don't know any other terms," Kirsten protested.

"I know. But I don't want a permanent location and a staff and all those obligations. I *like* my independence. It's part of who I am."

And she was giving it up for Connor. That uneasy feeling whispered through her. That stir of wanderlust.

"I'm not trying to change who you are," Kirsten insisted. "I've always envied you."

Surprise shuddered through her. "What?"

"You were always so free. The rules were different for you. You got to be the rebel! Deenie Baby. Who got away with *everything*. Who got to do whatever she wanted. You think I never wanted to go to Europe? To study art and drink café au lait?"

Deenie shook her head. "The rules were not different. And I didn't *get* to be the rebel. I just didn't let Mom and Dad dictate my life. It's not like it was easy."

"And you think my life was?" Kirsten challenged.

"I didn't say that," Deenie said.

"You were always pushing us away. Always throwing in our faces how free you are."

"If I do push you away, it's because whenever I'm with you guys, I have to constantly defend my right to be different. Which just makes me want to be more different. To prove that it's not *wrong*."

"No one said it was wrong. We just worry about you. How can you be happy without stability? We were all so worried about your future, and it's such a relief that we don't have to worry about you anymore."

Unease whispered through her, and Kirsten took advantage of her inattention to reclaim the rosé bottle. "What do you mean?"

"Just that we're happy for you. Peter kept saying you were bound to grow up eventually, but Peter's an idiot."

Deenie snorted at her sister's opinion of their only brother, who generally thought he knew everything about everything.

"But he was right this time. Somebody finally tamed Deenie!" Deenie's heart stuttered as Kirsten kept gushing. "You have a job, with an address, and a steady, responsible boyfriend. I actually knew where to send all your invites for the wedding stuff! How often have you even had the same address for six months? This guy. He's *changed* you. And Mom and Dad *love* him."

The unease had progressed to full-on alarm bells, clanging in her brain.

"I'm so proud of you. You're finally settling down. And I'm getting *married*!"

The last was shouted—and met with a round of *"Woo!"*

from the bridal party. But Deenie couldn't woo. She could barely breathe.

Had she changed for Connor? Had she become exactly what she'd always fought against?

"I'm so happy for you, Deenie Baby."

Kirsten dropped her head onto Deenie's shoulder, sighing contentedly. While Deenie wondered if this was what a panic attack felt like. Her chest was tight, and she couldn't get a full breath.

The urge to run thrummed beneath her skin.

She didn't know what she wanted right now. Everything was so tangled up. The independence she'd had before was compromised now by things she *should* do. She'd promised to be here for the wedding. She'd promised to stay with Connor. She'd promised...and now those promises held her hostage.

She reached for the rosé.

Chapter Thirty-One

It was the same ballroom. The same picturesque resort. What were the odds?

Connor stood in the same venue where he'd nearly married Monica sixteen months ago, and expected to feel something, some kind of regret or at least a flood of memory, but his thoughts were all on Deenie as he watched her pose for the wedding party photos.

He'd barely seen her all week. He told himself not to be paranoid. He had a new resolution: He was going to trust her. He wasn't going to read into every little thing. She'd been busy. The shelter was busy. Her dress business was slammed. She'd been conscripted to help with last-minute wedding favor stuff. And then there had been rehearsals and rehearsal dinners and practice sessions with the makeup artists and hairstylists. Of *course* he hadn't seen her. She wasn't avoiding him.

And he'd see plenty of her tonight. They were spending the night at the resort, along with most of the wedding guests. He'd dropped Max off at Furry Friends for the night before heading down to meet Deenie, who had been here at the resort all day, being curled and primped to a neutral shine. Even the pink in her hair seemed faded.

She was so subdued. Not a trace of glitter in sight as she stood in her muted gray bridesmaid dress.

He'd watched her all through the ceremony. She was playing her part well, and her smile didn't falter for a second, but he couldn't escape the unsettling feeling that she was pulling away. Mentally retreating from him and all of this.

The group shuffled and reshuffled for photo after photo— the bridal party, the groom's family, the bride's family. Inside, the guests were mingling and nibbling appetizers in the ballroom, waiting for the arrival of the newly married couple. Connor should be inside with them, but the only reason he was at this wedding at all was for Deenie, so he'd slipped outside to watch the photos.

He realized his mistake when Kirsten spotted him.

"Connor!" She thrust her bouquet imperiously in the air. "Let's get one with Connor."

"Oh no, that isn't necessary." He held up a hand in protest, but Kirsten's expression had turned cheerfully militant.

"You aren't going to deny a bride on her wedding day. Get over here."

They were taking pictures of Deenie's family with the happy couple—her parents, her siblings, her nieces and nephews. All of them were beaming at him as he approached, welcoming him to the family with eager smiles as Deenie's smile stayed perfect and the look in her eyes got even harder to read.

The photographer shoved him into place beside Deenie, even setting his arm around her waist, and Connor bent his head to her. "Are you okay with this?" he whispered—

even though he wasn't sure how to stop it if she wasn't because the photographer was already resuming his position.

"Shoulders back," the photographer called, making him straighten to his full height.

"You'll thank me, Deenie Baby," Kirsten gushed. "Can you imagine looking back on this in ten years and thinking, 'Why aren't there any pictures of Connor at Kirsten's wedding? I know he was there.'"

Connor nearly cringed—Kirsten wasn't helping. He looked down at Deenie, but she stared fixedly at the camera, smile locked in place.

"Eyes here! Big smiles!"

Connor obeyed the commands while the photographer rapidly snapped the photos, and then he was evicted from the photo session and sent back inside to await the wedding party with everyone else. He lingered, glancing back at Deenie, but she wouldn't meet his eyes.

He told himself not to be paranoid. He told himself it was all in his head.

He told himself that through the happy couple's big entrance, through dinner and toasts and the first dance and cake. He was trying to trust her. But something was off. Like her guard was up again, and she was only pretending to be happy she agreed to be with him. And he was pretending not to notice her pretending, because otherwise she would leave.

The band was playing a selection of jazzy old standards as a handful of couples danced and the bride and groom circulated, attempting to accept the congratulations of every one of their two hundred guests. And Deenie still hadn't said more than half a dozen words to him in a row all night.

She had to be exhausted. She'd been out here at the crack of dawn to start getting ready.

"It's almost over," Connor murmured as they sat at their table and she watched the couples on the dance floor. "Once they toss the bouquet, we can sneak away."

Deenie didn't respond. Her gaze had caught on a woman moving toward them with purpose. Her mother.

"Come on." Connor stood suddenly. "Let's dance."

She didn't speak, but she didn't resist. He led her onto the dance floor and into his arms as a new song began and the female singer began to croon into the microphone.

At least this was one place where things still felt right. Even if it still felt like he was trying too hard, doing everything he could to distract them both from the feeling that she was slipping away.

Deenie swayed in Connor's arms, the lyrics of the song wrapping around her. She knew this song—an old standard called "Something's Gotta Give," all about irresistible forces and immovable objects. The band had slowed it down, drawing the jazzy tune into something lingering and poignant, and emotion caught in Deenie's throat.

"It's our song," she drawled, making her voice sarcastic so he wouldn't hear the catch.

All day—hell, all week—her sister's words from the bachelorette party had haunted her.

Somebody finally tamed Deenie.

Her family loved him. Her sister had dragged him into the family photos like they were already engaged, like it was just assumed they were still going to be together in ten years.

He'd asked her to leap for him and she had...but in the back of her mind, the truth kept whispering. She was an unstoppable force, and he was an immovable object. Something had to give. And it had been her. *She'd* had to give.

She'd given in. Lost who she was. And why? Why was she doing any of this?

"You holding up okay?" Connor asked, shifting to draw her a little closer—and suddenly the fact that he was so considerate, so understanding, so freaking *perfect*, grated against her skin. She pushed away from him.

"I need to get some air." When he started to nod, like he would come with her, she bit out, "Alone."

She didn't look back as she pushed out into the warm June night. She shouldn't abandon him in the middle of her sister's wedding. He was only here for her. But the vise closing around her chest, squeezing off her breath, wouldn't let her go back inside.

She braced her hands on the stone balcony, overlooking the nighttime gardens, lit with carefully placed spotlights. The venue had been a point of contention between her mother and sister. The amenities weren't quite up to her mother's five-star standards—no spa, no Michelin-starred restaurant—but Kirsten hadn't been willing to compromise on the views. The stone bridges. The lush gardens. The mountainous backdrop.

The door opened behind her. "What are you doing out here, Nadine? Your sister's about to toss the bouquet."

Deenie didn't look back at her mother's voice. "I just need a minute."

"You can have a minute later. This is your sister's night."

"I know, Mom." She kept her eyes on the garden, trying to absorb its calm. *Zen. Think Zen.*

"People will notice if you aren't there for the bouquet."

"Will they?" She immediately regretted the snark.

"Your sister will notice," her mother snapped. "We all know you try to pretend you aren't part of this family, but the least you can do is catch a bunch of flowers."

"I know I'm part of this family." She couldn't escape it.

"You could have fooled me. You spent your Christmas with Bitty, and she doesn't even remember who you are."

The words stabbed and Deenie turned to face her mother, her back to the stone railing. "At least she *likes* me. At least she never makes me feel like I'm not good enough. You were the one who told me I should have said no when Kirsten asked me to be in the wedding."

"Because you're irresponsible!"

"No, I'm not! I have done *everything* you asked of me for this wedding, and you still cannot stop picking at me." She'd done nothing but work to make Kirsten's wedding perfect this week. She'd been the only person on the wine bus who *hadn't* made a fool of herself and now she was getting it from her mother? "When am I going to be able to do something right?" she demanded. "I've done it now, haven't I? Ticked off all the boxes on your success checklist? Stable job, stable relationship. Isn't this what you wanted? For me to become your perfect Stepford daughter? For someone to *tame* me? When is it going to be enough?"

"When you catch the bouquet!"

Deenie nearly screamed. Her mother wasn't hearing her. She *couldn't* hear her. And the one person who had always heard her didn't know who she was anymore. No wonder Deenie had lost herself.

"I'm sorry, Mom. I can't do that."

She strode away from her mother, down the flagstone steps into the garden, ignoring her mother's sharp "Deenie!"

Something had to give.

Chapter Thirty-Two

Her phone rang early the next morning and Deenie caught it on the first ring, rolling out of bed and making her way quickly to the tiny balcony so she wouldn't disturb Connor.

She'd hidden from her mother last night through the bouquet toss and missed waving Kirsten and Todd off on their honeymoon—but with two hundred other guests throwing flower petals, she doubted anyone but her mother noticed her absence. When she'd come back inside, only the diehards were still on the dance floor. Connor had already retreated to their room when she got there.

He didn't ask her where she'd been. He didn't accuse her of running out on him—which she absolutely had. He just asked if she was okay. And she'd felt like a horrible person as she briskly assured him she was fine and announced she was going to take a bath, shutting herself in the bathroom until she was certain he'd fallen asleep.

The sun was up, but the air was cool and dew still covered everything as Deenie shivered on the balcony, connecting the call. "Hello?"

"Nadine Mitchell?"

Deenie frowned at the name that only telemarketers used. "Who is this?"

"Ms. Mitchell, my name is Eileen Glenn. I work at the Summerland Estates."

The voice was gentle, with an aura of compassion that set off alarm bells in her heart. "Is everything okay?"

"I'm afraid I have some sad news."

Bitty. Deenie's heart seized hard.

"I'm so sorry, Ms. Mitchell," the voice on the other end of the line went on, gentle and soothing, a voice with practice at these kinds of calls, who knew the person on the other end had already guessed the truth. "It was quick."

Connor woke up alone, momentarily disoriented by the strange surroundings before his brain kicked in and he remembered where he was. Sun slanted into the room. He'd slept fitfully the night before, restless and incapable of getting comfortable, but he must have finally fallen solidly asleep at some point because, from the angle of the sun, he'd missed half the morning. He scrubbed a hand over his face, groggy from the uncharacteristic late start.

"Deenie?"

She didn't answer, and his hand brushed something on her pillow. A crinkle of paper.

He sat up, blearily studying the scribbled note, the words not making sense.

Sorry. Had to go.

He frowned at the sheet torn off a hotel notepad. Not quite a Post-it, but close enough. "Ouch. Too soon, babe," he called, kicking off the covers and walking to the partially cracked bathroom door. He shoved the door open all the way—and the room was empty. Even the toiletries that had been littering the vanity were gone.

Connor spun, looking to where Deenie's overnight bag had been exploding its contents all over the floor—because she was the least tidy person he'd ever met—but it was gone, too. The floor was spotless.

"No," he told himself when paranoia screamed in his ear. She wouldn't do this. Not exactly the way Monica had done it. She knew that would hurt him, and Deenie was never cruel.

He grabbed his phone and dialed her number, but it went to voice mail. He typed a quick text. *Where are you? Are you okay?*

But there was no response.

"Shit." Connor didn't bother to shower. He threw on clean clothes, tossed his things into his bag, and was on the road in under ten minutes. He and Deenie had driven two cars down to Castle Hill yesterday because she'd had to be there so much earlier than he had, but he hadn't considered she might leave without him in the morning.

Something was wrong. Something had to be wrong.

Deenie's powder-blue VW Beetle was crooked in the driveway of Furry Friends. Connor pulled up behind her, blocking her in, and jumped out of his car, racing up the porch steps.

He almost never went inside the farmhouse. Deenie came to his house so often, there was no need. He would visit the dog park Deenie and Ally had created out back. He'd drop by to pick up Deenie, but she'd almost always meet him outside. He hadn't been inside the farmhouse since their impromptu party after they'd demolished Ben's kitchen. The same day Deenie had made her outrageous proposal that they pretend to date. The day that had set everything in motion.

Ally opened the door before he reached it, her eyes worried. "She's upstairs."

Connor took the stairs two at a time.

The wide hall on the second floor had half a dozen doors. He didn't know which room was hers, but they were all open and he followed the sound of movement. "Deenie?"

She didn't answer. He nudged the door open farther, stepping over the threshold, and the sight of her hit like a sledgehammer to the chest.

Her eyes were puffy, her face chalk white. A tiny dog with little bows on its ears sat in the center of her fluffy white duvet, amid a pile of colorful clothes. A large purple backpack sat open beside the dog. Deenie roughly shoved clothing inside the bag.

She was packing.

She wasn't ready to see Connor. She'd known she *would* see him. She wasn't going to run off and leave him without explaining. He deserved more than that. But she wasn't ready to see him yet. She hadn't mentally composed what she was going to say to him. She hadn't figured out how to excuse what was about to happen. How to explain that it was for the best. For both of them. She didn't have her angle.

All she had was grief.

"Deenie. What's going on? What happened?"

His voice seemed to be coming from a great, foggy distance. She stared at the wadded-up leggings in her hands. "I'm packing," she said, her voice sounding rusty and thick. *Focus on the task.* She had a purpose. A goal. She had to finish this.

She couldn't look at him, but she knew he was there, the height of him filling the room, his concern a heat at her side. "Did something happen with Bitty?"

Deenie flinched, her hands tightening on the leggings. She shoved them into the bag. "It was Mr. Burke. He had a stroke. They said it was quick. He didn't suffer."

She'd been at the Estates all morning. She'd left Connor sleeping and gone immediately to collect JoJo and discuss arrangements with the staff, forcing her tears back, even when the staff had cried and squeezed her hands and told her how lovely they all thought he was. They'd treated her like she was his family. And maybe she was.

She'd gone to Bitty then. Never planning to tell her about Mr. Burke. She wouldn't remember him. She didn't remember Deenie. She'd lain in her bed, not even aware Deenie was there, lost inside a world of her own, and Deenie had realized her aunt wasn't coming back. Physically, she might still be there, but mentally she'd slipped away, like silk slipping through her fingers, the slinky fabrics her aunt had taught her to sew.

It was all over now but the crying. Deenie had been in denial of that fact for weeks, but the reality had shuddered home in a rush. There wouldn't be any more good days. There hadn't been for a while. The truth was right there in the sympathy in the nurses' eyes, staring her in the face.

Connor stepped closer. "Deenie, I'm so sor—"

"Don't." She shoved past him, hurrying toward her underwear drawer. She would need underwear. Underwear was important. Much more important than his voice filled with the sympathy and understanding that was going to break her.

I'm not handling this well.

The thought echoed, strangely clear and distant, like a piece of her had broken off and was analyzing from the outside—but at least that piece was calm. She liked the calm.

"Where are you going?" He wasn't trying to push his sympathy on her now. That was good.

"Rome. He told me to take an adventure." *You can't put more life in the bank.* What did that even mean?

He'd left her JoJo. And a note. Tucked into a drawer for "when it happens." He didn't have any family to speak of. He'd left everything to a nephew of David's, a few charity bequests, and to her. He'd told her she wasn't allowed to spend the money on anything practical.

There would be a will. There would be the business of cleaning out his apartment. There would be practicalities. But first...

"I got a good deal on a last-minute ticket, but the flight leaves tonight. I have to pack." She grabbed handfuls of underwear, his silence feeling like a condemnation. "I was going to come see you. On my way to the airport. I wasn't going to leave without talking to you."

"When are you coming back?"

She shook her head, carrying the underwear over to her bag, keeping her eyes on her packing. "I don't know."

She couldn't look at him. If she looked at him, everything would push through. She would feel it all. She couldn't feel it all. Not right now. She had to push it away. Had to do something. Had to escape.

But his voice wouldn't let her. "You bought a one-way ticket? What about us?"

The words seemed to echo in the room as he clung to calm. She was upset. She'd loved Mr. Burke. She didn't mean this.

But she wouldn't let him touch her. Wouldn't let him get within two feet before she rushed to a different part of the room to get something else to shove into that damn pack. The tiny dog sniffing each new addition.

He could have stopped her. He could have easily restrained her, pulled her against his chest, and wrapped her in comfort, but this was Deenie. He wasn't sure what she would do if he tried to physically hold her in place. She might never forgive him.

She shook her head, rejecting his words. "You don't need me anymore. Max is trained. You made partner. I fulfilled the contract."

"Screw the contract," Connor snapped. "I don't care about the contract. Deenie, look at me!"

She went still, turning her face toward his—and the

look in her eyes was already a million miles away. History was repeating itself. She was pushing him away. She was leaving him.

Only this time he could plead his case. This time he could be rejected to his face.

"*Talk* to me," he urged.

"What is there to talk about? We were never going to work. We both know it. I was always going to need to get away."

"That's a self-fulfilling prophecy. You don't have to go—"

"Yes, I do!" she shouted, the words echoing off the high ceiling. "This isn't me. You've made me into *you*. Aren't you proud of yourself? You *tamed* me. Turned me into a grown-up."

"I never wanted you to change—"

"Then why did you ask me to stay?"

"Because I love you!"

"No, you love who you want me to be. And I gave in to you. I tried to be that person. But I stayed too long. I started to forget who I am. I started to want the house and the yard and the kids when that has *never* been me. I *changed* for you. Because I—" She broke off, the rush of words stopping in her throat. She took a breath, reclaiming her calm, her next words as cold and smooth as ice. "It was all pretend. We fell for our own ruse. None of this is real."

"It was real to me. It hasn't been fake for a long time. I'm not sure it ever was."

Her breath caught, and for a second, he thought he had her.

"Deenie. *Please*." He took a step closer—and a steel door slammed in her eyes.

"No." She spun away, moving quickly around the room, packing at warp speed now. "That's even worse." Toiletries jammed into the bag. A long scarf. The tiny dog on the bed watched it all with shiny black eyes. "My family is so happy that I'm with you. They can see me turning into you. Changing my hair, changing my clothes, my behavior, until finally I'm exactly who they wanted me to be."

"I never wanted you to change. I love the pink. I love the glitter. I love *you*."

"Stop *saying* that!" She whirled, throwing a wad of socks at him. "You don't want me! You want someone who fits into your plan. You don't want to make a plan with me. You want me to accept yours. And I won't do that."

"You said you would stay."

"You shouldn't have asked me." The sound of the zipper was loud in the room.

Panic stabbed into Connor's chest. She was leaving. Really leaving. He'd pleaded his case, he'd freaking *begged* her to stay, and she was still going.

"I promised myself I would never be with someone who made me feel like I wasn't good enough. Who made me feel like I had to change—"

"I *never* wanted you to change!" Why wouldn't she *hear* him?

"I can't be what you want."

"I want *you*."

"No, you don't. You just want me to stay."

She swept up the backpack and the tiny dog, walking out the door, and nothing Connor said or felt could stop her.

He stood in the bedroom that still had so much of Deenie in it—the gauzy pink drapes, the sewing machine strewn with the glittery fabrics that were constantly leaving debris on everything she touched, the discarded neon leggings that hadn't made the cut to go to Europe.

Outside, a car door slammed.

"Shit." He raced out of the room and down the stairs, across the living room, bursting out onto the porch. "Deenie!"

Her car was still there. But the Furry Friends truck was pulling onto the street—Deenie and Ally visible in the front seat. He ran down the driveway, waving his arms—knowing he looked like a fool, but if she looked back, if she just saw him waving like an idiot, she would change her mind.

Wouldn't she?

He stopped when he reached the street, breathless, even though he hadn't been running that far. Gravel crunched beneath his feet.

He hadn't chased Monica. He hadn't begged her to stay. He'd never had the chance, but somehow telling Deenie he loved her and still having to watch her drive away was worse. Or maybe it was always going to be worse because it was Deenie. Because he had never loved Monica the way he loved her.

Monica had fit his life. They'd gotten along. But when she left, he'd mourned his *plans* more than he'd mourned the loss of her. He'd always prioritized the future over the present. Goals over impulses. He had made his plans and tried to fit a woman into them, just like Deenie accused him—but she'd blown up his neatly ordered life. She didn't play by his rules. And he'd loved it.

Who was going to argue with him about movies and tell him when he was being too stiff? He didn't want someone who checked all the boxes, any of those *suitable* women.

He wanted Deenie more than he wanted the vision of his future he'd been chasing for the last two decades.

But how could he prove that to her? How could he show her he wanted to be the one to change for her? That he *had* changed for her. That all that mattered to him now was arguing his way toward compromise, because he'd finally found someone he couldn't live without.

The memory of dancing with her last night echoed in his mind, the lyrics of "their song" taunting him. She was an irresistible force. He'd been an immovable object.

But he would move for her.

Connor ran back to his car.

Chapter Thirty-Three

Deenie sat in the passenger seat of the Furry Friends truck with her bulging backpack pressed against her knees and JoJo cuddled on her lap. The soft-sided pet carrier that JoJo would travel in sat beside her on the seat, but she needed the silky, sweet comfort of JoJo in her lap right now.

She was making the right choice. She was at least seventy percent certain she was making the right choice. Sixty minimum. But Connor's words kept echoing in her head.

Ally sat beside her, focused on driving, very carefully not saying anything—though Deenie could feel all the things she didn't say filling the cab. Invisible fumes of judgment.

She should have driven herself. Or taken an Uber. But an Uber all the way to the Burlington airport was stupidly expensive, and she hadn't wanted to leave her car in airport parking indefinitely. Normally she would take the time to put it in storage properly. She would pack all her things so she wasn't leaving Ally with a guest room strewn with sewing machines and princess party debris.

Normally, she wouldn't be fleeing the country on less than six hours' notice.

No. Not fleeing. *Adventuring*. Mr. Burke had told her to have an adventure for him. But this didn't feel like one. She didn't feel liberated. She felt miserable.

She'd been in Pine Hollow too long. That was all this was. That was the only reason she'd started fantasizing about domestic life with Connor. She hadn't *actually* fallen in love with him.

But then why did it feel like her heart was breaking?

It was Mr. Burke. Of course she was broken. She was *grieving*. But she also felt like she was letting him down somehow. Like he would be disappointed in her. She pulled the letter he'd left her out of the top of her backpack, smoothing out the creases she'd already put in the pristine stationery.

Nadine,

I know when you read this it will feel like it happened too soon, but don't grieve too much for me. I'm ready to be with David again. I had a good run and more happiness than I could have hoped for in one lifetime. Thank you for making these last few months feel like life again, full of possibility, even though the clock was winding down.

I don't have much family, as you know, so I'm leaving you a little something. Promise me you won't be practical with it. I would be so disappointed if you didn't use it to seize life with both hands. You can always put more money in the bank, but you can't put more life in the bank—and

never let Bitty claim she came up with that herself. It
was all David.

I hope you have so many adventures, Nadine, but mostly
I hope you never let fear hold you back from happiness.
Be brave. Chase your dreams. Be only yourself in a world
that tries to make you into everyone else. And all those
other silly platitudes.

Remember me, from time to time, as a nosy old man who
told you what to do, even when you always knew exactly
what to do. And take care of my JoJo.

With my love,
James Alexander Burke

Deenie cuddled JoJo closer, tears slipping silently down
her cheeks.

"Deenie?" Ally asked gently. "Are you sure this is what
you want?"

Ally. Who tried so hard not to pressure her into staying,
even when she made it clear that Deenie was welcome.
That Deenie was wanted. That she had a place, if she only
accepted it.

And then there was her sister, who had wanted her in
the wedding, who had invited Deenie, even when she kept
pushing her family away, running away...

And Connor...

Deenie shook away the thought of him, focusing on the
letter again through vision blurred by tears.

Mr. Burke wanted her to chase her dreams. So why did it feel like she was running from one?

She'd promised herself she wouldn't let the fear of not fitting in rule her life, but was she letting a different kind of fear control her now?

She was so scared of not being good enough. Of not being accepted for who she was. Of not being loved. But Kirsten loved her. Ally loved her.

And Connor...

He'd never made her feel like she wasn't good enough. He'd made her feel like sunshine. And yes, he'd wanted her to stay, but not because he was trying to put her in a box. He'd never asked her to pretend to be anything she wasn't. She was the one who'd wanted to pretend to be something else—an accountant or a financial adviser. He'd wanted her on his arm as a princess party planner and a dog trainer. He'd wanted *her*.

He'd loved her.

And she'd thrown it in his face. She'd run away. Even though she knew—she *knew*—that was the worst possible thing she could have done to him.

Deenie's heart clutched, her throat squeezing.

"We have to go back."

Ally jerked the wheel, startled by the volume of Deenie's declaration. "Really?"

"I'm in love with Connor. We have to go back."

A broad grin spread across Ally's face as she executed a U-turn. "It's about time."

Chapter Thirty-Four

The love of her life was missing.

His car was long gone from Furry Friends when she and Ally finally made it back. Ally took her to his house, but the door was locked and the security system armed.

She'd wanted to talk to him in person, but if she couldn't *find* him, that proved problematic. She tried his cell, but it rang through to voice mail. They retreated back to Furry Friends to plan their next steps while Deenie called again—getting voice mail again.

"Do you think he's at his mom's?"

JoJo wriggled on the seat beside her, yapping excitedly at her urgency.

"Let me see if Ben knows where he is," Ally offered—fully invested in the chase. They pulled into the gravel drive in front of Furry Friends to the usual explosion of barking from the barn.

Deenie leapt out of the truck and raced to the kennels, emerging again a moment later. "Max is still here!" she

shouted to Ally, who held her phone to her ear, her eyes
wide. "What? What is it?"

Ally pointed to the phone. "He's on his way to *Rome*."

This was, without a doubt, the most reckless thing
Connor Wyeth had ever done. He moved past security,
toward the gate, with just his overnight bag and a
fraying sense of optimism, keeping his eyes peeled for
Deenie.

She had to be on the same flight. There was only one
flight out of Burlington that would connect to a flight to
Rome, via JFK. He just hoped she was happy to see him.
He was very aware this could backfire on him in a big way.
What if she hated him for chasing her to Rome? What if she
was trying to get away from him?

He shook away the panic, closing in on the gate. If she
didn't want him there, he'd get on the first flight home. He
could even turn around at JFK. He hadn't checked any bags.
But he had to try.

Hopefully, when she saw him, she would think this was
romantic and not stalkerish.

It might be stalkerish.

She wasn't at the gate.

Connor frowned, glaring at the deadweight of his cell
phone. He'd forgotten his charger. *This* was why he made
packing lists and prepared for things. So he didn't end up
searching the airport for someplace to buy a charger in the
five minutes before his flight was set to board.

He'd thrown everything into his overnight bag in a frantic
rush, barely remembering to grab his passport. He'd been

booking the last-minute flight on his phone as he ran out the door—and hadn't even thought about chargers.

He would definitely have words with Deenie about giving him more than fifteen minutes' notice next time they planned an international trip—provided there was a next time. God, he hoped there was a next time.

The gate agent called preboarding, and Connor went alert, watching the people mulling around the gate for a telltale flash of pink. But she wasn't there.

Had she gotten on another flight? Could he find her in Rome? He didn't know where she'd be staying or if her phone would work internationally. She must have some way of keeping in touch. Ally would know. All he had to do was get Ben to get Ally to tell him where her friend was so he could stalk her on a foreign continent...

Connor watched the passengers begin to trickle onto the plane.

He'd lost his mind. What was he doing here? This wasn't him. He planned things. And he certainly didn't jeopardize his career to run off to *Rome* on literally no notice.

Davis had been startled—to put it mildly—when Connor had called him from the car on his way to the airport and asked for the week off. Connor had plenty of vacation days in reserve, since he hadn't taken a day off in over two years. His work would be fine, and Davis knew it—he was always working well ahead of his deadlines—but it wasn't a good look for someone who was angling for partner to abruptly leave the country immediately before the partners made their final decision.

He knew he was putting his promotion at risk. And he couldn't make himself care.

The word *partner* had always represented success to him.

He'd seen the partners at the Pine Hollow firm where his mother worked as the epitome of success. He'd thought, in his nine-year-old brain, that if he could prove he was rich enough, successful enough, *perfect* enough, that nothing in his life would ever go wrong. No one would ever leave him. And on some level he'd never lost that belief.

He'd thought somehow that making partner would magically solve all his problems, but of course it wouldn't. That was never what was missing. His mom was happy as a paralegal. He would be happy as an associate. Or a partner. Or a dog walker.

As long as Deenie didn't leave.

It was terrifying, being so completely out of control. This feeling that his entire happiness rested in someone else's hands.

And maybe it didn't. Maybe that was dramatic. Maybe he would survive the loss of Deenie. Survive the sucker punch of another woman vanishing on him—of another goddamn note.

But he didn't want to have to.

He wanted Deenie.

Connor took his place in line to board the plane.

Deenie had always been a sucker for those scenes in movies where someone went sprinting through the airport, desperate to catch their love before they flew away forever.

It turned out being the one doing the sprinting was *incredibly* stressful.

She was late.

She'd driven herself to the airport. In part because she

wasn't planning to leave her car in long-term parking—
she was just getting Connor and bringing him back to Pine
Hollow—but also because she'd known she was going to
want to speed the entire way and hadn't wanted to saddle
Ally with a speeding ticket just because she'd been too
foolish to recognize a good thing when he was standing
right in front of her telling her that he loved her.

She didn't know how far ahead of her he was—she and
Ally had been halfway to Burlington before she'd come to
her senses—but she knew what time her scheduled flight
departed, and she assumed he'd gotten on the same flight. It
was the last flight out that evening. If she missed it, he'd be
in Rome without her.

And if she didn't run, she was going to miss it.

Deenie parked in the closest lot—and ran. She'd yanked
the toiletries too big to go through security out of her bag
one-handed as she drove. She was cutting it too close to
check a bag. She'd even left little JoJo with Ally, making
Ally promise to take good care of her until they got back.

Deenie tried Connor's cell one more time as she waited
in the TSA PreCheck line. He still wasn't answering his
phone.

She cursed under her breath, disconnecting the call in
time to toss the phone into the little bin and rush through
security.

On the other side, she grabbed her phone and her bag
and ran.

She really needed to work on her cardio.

She was huffing for breath when the gate came into
view. Empty of passengers. The gate attendant calling final
boarding. Reaching for the door behind her to close it.

"Wait!" Deenie shouted.

She poured on an extra burst of speed, thundering up to the gate.

The gate agent smiled. "Just in time. It's your lucky day."

"I hope so," Deenie wheezed, hitching her bag up on her shoulder as she scanned her boarding pass.

She rushed onto the jetway, the door closing behind her. Hopefully, they would open it for her and Connor to get off the plane before it took off, or it would be a long drive back from New York.

Her feet thumped down the jetway—and then the open plane door was in front of her.

Moment of truth.

What if he'd changed his mind? What if he'd caught a different flight or had decided she wasn't worth chasing after all? What if he'd realized she wasn't worth the trouble?

Deenie stepped into the aisle.

The plane was nearly empty. He wasn't in first class. She couldn't imagine Connor traveling any way *other* than first class. Had she been wrong?

"Miss?" The flight attendant spoke behind her. "You need to take your seat."

"Right," Deenie whispered, the first hint of dejection shivering through her.

She'd been so sure he would be here. When Ben said he was coming after her, it had sent a shock of elation rushing through her. But now all that giddy optimism fizzed away like the bubbles on stale champagne.

She trudged down the aisle, losing more hope the farther back she went in the plane.

He wasn't here. She was almost to the last row—

"Deenie?"

Her heart stopped. *Connor.*

Chapter Thirty-Five

D eenie had been in such a hurry to *get* to Connor that she hadn't planned what she was going to say to him when she did.

He sat in the second-to-last row, in the window seat, his long legs tucked up awkwardly. He unbuckled his seat belt, moving to stand.

A flight attendant moved toward them from the service area at the back of the plane. "Ma'am, we're going to need you to take your seat. Do you need help with your bag?"

"We're not staying," she blurted to the flight attendant—though her eyes never left Connor's face. "I came to get you. I went back, but you weren't there. I want to stay. I want to be with you."

"Ma'am..." The flight attendant stepped forward.

"Deenie..." Connor was on his feet, hunched beneath the overhead bin.

"I love you."

The flight attendant hesitated, her gaze flicking back and forth between Deenie and Connor—declarations of love evidently not covered by their handbook.

The attendant from the front of the plane began moving down the aisle toward them.

"Let's go home," Deenie begged. "I'm so sorry. I never should have run."

Emotion shifted in Connor's eyes, settling into an amber resolve. "No."

"What?" Her heart stuttered. Did he not want her anymore? After he came all this way? Why was he on this plane?

He stepped into the aisle with her, straightening to his full height, his devastating dimples winking down at her. "I want to go to Rome."

She frowned, irritation flashing. "We don't have to," she insisted. "I want to stay. You win."

The other flight attendant arrived. "Is there a problem here?"

"We're getting off the plane," Deenie said.

"No, we aren't," Connor countered, almost in the same breath. He took Deenie's bag, stowing it in the overhead compartment in an unfair display of deltoids, speaking the entire time. "You were right. I tried to fit you into a space I'd already made in my life, but you have never fit the mold. And I wouldn't want you to. I don't want the women who check all the boxes. I want you. And I want Rome."

He stepped back into his row, pulling her with him, and Deenie was too shocked to resist.

"My life needs more spontaneity. More adventure. And a lot more glitter. I need *you*, Deenie. Arguing with me and pushing me out of my comfort zone and making everything brighter."

"I need you, too," she whispered, settling into the seat beside his. She couldn't take her eyes off him, even as he buckled her seat belt, his eyes glinting. "To keep me grounded—which isn't always a bad thing—and remind me not to spite myself by throwing away the good things just because someone else thinks I should want them. But, Connor, we don't have to go all the way to Rome to prove it—"

"Yes, we do. You were willing to stay for me. I need you to know I'm willing to go anywhere for you." His dimples flashed. "And I've never been to Italy."

Her eyes flared. "No! Really?"

His gaze met hers, thickly lashed and unfairly gorgeous. "Show me the world, Deenie Mitchell?"

Her heart melted as the jet engines began to hum. "I can't think of anything I'd like more."

And then he sealed it with a kiss. The *perfect* kiss. And Deenie felt…perfect.

Epilogue

Connor didn't have the best track record with weddings. They seemed to make the women in his life flee the country. But as he watched Deenie bouncing in the middle of the dance floor with Ally as they belted out the lyrics to an eighties power ballad, he couldn't think of any place he'd rather be.

She'd touched up the pink in her hair and even added sparkly strands of what she called "hair tinsel" for the occasion after he'd asked if there was any way she could be *more* covered in glitter. He should have known she would take it as a challenge.

Deenie never backed down from a challenge. Or an adventure.

They'd spent a week in Rome, walking through piazza after piazza, celebrating Mr. Burke's life with *limoncello* toasts at sidewalk cafes, eating entirely too much Italian food, and zipping around cobbled streets on a Vespa, just as Deenie's Aunt Bitty had during her own Roman holiday. Connor hadn't had time to make lists of all the things he wanted to see before they arrived and he'd barely had any clothes, but he wouldn't have changed a minute of their impulsive, disorganized trip.

They were already talking about where they would go next. He was pushing for Paris, but with the way Deenie's eyes glittered when she talked about Iceland, he had a feeling they would be checking out some glaciers before long.

It had been strange, taking a whole week away from work, but Davis had covered for him, and he came back refreshed—and to the partner position. A position it no longer felt like he had to play a part to deserve. He'd somehow become the person he'd been pretending to be. Thanks to Deenie.

The song ended, and she bounded over to their table at the edge of the dance floor, breathlessly flinging herself onto his lap. His arm closed naturally, possessively, around her waist.

"Careful," she announced, pausing to drain her water glass. "Ally just told me she's going to start chucking flowers soon. We might want to clear the area."

They'd carefully avoided the topic of marriage. He'd put his five-year plan on the back burner—but he'd taken a page from Mitch's playbook and started carrying around an engagement ring, just in case. And right now, with their best friends tying the knot and love in the air, he was feeling daring.

He leaned forward until his breath brushed her ear, amid those pink sparkling curls. "I dare you to catch the bouquet," he challenged, loving the flash of interest that fired in her blue eyes when she whipped her head to study him. He held her gaze. "Really fight for it. Claw their eyes out. Take no prisoners."

"I would *never* make such a scene." She fluttered her lashes innocently.

He closed the inches between them, catching the smile on her lips, because he couldn't resist.

She was still smiling when he pulled back. "You have glitter on your cheek."

He swiped where she indicated, seeing the sparkle on his fingertips. "You marked me."

"You're mine now."

He rubbed the glitter back onto her skin, then drew his finger slowly along her jaw. "I've been yours since that first night in the Jacuzzi," he murmured. "When Max doused you."

Her eyes widened with mock shock. "That's so funny! That's when I started falling for you, too." She leaned closer, lowering her voice intimately. "It is a *beautiful* Jacuzzi."

His snort of laughter was drowned out by the emcee calling all the bouquet hopefuls to the dance floor.

Deenie glanced toward the dance floor, then back into his eyes. "If I catch the bouquet, I get to plan any weddings that result. And you should be warned, it is highly likely that will entail Vegas and an Elton John impersonator. And you'll never know when it's coming," she described with relish. "I'll just spring it on you one day. You won't even have time to get a tux. We'll be on the way to the airport and *boom*. Flip-flop wedding."

Connor smiled at the threat. He didn't think she was serious, but he could think of worse ways to tie the knot. Eloping sounded *much* better than a big buildup to another elaborate day. Life with Deenie would always be an adventure.

And he couldn't wait.

"Deal."

Her eyes lit at his words. "Oh, it is *on*."

She kicked off her shoes and flung herself off his lap, bouncing to the center of the knot of people on the dance floor. She looked back over her shoulder, pointing two fingers toward her eyes and then at him before turning back to focus on the bouquet, rocking back and forth, her weight on the balls of her feet like a shortstop waiting for the pitch.

Ally wagged the bouquet, taunting the assembled singletons, then turned and sent it sailing over her shoulder. Eager bouquet-seekers leapt into the air, hands thrust high. One woman in a navy dress tumbled into a redheaded bridesmaid, and the entire pile collapsed to the floor.

The crowd gasped.

The bride laughed so hard she would have fallen over if her groom hadn't steadied her.

And a single arm thrust triumphantly out of the squirming pile, holding the bouquet aloft.

And if the maid of honor bellowed, "Vegas, baby!" at the top of her lungs as she emerged victorious, no one thought anything of it. She'd always done things her own way.

And Connor couldn't wait to see what she did next. His very own princess/dog trainer/seamstress/rebel/love of his life. Some things were too good to be planned.

Acknowledgments

Huge thanks to the entire team at Forever, who are always a delight to work with and have been invaluable in launching this book into the world. Estelle, Joelle, Stacey, and Sabrina, thank you. And a very special thanks to my editor, Leah, who makes the hard conversations easy and introduces me to the best reality TV addictions—if I start pitching you *Alone* romances, you have no one to blame but yourself.

As always, thanks to my agent, Michelle, the biggest cheerleader for my work, and to my writer friends who always lift me up and talk me down when I'm in a brainstorming spiral, especially Kim Law, the Hallmark cohort, and the Rubies. Special thanks to Leigh, Kali and the kiddos, Jane, and Mili, for teaching me the gospel of glitter—and making sure I knew *all* the lyrics to *Frozen* and *Coco*.

All my love to my *ohana*.

And, finally, thanks to the wonderful folks at *Wait Wait...Don't Tell Me*, the NPR news quiz, for keeping me laughing through quarantine and introducing me to the concept of the Public Domain Party Princess.

Read on for a preview of the first charming and
heart-warming Pine Hollow book from
Lizzie Shane!

The
Twelve
Dogs of
Christmas

Available now from

HEADLINE
ETERNAL

Chapter One

The residents of Pine Hollow, Vermont, liked to think of it as the Mary Poppins of towns. Practically perfect in every way. Which was cute and all—as long as you weren't one of the town council members responsible for making sure everything *stayed* perfect. After two solid years of listening to every little complaint, Ben West figured he'd now sufficiently paid for any crimes committed in a past life.

And Christmas...Christmas was the worst.

The town went nuts for the holiday every year—and Ben's phone exploded with demands from overly enthusiastic citizens. More lights for the tree lighting. New garland for the library. More padding for the Santa costume since their regular jolly elf impersonator had started running marathons over the summer and lost fifty pounds.

It all had to come out of the town budget—which meant it all went through the town council. And Ben had the dubious distinction of being the swing vote on that council.

He was lucky if he could walk from the house to Astrid's school to work without being stopped half a dozen times with a cheerful, "Oh, Ben! I was hoping I would run into you!" And his phone never seemed to stop vibrating.

Right on cue, a snippet of the *Jaws* theme music *duh-duh*ed from his pocket, alerting him to a new email in his council account. He ignored the sound as he crossed the kitchen, making a beeline for the Keurig. Town business before caffeine was never a good idea. Though maybe this time it wouldn't be anything he needed to deal with. Maybe it would be a Christmas miracle, and someone would be offering a solution rather than heaping another problem onto his plate.

The ominous *Jaws* music came again as he popped in the K-Cup and pushed the button, waiting for the machine to groan to life and dribble salvation into his cup. But nothing happened. He bent closer, studying the face of the machine. It was lit up, just like it was supposed to be. Everything looked fine, but when he pushed the button again—nothing.

The Keurig sat there, silently taunting him, and Ben found himself confronted by the horrible catch-22 of needing caffeine to figure out what was wrong with the machine that was supposed to give him caffeine.

"Morning, Uncle Ben!"

He grunted something vaguely g'morning-ish as his niece bounded into the kitchen.

Astrid, apparently unaware of the imminent caffeine crisis, pulled open a cabinet. "What do you think? Cupcakes, brownies, or gingerbread?"

Ben turned his head just enough to study her as she pulled cereal out of a cupboard. Astrid was that terrifying creation—a morning person—but she didn't usually ask him for sweets over breakfast. "None of the above? Too early for sugar."

"For the bake sale?" Astrid reminded him as she dropped a box of cornflakes on the island. "The Christmas fair? Everyone has to sign up to bring something."

"Right. The fair." Ben turned his attention back to the Keurig. It was plugged in. It had water. What if he turned it off and turned it back on again like rebooting a router? That should work, right? "That's soon?" he asked absently.

"A week from Sunday." Astrid gathered milk and blueberries from the fridge, taking her entire haul to the island. "We have to turn in the forms today, and we can't do cookies because Merritt Miller said she's doing cookies this year and her aunt runs the bakery so hers are going to be, like, the best cookies ever in the history of cookies and anyone else who does them is going to look pathetic." She poured flakes and milk and blueberries into her bowl, pausing with her spoon poised. "Have you *seen* the cookies they sell? They're like, *amazing*. So we have to do cupcakes or brownies or gingerbread or something, and I don't know what to put."

Ben opened his mouth, but no answer came out, his noncaffeinated brain completely empty of inspiration. *Brownies, cupcakes, or gingerbread?* "Uh…"

If someone had told him two years ago that some-day the question of Christmas fair baked goods would be more complicated than the riddle of the Sphinx, he would have laughed them into next week—but a lot of things had changed in the last two years. His obnoxiously perfect overachiever sister and her most-reliable-man-on-the-planet husband were gone. Astrid was his responsibility. And he was now on a Facebook group for parents in Astrid's class, which seemed to double as a master class in passive-aggressive mommy shaming—or uncle shaming, in his case.

Brownies, cupcakes, or gingerbread—whichever he chose, he needed to be prepared to defend that choice with the latest child nutrition studies, or he'd be shredded on the group. Were they gluten-free? Were they prepared on a surface a nut had touched in the last two decades? How many grams of sugar? How many carbs? Were the eggs from organic, cage-free, happy chickens with a quality of life that would rival his own? Had an ancestor of the dairy cow that produced the milk once been given antibiotics?

He wanted to be a responsible guardian. He wanted Astrid to be healthy and happy, which meant worrying about all the things that he was supposed to worry about. But sometimes it seemed like there was no winning except for the oh-so-helpful people who wanted to tell him he was doing something wrong—because he was *always* doing something wrong.

Brownies, cupcakes, or gingerbread?

He needed coffee for this decision.

Every choice had become an important one the second he'd become Astrid's guardian, but this felt like he was being set up to fail. Why were they constantly doing bake sales if half the parents thought sugar and flour were poison? Sometimes he just wanted to wear a T-shirt to drop-off with I SURVIVED HIGH-FRUCTOSE CORN SYRUP on the front in block letters, but he wasn't sure he'd live to tell the tale. This parenting stuff wasn't for the faint of heart.

"We can just do brownies." Astrid spoke to his back as he faced the useless coffee maker. She didn't sound upset, but the *just* dug into his chest.

Katie never would have done *just* anything. She was Supermom, Queen of Bake Sales, but she'd also had a wicked sense of humor and never taken herself too seriously. She was the kind of mom every kid wanted to grow up with. She was the mom Astrid *should* have grown up with, but now his niece was stuck with him and his less-than-stellar baking skills. And he refused to let her down.

"Nah, let's do something fun," he insisted, forcing cheer into his tone, as if his entire neural network wasn't begging for coffee. "How about gingerbread?"

He'd never made gingerbread a day in his life.

Please let gingerbread be easy.

"Really?"

The note of disbelief in Astrid's voice had him doubling down. "Yeah. How hard can it be?"

His niece grimaced. "Maybe we should do the brownies."

"Are you implying I can't do gingerbread?" *I might not be able to do gingerbread.*

"Kinda."

Ben huffed out a laugh at her honesty. "We're doing it. Gingerbread." His phone *duh-duh*ed another *Jaws* warning, and he resisted the urge to fish it out of his pocket, catching sight of the clock on the microwave. *Crap.* "You gonna be ready soon? We're running late." Again.

Astrid was already dressed in her school clothes, but he was going to have to hurry to find a clean-enough work shirt if he was going to get her to school on time. The washer had been on the fritz for the last two weeks, and he was running out of clean options. With the Thanksgiving holiday messing with schedules, the only time the repairman had been able to come out had conflicted with Astrid's parent-teacher conferences, so they were making do with sink laundry until he could reschedule.

Just another of the many things he wasn't quite keeping up with. And now he had to add fixing the Keurig to the list.

How novel it must be to actually have enough hours in the day. He vaguely remembered what that felt like, though the memory was distant.

Astrid slid off her stool, taking her bowl to the sink. "Brownies are cool, too..."

"Have a little faith in your elders."

"I have faith. I just also remember last year."

Ben opened his mouth to refute her—somewhat warranted—concerns, but his cell phone rang, cutting off his defense. The words *Boss Lady* flashed on the screen. *Saved by the bell.* He plucked the phone off the counter, connecting the call. "Hey, Delia. I can't talk long. I've got to get Astrid to school."

"Did you get my emails?" The mayor's voice

reverberated against his eardrums. Delia Winter had one volume: bullhorn. And one mode—impatient. Her question explained the *Jaws* warnings. She'd probably been sending a new email every five seconds—she never could wait to get a reply. But she loved the town, and no one had done more for Pine Hollow than she had. Delia charged on before he had a chance to answer. "I think I have a solution for the budget shortfall."

"Great."

"It's the dog shelter," Delia boomed.

Ben flinched, but thankfully, Astrid didn't seem to have overheard anything from the other side of the island, where she was packing her lunch. His niece had been hinting at wanting a dog for months. Ever since her tenth birthday. And he'd been shutting her down every time. Now it had gotten to the point that even the mere mention of the infamous *D-O-G* word was enough to restart the argument that never seemed to end.

"Just a second, Delia," he said. He mouthed, *"Five minutes,"* at Astrid and rushed out of the kitchen like he was being chased, stubbing his toe on the loose trim on the second stair and swearing under his breath at the reminder of yet another thing that he hadn't gotten around to fixing in the creaky old house.

Delia waited her obligatory one second and forged on. "The funding for the animal shelter was always part of the mayor's discretionary budget. So we just reallocate it. I don't know why I didn't think of it before."

"Won't that hurt the shelter?" he asked, keeping his voice down so it wouldn't carry to Astrid. He'd never gone to the shelter himself, but he had a vague image of a nice older couple on a piece of land at the edge of town.

"We'll fund them until the end of the year to give them time to find homes for the dogs. Rita and Hal are getting up there, and their granddaughter had to come up from the city to help out, but I'm sure she'd like to get back to her own life—and rumor has it Hal and Rita were looking to move out to the Estates but couldn't because of the dogs. Everybody wins."

Ben found a shirt that passed the sniff test and pulled it on. It felt like there was a catch about this perfect solution he wasn't seeing, but he couldn't put his finger on it.

"We have to find the money to fix the rec center roof somewhere, and this is the thing that impacts the town as a whole the least," Delia boomed. "It's not like we can cut schools or the firehouse. And the last time we tried to cut the budget for the Christmas tree lighting, I thought we were going to have a riot. This is the obvious choice."

"Right…" His socks weren't going to match today, but did people really look at socks?

"So I have your vote? We can pass the budget this afternoon, notify the shelter, and recess for the holidays if you're onboard."

He hadn't known what he was getting into when he'd volunteered to take over the rest of his brother-in-law's four-year term on the city council. He'd only been thinking that Paul's and Katie's responsibilities were his responsibilities now and that the consistency would be good for Astrid. But two years of budgets and zoning disputes had shown him the error of his ways. "Recess for the holidays" was the most tantalizing phrase he'd heard in a long time.

He loved Pine Hollow, but one less thing on his list sounded like heaven.

"Sure." He shoved his feet into his shoes and grabbed his laptop bag. "It makes sense." He charged down the stairs, dodging the loose step this time. "I've gotta go, Delia."

"I'll see you later. Thanks, Ben!"

Astrid was waiting at the bottom of the stairs, already wearing her puffy down coat and her backpack—and making him feel like even more of a screw-up as the so-called parental figure.

"You all set?" he asked, even though she obviously was. He grabbed his coat off the hook by the door, checking the time on the grandfather clock in the hall. If they hurried they would make it—and then he could grab a coffee at the Cup before he had to be at work. He pulled open the door, holding it for Astrid to pass through and feeling like he'd dodged a bullet—or an entire firing squad—until he fell into step beside his niece on the front walk and she tipped her head at him innocuously.

"What's going on with the dog shelter?"

Look out for

*To All
the
Dogs I've
Loved Before*

Coming soon from

**HEADLINE
ETERNAL**

HEADLINE
ETERNAL

FIND YOUR HEART'S DESIRE...

VISIT OUR WEBSITE: www.headlineeternal.com
FIND US ON FACEBOOK: facebook.com/eternalromance
CONNECT WITH US ON TWITTER: @eternal_books
FOLLOW US ON INSTAGRAM: @headlineeternal
EMAIL US: eternalromance@headline.co.uk